FIRSTBORN SONS

PROFILE

FIRSTBORN SON:	Walker James
AGE:	28
STATS:	6'2", lean, well muscled. Jet-black hair. Piercing blue eyes. Chiseled, gorgeous features.
OCCUPATION:	International spy
AREA OF EXPERTISE:	Antiterrorism
PERSONALITY:	Tough but charming
FAVORITE SPORT:	Climbing isolated mountains and rappelling down canyon walls
MOST CHARMING CHARACTERISTIC:	His slow, wide, devastating grin
BRAVEST ACT OF COURAGE:	Going back into a building he'd set to detonate to assist an injured team member
PREFERRED ROMANTIC SETTING:	A certain balcony in Venice dancing beneath the stars
GREATEST PASSION:	An exotic Moroccan beauty he's been unable to get out of his mind—or his heart

Dear Reader,

The year is almost over, but the excitement continues here at Intimate Moments. Reader favorite Ruth Langan launches a new miniseries, THE LASSITER LAW, with *By Honor Bound*. Law enforcement is the Lassiter family legacy—and love is their future. Be there to see it all happen.

Our FIRSTBORN SONS continuity is almost at an end. This month's installment is *Born in Secret*, by Kylie Brant. Next month Alexandra Sellers finishes up this six-book series, which leads right into ROMANCING THE CROWN, our new twelve-book Intimate Moments continuity continuing the saga of the Montebellan royal family. THE PROTECTORS, by Beverly Barton, is one of our most popular ongoing miniseries, so don't miss this seasonal offering, *Jack's Christmas Mission*. Judith Duncan takes you back to the WIDE OPEN SPACES of Alberta, Canada, for *The Renegade and the Heiress*, a romantic wilderness adventure you won't soon forget. Finish up the month with *Once Forbidden...* by Carla Cassidy, the latest in her miniseries THE DELANEY HEIRS, and *That Kind of Girl*, the second novel by exciting new talent Kim McKade.

And in case you'd like a sneak preview of next month, our Christmas gifts to you include the above-mentioned conclusion to FIRSTBORN SONS, *Born Royal*, as well as *Brand-New Heartache*, award-winning Maggie Shayne's latest of THE OKLAHOMA ALL-GIRL BRANDS. See you then!

Yours,

Leslie J. Wainger
Executive Senior Editor

Please address questions and book requests to:
Silhouette Reader Service
U.S.: 3010 Walden Ave., P.O. Box 1325, Buffalo, NY 14269
Canadian: P.O. Box 609, Fort Erie, Ont. L2A 5X3

BORN
IN
SECRET
Kylie Brant

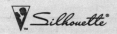
Silhouette®

INTIMATE MOMENTS™

Published by Silhouette Books

America's Publisher of Contemporary Romance

Special thanks and acknowledgment are given
to Kylie Brant for her contribution
to the FIRSTBORN SONS series.

For all our extra kids—who fill our house,
empty our cupboards and warm our hearts

 SILHOUETTE BOOKS

ISBN 0-373-27182-4

BORN IN SECRET

Visit Silhouette at www.eHarlequin.com

Printed in U.S.A.

Bound by the legacy of their fathers, six firstborn sons are about to discover the stuff true heroes—and true love—are made of....

Walker James: This darkly handsome spy learned the hard way that beautiful women are lethal if not kept at a distance. Now, working side by side with his stunning former flame to locate a deadly virus—and keeping a tight rein on his traitorous desires—could prove to be his ultimate undoing!

Jasmine LeBarr: As she aligns herself with the only man who can make her tremble with his merest touch, Jasmine is caught off guard by the emotional storm raging inside her. Now it's anyone's guess who will emerge victorious in this turbulent battle of wills....

Captain Richard Sutter: This seasoned mercenary is working behind the scenes to pave his firstborn son's future. But at what cost?

The Brothers of Darkness: The sinister terrorist organization has been using the bad blood between the powerful Kamal and Sebastiani clans to their own advantage....

Sheik Rashid Kamal: Will this missing royal heir make it back alive to claim his rightful legacy—and his child?

A note from talented writer Kylie Brant,
author of over ten novels for Silhouette Books:

Dear Reader,

Being asked to be part of a continuity is always a special thrill.
And the concept behind the Intimate Moments FIRSTBORN
SONS series intrigued me from the first. Who could resist
heroes who put honor above all else and the very special
heroines who teach them the power of true love?

In *Born in Secret,* Walker James and Jasmine LeBarr are
paired to track down the deadly anthrax virus before it can be
used to destroy an entire country. Their dangerous mission is
complicated by their memory of the night they spent together
three years ago. This time, though, they're both convinced they
can walk away from each other unscathed. What they learn,
however, is that the peril of their assignment is matched only
by the danger to their hearts!

My writing shares time with my full-time teaching job, husband
and five children. Now that two of my kids are grown (well,
sort of!), we juggle only three athletic calendars each season.
These days, the most time my husband and I spend together
is sitting on a bleacher at a game of some kind! We're also
veterans of emergency-room visits, usually the result of the
aforementioned sports. But when the games are over I can close
the office door, turn on the computer and dream away. And in
between the frequent interruptions of phone and family, Walker
and Jasmine's story unfolded.

I hope you enjoy their story!

Sincerely,

Kylie Brant

Readers may contact me by snail mail at P.O. Box 231, Charles
City, IA 50616, or by e-mail at kyliebrant@hotmail.com.

Prologue

"No one can know that I'm involved. Not even your agents."

Richard Sutter picked up a crystal decanter of aged Scotch and splashed two generous fingers into each of a pair of cut glass tumblers. He handed a glass to his friend, and then sank down into one of the matching rich leather armchairs. At the first taste of the smooth liquor, he gave a small sigh of appreciation. It was a moment before he noticed that his guest had failed to follow suit.

"What's the matter? Those terms not to your liking? I'm paying you a king's ransom, you old reprobate. I'm entitled to a few conditions."

The remark had Dirk Longfield's mouth curving, but his gaze remained speculative. "No problem. Just wondering what's behind your need for anonymity." At the silence that followed his words, his brows skimmed upward and he tipped his glass to his lips. "And I'm quite aware that you're not going to enlighten me."

Raising his glass in a mock salute, Richard drank. "An astute observation." His friend knew better than to waste time asking questions that wouldn't be answered. They were both comfortable in the shadowy world of secrecy.

"Do you think you'll have trouble getting Walker James to take this assignment?" His casual tone belied the purposefulness of the question.

Dirk hooked an ankle over his knee. "Trouble? No. Walker will do it for me."

The certainty in his remark brought Richard a sense of relief that was only mildly tinged with jealousy. He focused on the first emotion and tried to ignore the second. The assignment would proceed as he'd planned. That was all that mattered. He thought it, and tried to believe it. "Good. From what I've observed, James is becoming one of the best in the business." He waited with interest for his friend's reaction.

Dirk tensed, straightened a bit in his chair. "*Becoming?* Walker *is* the best. The boy's instincts are uncanny, and he's a bloody genius when it comes to circumventing security. There's no one in the field better suited for the task you outlined."

For all the pride in his tone, Dirk sounded like Walker's proud father, something both he and Richard knew he was not. "I assume you have someone in mind to partner with James."

Nodding, Dirk raised his glass and sipped. "Another agent I highly recommend. Not as experienced as Walker, but very resourceful, and rapidly earning a reputation. I have no doubt they'll execute the mission perfectly."

"I hope so. Because we both know the ramifications if they fail." The two men shared a silent look of understanding, then raised their glasses. To the mission. To success.

* * *

Long after Dirk had left, Richard remained in his study, contemplating the faded network of scars on the back of his hands. His gaze was turned inward, on a bittersweet journey of memories that he rarely indulged in. The hard living he'd experienced in his sixty-two years hadn't come without regrets. Decisions made decades ago, even viewed from the distance of time, could still haunt.

With effort he climbed out of memory's abyss and into the present. He trusted Dirk to do as he'd promised, and had no doubt that very soon Walker James would be flying to the Middle East to begin the assignment. Richard thought it was a mission that Walker would relish and excel at. And since Richard's involvement would be kept secret, there was no reason to believe he wouldn't accept the job.

It occurred to him then that Walker bore more resemblance to Dirk Longfield than he did to his own father. He tried not to let that bother him, wished that it didn't. They both had black hair, although Dirk's was now threaded with gray. Walker's eyes were a shade lighter than Dirk's midnight-blue, and his regard even more piercing. But the real cause for jealousy wasn't for the two men's similarity in looks, it was for their relationship. Richard knew that Walker considered Dirk his father in every sense that mattered.

And that fact was his biggest regret of all.

Chapter 1

At heart, Walker James would always remain a thief. The acknowledgment brought him no shame. He'd been a damn good one in his delinquent youth. If his illegal career had been cut short by Dirk Longfield's interference, well, the talents he'd acquired along the way had been equally useful in the alternative path he'd chosen. Or perhaps, he mused sardonically, it had chosen him. It was doubtful that many people made the conscious decision to become a spy.

He prowled Dirk's well-appointed office, his muscled frame moving soundlessly. For once he failed to be amused by his mentor's choice in collectibles. A Ming dynasty vase stood side by side with a chipped and faded replica of Mickey Mouse. A Picasso adorned one wall, hanging next to a scarlet sunset painted on velvet, artist unknown. Beneath his feet was a rich faded tapestry rug dating from the regime of Catherine the Great. And behind the acre-long walnut desk was a well-known wall hanging of canines cheating at poker.

The rare beside the common. The tacky and the price-less. The collection invited a guest to make all manner of judgments about the collector. They would likely all be wrong. After ten years of friendship with Dirk, Walker knew the man acquired chiefly for whimsy. The value of an object meant far less to him than the fact that it had caught his fancy. Walker didn't share the sentiment, but he understood it. Just as he understood the man who had currently been keeping him waiting for—he checked his watch again—twenty minutes.

When he'd received the phone call from his mentor, Walker had been on his way out the door for some well-deserved rest on a tropical beach, preferably a nude one. Although he'd meant to travel alone, he hadn't intended to stay that way for long. There had been a lot of creature comforts that he'd gone without for a while, and sex was one of them. He'd hoped to take the next couple weeks remedying that.

But then he'd spoken to Dirk and plans had changed. The airline ticket had remained lying on top of the gateleg hallway table in his Philadelphia penthouse, and he'd driven down to Virginia immediately. Loyalty was an innate part of his makeup. Which explained why he was currently cooling his heels in this gallery of contrasts instead of sitting on a white sand beach, sipping rum and oiling a well-endowed blonde's butt. He glanced at his watch again. Patience would never be one of his strengths.

The door opened then and he turned a jaundiced eye toward the man strolling toward him. "For a guy who was in such a hurry to get me here, you seem to have developed a sluggish sense of time."

Dirk merely shot him a good-natured smile and clapped an arm around his shoulders. "You're looking good, kid." He reared back, pretended to study the younger man's face.

"A few more lines, maybe, but you needed to toughen up that pretty-boy face of yours."

An unwilling smile tugging at his lips, Walker returned the man's embrace. "It's only been three months. I couldn't have aged that much." If he had he would only count it as a blessing. The movie star good looks he'd been cursed with at birth didn't exactly make his an anonymous face. That was a damn nuisance in his line of work.

Gesturing the younger man to a chair, Dirk seated himself. "You probably should have. The way I hear it, you barely managed to escape your last mission with all your limbs intact." His casual tone didn't quite mask the concern in his voice.

Walker shrugged. "Let's just say I have a renewed respect for explosives." Although he hadn't walked away from the job unscathed, he *had* walked away. It was an important distinction. "The mission was successful."

Dirk's mouth quirked. "I never doubted it. Which leads me, indirectly, to why you're here. I have a job to propose, one that calls for the best. Naturally I thought of you."

"I learned from the best." Walker's quiet answer was more than just factual. It was Dirk who had introduced him to the shadowy world of espionage…a world where right and wrongs weren't always black and white, but more often a mottled shade of gray. He'd found it a comfortable enough fit.

Inclining his head to acknowledge the compliment, Dirk went on. "How much have you heard about the trouble brewing between Montebello and Tamir?"

"In which decade?" Walker asked dryly. The two small Middle Eastern countries had been feuding on and off for more than a century. "Seems like I heard something recently about Sheik Ahmed Kamal's son being missing and him holding King Marcus Sebastiani responsible."

Dirk's expression was serious. "The king's oldest daughter is pregnant by Kamal's son, Rashid. He was last seen in the company of the princess, so when he came up missing Kamal immediately blamed Sebastiani. The sheik threatened to retaliate by taking over Montebello."

Walker let out a soft tuneless whistle. Since Montebello was situated in a strategic military location, the ramifications were clear. "So the U.S. wants to protect their interests there, discreetly of course, while keeping the peace."

"Partially." Dirk hesitated for a moment, seemed to choose his words carefully. "There have been threats on Sebastiani's family—bombings, attempted kidnappings—and the king believed Kamal was behind them. New intelligence indicates that the sheik wasn't responsible at all, but a rebel faction housed in Maloun called the Brothers of Darkness."

"I've heard of them. They're rumored to have at least one terrorist cell here in the states, near L.A." He frowned, searching his memory. "Seems there was something recently about a U.C.L.A. scientist being questioned about a possible connection with them."

"Dr. Sinan Omer. He's suspected of taking a shot at Princess Christina Sebastiani while at a conference out there. We think the Brothers have been heightening the strife between the two countries as a cover. Our sources in the Middle East tell us the organization is close to developing an anthrax virus to use against Kamal's people. They intend to overthrow the sheik's government and bring their own leader into power there."

"Biological warfare." Walker said the words, felt chilled. If the organization succeeded, he doubted they'd be content with oil rich Tamir. The entire Middle East would be at risk. The repercussions would be felt around the world.

He looked at Dirk. "What do I do?" That simply, that easily, he was committed. He could think of nothing he wouldn't do for this man, who'd stepped into his life and changed its direction. But there was a larger, more encompassing matter at stake. Over the years, much to his dismay, Walker James had developed a conscience.

He blamed Dirk for it, of course. It was a damn bother most of the time, and he'd never grown entirely comfortable with it. But the work he'd done first for Dirk, and then with his own team, hiring out to the trouble spots in the world, had taught him to value peace. It was a quality found too infrequently for him to be indifferent to it.

The older man looked pleased, and a bit relieved. "Before I go into the whole plan, I should tell you that you'll be paired with a partner. I was briefing her before you arrived. I'll get her so we can all discuss the job together."

Before Walker could respond, Dirk strode to the door, pulled it open and disappeared. He rose, stared after the man, something about his behavior striking him as odd. There had been an almost furtive quality to it, which was ludicrous. Dirk had never been anything but up-front with him.

Shaking off the feeling, he strolled to his host's desk and picked up a chunk of jade used as a paperweight. It was new since Walker's last visit, and he hefted it, examining it critically. Worth about twenty grand on the open market, he calculated, probably half that to a fence. The assessment was as natural as breathing. He may have gotten his life straightened out a decade ago, but he prided himself on keeping up on the trade.

Hearing a sound at the door, he turned, ready to ask Dirk about the jade. And instead stared in disbelief at the woman accompanying the older man. Fate, he'd always thought, was merely the acts of a whimsical god. And right now that god was having a good hard laugh at Walker's expense.

"What's she doing here?" His voice was flat. He was afraid, very much afraid, that he already knew the answer to that particular question.

His fear was confirmed when Dirk skirted his gaze and said, just a shade too heartily, "You remember Jasmine, of course. She'll be your partner on this case."

Walker glanced at the woman and saw her looking at him, her beautiful, exotic face composed. As if she didn't remember the one night they'd spent together. How completely she'd surrendered; how perfectly they'd fit.

And how easily she'd betrayed him the next day.

He gave her a careless nod. "Jasmine...LeBarr, isn't it? Sure I remember. It's been...what? A couple years? In Barcelona?"

"Closer to three, I believe. And it was Venice." Her English still held the slightly formal style of those not born speaking it, though her accent had faded to a mere lilt layering her words. Her voice was the same, warm sin wrapped in seductive velvet. Such a lovely voice for someone so unscrupulous. It had lingered in his memory far longer than he'd like to admit. The admission was bitter.

His attention switched to Dirk. "Get rid of her."

"What?"

"Get rid of her, or find someone else to take my place. I don't lay my life on the line with a partner I don't trust absolutely. She doesn't come close to fitting the bill."

Clearly taken aback, Dirk cleared his throat. "Let's all sit down, shall we? We can work this out."

"I do not think Walker can be convinced, Dirk." Jasmine's tone was coolly amused. "From what I remember he does not like to listen to reason."

His gaze narrowed. "No offense, sugar, but I don't happen to have a death wish. And going into a terrorist stronghold with a woman of your, uh, *experience* doesn't exactly fill me with confidence." He was gratified to see her lovely cheeks flush with reaction to his innuendo. She glared at him.

"Now, Walker...surely you haven't held a grudge all this time just because Jasmine outmaneuvered you the last time the two of you met up."

Dirk's voice, damn him, was amused. But then, he would only know about the mission that had pitted Walker and Jasmine against each other, not about their brief relationship. Walker was in no mood to enlighten the other man. "I don't need her. I can do the job alone."

"No, you can't." Gesturing Jasmine to a chair, Dirk waited for her to be seated before sitting beside her. The fact that Walker remained standing didn't seem to bother him in the least. "It's taken some very delicate negotiation to hammer out a plan with Sheik Ahmed Kamal. He's touchy and has never made any secret of his distrust of westerners. He'd never agree to having this operation rest solely in the hands of an American."

Knowing that Dirk was right didn't make the words any more palatable. Walker paced, hands jammed into his pockets. The sheik's bias against the western world was well known, and second only in intensity to his distrust of King Marcus. Walker was rapidly getting a sense of finality about this whole thing. But that didn't stop him from trying one last time. "You can get someone else to take her place then. Preferably someone with a few more years in the field than she has."

"That's not possible. Sheik Kamal has already approved

Jasmine for the job. In fact, he seemed quite pleased that she would be included.''

''Another sucker duped by your charms, Jaz?'' It was nasty and low, but at the moment Walker was feeling nasty, and he was feeling low.

''I had the privilege of staying at the sheik's home as a guest of his daughter, Leila, just last year.'' Jasmine's words were even, her gaze unwavering. ''He is a man of great pride. It will be difficult for him to remain in Tamir while others fight what he believes to be his battles. I think we must handle him with care.''

''Jasmine's right. And if you'd stop prowling around the room, and listen, you'll understand why.'' Dirk waited until Walker took a seat before continuing. ''We've suggested to Sheik Kamal that he pretend to send a dignitary to Maloun to hammer out an accord between the prime minister there and Kamal's country. According to our sources, the government is little more than a front—the Brothers of Darkness hold the real power. Once there, you'll arrange for the prime minister to introduce you to the rebel faction leaders and get yourselves invited to their stronghold under the guise of completing the negotiations.''

The explanation sounded a death knell for Walker's hope to have Jasmine replaced on this mission. ''Don't tell me. She's going to play the part of the dignitary.''

Dirk inclined his head. ''Exactly. With her coloring and background she's admirably suited to the job. You'll go along as her driver and personal assistant. While Jasmine engages the leaders in the phony trade talks, you'll be searching the grounds for information about the location of the virus.''

Walker considered the idea. The thought of playing servant to Jasmine wasn't especially appealing, but he'd be the primary engaged in the search, so he supposed he could live with the situation.

He glanced at her, observed the knowing tilt of her lush lips. She expected him to refuse, he realized; expected his pride and ego to make the decision for him. Since he had an ample supply of both, perhaps it was a reasonable assumption.

And it certainly wouldn't be the first time that Jasmine LeBarr had misjudged him.

"It could work," he conceded, and paused a moment to enjoy her expression of consternation before addressing Dirk again. "Developing an anthrax virus is a huge undertaking for a Third World country like Maloun. How do we know the Brothers are developing the virus themselves? They could have contracted the job out."

Dirk was shaking his head before Walker had finished speaking. "Our government gathers intelligence on all countries and groups who try to produce deadly biological agents. The few who have been successful are monitored very carefully. None of them has ties with Maloun, and we're guessing the Malounians wouldn't make those kinds of inquiries and risk having their plans leak out. No, they're directly involved in the development. We know they haven't lacked for money. A man by the name of Amin Qadir was recently arrested. It's suspected he was one of the major sources of funding for the group. The only questions remaining are how far along the virus is and where the work·is being done."

"The development of this virus you speak of, Dirk, would require highly skilled scientists, would it not?" Jasmine's smoky voice curled through Walker's senses and had an immediate, unwelcome affect on his hormones. He found the involuntary response damn irritating. "They would need technical equipment, expensive supplies..."

''They have to have a lab somewhere,'' Walker concluded flatly. Oddly restless, he rose again to cross to Dirk's desk. Leaning against it, he surveyed the other two. ''And their little venture is taking some big financing.''

Nodding, the older man said, ''The Brothers of Darkness would be the only group in the country powerful enough to provide all of those. You'll have to go through them to locate the virus. Once you do, I want you to confiscate it, then get the hell out of the country.'' A flicker of concern crossed his face before it was smoothed away. ''The group is known for being particularly brutal with those who cross them. A couple of years ago it was rumored that one their members was thought to be selling information on the group to the Pakistani government. He vanished, only to show up a month or so later on the palace grounds, disemboweled.''

Silence stretched, thick and elastic. Walker appreciated the man's warning, but it wouldn't change the outcome of this meeting. He'd been committed the moment Dirk had contacted him. ''When do we start?''

''Immediately. As soon as I contact Kamal he'll send his private jet for you. You'll have time to go out and pick up anything you think you might need.'' His handsome face creased with a surprisingly youthful smile. ''And if there are any odds and ends that you're lacking for the job, I can probably supply them.''

Walker was well aware of the *odds and ends* Dirk kept in his warehouse of high-tech gadgetry. He wouldn't mind taking a look. The man had an incredible knack for getting his hands on tools still in the prototype stage. ''I can be ready.'' He sent a lazy glance Jasmine's way. ''How about you?''

If she'd been affected by Dirk's warning, it didn't show in her expression. Her gaze met his in a silent challenge before turning to the older man. "I am sure Kamal is anxious for your call. There is no need to make him wait any longer."

Slapping his hands on his knees, Dirk rose, and after a moment, she followed suit. "I'll do it right now. Then the three of us can relax and catch up for a few hours. If you'll excuse me for a few minutes?"

Walker waited until the man had strode out the door before focusing on Jasmine. She was, if anything, lovelier than the last time he'd seen her. The scarlet suit she wore showcased her endless legs and hugged her generous breasts. She still wore her long thick hair straight and loose to swing around her shoulders. He remembered how it felt draped across his chest; wrapped around his fingers. And because the memory burned, he gave her a mocking smile.

"Red's a good color on you, Jaz. You should wear it often."

She lifted an elegant brow. "Compliments, Walker? I do not remember that you were so flattering the last time we spoke."

"Yeah, I was hard on you." Hands still in his pockets, he strolled over to her, noted her almost imperceptible reaction when he deliberately invaded her space. At five foot nine she was five inches shorter than him, and he dwarfed her when he stood this close. She was incredibly feminine, with a delicate bone structure. It was an effective disguise for a woman trained to kill a man in half a dozen different ways.

But her real danger would come not from her skills but her ability to get people to trust her. To underestimate her. Then when she turned out to be something far different from what they expected, she had the element of surprise. He could attest that she used the quality to her advantage.

He crooked a finger, ran his knuckle lightly along her

delicate jaw. "I shouldn't have said those things back then. I was angry."

Her eyes flickered warily, and this time she did take a step backward. He followed, maintaining the contact. Intent. Predatory. His thumb skated lightly across her lips. He felt each word as she formed it.

"You were furious."

"Yes." The word was a whisper of a sound uttered only inches from her mouth.

She moistened her lips. "You are still angry."

Walker cupped her face with both hands and brushed his lips against hers. Once. Twice. Again. "Do I seem angry to you?"

Her fingers locked around his wrists. When his mouth settled against hers, her grip tightened but she didn't push him away. He pressed her lips open and let her sweet unique flavor race through his system and fire his blood. When he traced the sensitive inner seam of her lips he was reminded of the silkiness of her mouth and dove deeper. He stroked her tongue with his, forcing her to respond to him. And when she did, when her fingers turned caressing on his wrists and her mouth opened avidly under his, he lifted his lips from hers to murmur, "No, I'm not angry. There's no point. You can't help what you are."

He toyed with the ends of her hair as he waited for his words to register. But then her eyes fluttered open, the look in them dazed, drugged, and lust punched him hard in the gut. And when comprehension chased those feelings away, a deeply primal part of him mourned.

"What…" He distracted her from her words by dropping a kiss at the corner of her mouth. "And what am I?"

"An opportunist." His lips skimmed the curve of her cheek. "A woman who'll go to any lengths to get what she wants." He felt her tense and with a twist had his hands free to capture her wrists before she could use her nails on him. "Hell, you're not the first woman to use sex to get what she wants. Guess I should be grateful you screwed me literally as well as figuratively."

She was faster than he remembered. He easily dodged her swiftly raised knee, but not the stomp on his instep. Even as he winced he was grasping both her wrists in one hand before she could try to flip him over her back, and yanked her closer to defuse the danger.

They were pressed together, legs, hips, chests; a solid length of heat pulsing between them. Even now he knew better than to underestimate her. "Still carry that stiletto around your thigh?" Without waiting for an answer, Walker slipped a hand under her skirt, skimmed his fingers over her silky leg and found the weapon strapped around it. She tossed her head, glaring at him murderously. Old grudges couldn't lessen his appreciation of the picture she made with storms brewing in her dark eyes. "You always did have a temper, Jaz."

"And always you had the head of a pig."

He interpreted her insult with very little difficulty. "I may be pigheaded, but I'm not stupid." With no little reluctance he removed his hand from her thigh. "I know how you operate now, and I'm putting you on alert. You'll do things my way in Maloun. An assignment like this can have only one leader, and it's going to be me." Watching the mutinous expression settle over her face, he gave her a slight shake. "I mean it. We can't be pulling in two different directions. We're going to have to come to some terms."

"As usual the terms must be yours. I understand exactly."

He might have believed her if her voice wasn't so defiant. As it was, he had the distant observation that her

accent still became more pronounced when she was upset.
"I'm the one who's going to be taking most of the risks.
I have to be able to call the shots."

"We will work as a team, as Dirk hired us to do." Her
eyes flashed at him. "You must learn to control your temper and your ego if we are to be successful."

She pulled away and he let her go. There could be nothing more accomplished now, at any rate. Not with both of
them at each other's throats. But he'd made his point, so
he turned and headed for the door.

Before he walked through it, though, sheer deviltry had
him turning back again. "Oh, and Jaz?" He waited for her
to look at him before smiling mockingly. "You definitely
kissed me back."

Chapter 2

Jasmine hesitated outside the door of Walker's temporary quarters in Sheik Kamal's palace. She'd faced the leaders of an international smuggling ring with far more equanimity than she felt right now. She'd known those men were dangerous, that her life had been in jeopardy. She'd been comfortable relying on her own skills to ensure her safety. It was telling that she regularly risked her life without a qualm, but had to summon the courage to approach Walker in his bedroom.

The man was every bit as dangerous as any she'd brought down, but it wasn't her life she feared for around him, it was something far more fragile. He'd bruised her heart once with his callous dismissal of her. She'd never allow herself to be that vulnerable again.

The silent vow made it a bit easier to raise her hand, to rap on his door. She was disconcerted when he pulled open the door and she was confronted by his partially nude body.

Her gaze skated over his bare chest, then lowered to the jeans that rode low on his lean hips, unbuttoned to reveal his hard flat belly. Averting her gaze, she scrambled to summon a steady voice. "I can come back later."

"No, come on in. I could use your help."

Reluctantly she followed him into the room. It was a moment before she noted the fresh angry-looking scar running down the center of his back, only centimeters from his spine. A gasp escaped her before she could prevent it. "What happened?"

He didn't halt on his way to the adjoining bathroom. "After setting the explosives on the last job, a member of my team caught a bullet as we were pulling out. I dropped back to give him a hand, and we were still a little too close when it detonated."

His succinct summary was all the more chilling for its casual delivery. "You went back into a building that was set to explode?"

One large shoulder lifted in a shrug. "I'm responsible for my team."

Yes, she thought, nausea curling through her stomach, he would be responsible. Whatever else she thought of Walker James, she'd never doubted his skill. His dedication to the men who worked with him. Her eyes shifted back to the raised, puckered wound on his back. It wouldn't be the only physical reminder he carried of the danger he routinely courted. His body was a map of faded scars acquired in the act of carrying out various missions.

He was something of a legend in the shadowy world they shared. The Ghost, he was called, for his ability to slip in and out of seemingly impenetrable places. His skill with security was matched by a cunning that kept his services in high demand. Certainly his reputation had been part of her admiration for him, her pleasure when he'd shown an unmistakable interest that time in Venice.

She'd learned the hard way that he was just as skilled at slipping under personal defenses, as well. Of using his looks and personal magnetism to defuse normal wariness and invite intimacy far too quickly, far too blindly. She may not have completed a formal education, but she never needed to review the same lesson twice. And if she did, she had only to remember their parting in Venice. The memory still throbbed like a wound.

"Will you come here a minute?"

From the slight edge in his tone, she realized he'd had to repeat himself. She poked her head in the bathroom to find him standing in front of the sink, his hair freshly doused.

"Put this ointment on my back, would you? It's harder than hell for me to reach."

Jasmine hung back, strangely loathe to comply. "Where are the bandages? We could put the ointment on them and then cover the injury."

"Yeah, that's what I was doing, but I'm not going to wear the bandages anymore. Too much trouble."

She opened her mouth, then closed it again. It would do no good to argue with him. She'd learned long ago that he had a will of iron. There was probably no real danger even if the wound didn't remain sterile. Against the stubborn blood that flowed through his veins, an infection wouldn't stand a chance.

Aware that he was watching her in the mirror, she approached and took the tube he held. With more concentration than the act required, she squeezed out a generous amount and applied it to his wound.

His muscles tensed under her touch. It was an effort to keep her mind firmly in the present and away from the time when her hands had roamed his body freely, with an eagerness that still had the power to embarrass her. She struggled to keep her face impassive as she completed the task, then stepped away. Noting a bowl beside the sink filled with an unfamiliar substance, she asked him about it.

"It's coloring." Even as he spoke he scooped up some of the stuff and rubbed it over his wet hair carelessly. "I'm going to lighten my hair for the assignment. It washes out in less than two weeks. That should give us enough time."

Studying the glop he was working into the strands, she said, "Perhaps I should do the same."

"It isn't necessary. You're expected to pass as a native of Tamir. Your coloring is perfect for this job."

He was right, of course. It also made it difficult for her to change her appearance for each assignment. She had to rely on discreetly applied makeup to add subtle lines, to alter her jawline. Maloun was a highly conservative society with little evidence of western influence. The traditional dress she would be required to wear lent ample opportunity to alter her body type. She'd have to rely on those techniques to mar an accurate description of her.

"I mean, I could change my hair. Perhaps cut it before we leave."

"No!"

The vehemence in that single word startled her. Her gaze met his in the mirror. But his voice was nonchalant enough when he explained, "Women have the advantage of being able to just pull their hair up to achieve a different look. Believe me, sweetheart, your hair is going to be the last thing any man concentrates on."

While she struggled with his meaning, Jasmine watched Walker cover the hair on his arms with the same mixture, then apply it to his chest. The matching color would make his alteration all the more convincing. She noted the face he made as he rubbed the stuff on his torso. "Wouldn't it be easier to just shave the hair off?"

One side of his mouth lifted. "Easier? Yeah. But the only time I tried that I almost went nuts while it was growing back. It itched like crazy. I've decided this is more work, but much more comfortable later."

He bent over the tub that was easily large enough to host a small dinner party, and turned on the gold-plated taps. With his head shoved under the faucet he said, "Get me a couple towels and washcloths, will you?" She did so, then returned to the bedroom. There was something much too cozy about watching the man engage in his preparations. Their assignment was complicated enough by their previous brief relationship. There would be no place for emotion in this job.

She distracted herself by studying the quarters he'd been given. It was opulent, like the rest of the palace, with a huge lake of a bed covered with rumpled satin sheets. Pillows lay strewn around it. Walker liked to sleep sprawled out, she recalled. At least he had in the little time they'd spent sleeping their one night together. Although she'd awakened to find herself close to the edge of the bed, she'd been in no danger of falling from it. He'd been holding her much too closely for that.

To shake the memories from her mind, she crossed to the large desk. Its top was strewn with papers and maps. When he rejoined her minutes later she was absorbed in them.

Without turning around she folded a map over to reveal the one beneath. "How will we travel to Maloun?" While she'd spent every hour they'd been in Tamir trying to learn as much of that country's history as possible, Walker had been taking care of the physical details of the assignment.

"The sheik's jet will fly us to Redyshah, the capital city. That's where the prime minister's quarters are located." He stepped to her side, indicated a spot on the map. "The airport is in the northernmost part of the city. One of our operatives will have a car waiting for us, outfitted with some supplies I ordered."

She nodded. "You will have ample opportunity to demonstrate your skills as my driver. I hope you are up to the challenge. As your passenger, I will have very exacting standards."

Her attempt to needle him failed. He merely crowded closer to her, reached to flip a map over. "I'll be at your service, Jaz. In whatever areas you require."

He was tantalizing her intentionally. The knowledge was the only thing that kept her from moving away. She was unwilling to display even that slight hint of weakness. Studying the maps, she gave every indication of ignoring him. Maloun was Tamir's closest neighbor, located on the nearby Arabian Peninsula. The northern and central parts of the country, she noted, appeared mostly desert, with the country growing hillier where it was edged by water. She wondered in what part of the country the Brothers were housed.

In a movement she hoped seemed casual, she turned, faced him. "When do we leave?"

"A few hours." He'd lightened his brows, too, she observed. He would probably also wear contacts to change the color of his eyes. She wondered if it ever seemed odd to him that while other men put on a suit and tie to go to work, he had to become someone else entirely.

But that thought was quickly followed by another. She couldn't see Walker James wearing pinstripes and keeping banker's hours. There was something much too elemental, too primitive about him for that. He would be attracted to danger, to excitement. If he hadn't turned to espionage, he'd be engaged in something else just as risky.

"Let's go over our covers again."

She stifled a sigh. They'd been over their stories so often she could repeat hers backward. "My name is Rose Mahrain. My father was the Tamir ambassador to America and we divided our time between Washington, D.C., and Tamir. My husband was also in government, until his death two years ago. When Sheik Kamal offered me a diplomatic post, I eagerly accepted. This will be my first assignment out of the country, and I am naturally anxious to do well." As was usually the case, the cover could be substantiated, at least on the surface. If an inquiry was conducted, it would be discovered that the details corresponded exactly with a woman by that name, who had been sent out of the country for the course of this assignment. Except the real Rose Mahrain had been offered no such post.

As Englishman John Logan, Walker, too would have a cover that would withstand scrutiny. She found herself anticipating the character he would adopt, complete with accent.

"How did your husband die?"

The continued questioning annoyed her. She was not a schoolchild reciting a memorized lesson for a critical teacher, although she'd certainly repeated this one for Walker often enough. A hint of mischief seized her. "He died in bed." Her improvisation earned her a narrowed look. "I am a woman of great...needs. I pleasured him to death."

There was a long pregnant pause. "Stick to the script," Walker advised finally. "This job is going to be complicated enough without you being deliberately provocative. You may get a response you hadn't counted on."

"I have no intention of provoking a response from our targets!"

"I was talking about me."

Her throat abruptly went dry. There was an all too familiar heat in his eyes that she hadn't meant to ignite. This tension between them was causing her to act out of character. In every job she prided herself on her ability to remain cool. But something about Walker brought out an unfamiliar impulsivity. The last time she'd given in to those impulses, she'd gotten badly burned in the process. She'd do well to remember that the next time she was tempted to drag a response from him.

To distract them both, she rounded the desk to cross to the window. "What have you learned about the prime minister?"

"His name is Hosni El-Dabir. He's a career politician, so he'll be well acquainted with Sheik Ahmed Kamal and his family, even though the two countries don't have much to do with each other. If he brings up a subject you aren't completely familiar with, you'd be better off to admit ignorance. He'll know if you bluff."

"Thank you so much for the advice," she said with mock politeness. "I do not know how I manage without your wisdom on other assignments."

Still wearing a slight frown, he looked at her. "Don't get bitchy, Jaz. I'm not belittling your ability, just giving you some facts. This thing isn't going to work if we're at each other's throats all the time."

Since she had thought much the same, she was ready to agree with him. Perhaps even to suggest some sort of truce. But the suggestion he made next drove all other thoughts from her mind. She gaped at him, doubting she'd heard correctly. "What did you say?"

"I said maybe we should just spend an hour or two in

bed and get it out of our systems." When she couldn't seem to manage an answer, he went on. "Sexual tension can be a distraction, one we don't need. A couple of hours burning up the sheets would go a long way toward relieving that."

She couldn't remember ever being propositioned quite so passionlessly. The offhand crudity left her speechless. But in the middle of summoning a blistering retort, she caught the flicker of anticipation in his eyes. He wanted a reaction from her, she realized. *Any* reaction.

So instead of giving him the response he was looking for, she merely arched a brow. He'd never know what her cool, mildly amused tone cost her. "I am afraid I must turn down your charming proposition. One night with you was more than enough." She turned and made her way to the door. "I will be ready to leave in two hours. We can meet at the front doors." Her hand was on the knob when she paused and looked at him over her shoulder. "Oh, and Walker? You could never be a distraction to me. My taste for loutish Americans was completely erased three years ago."

She pulled open the door, sailed through it with queenly grace. The only thing that marred her departure was knowing that he watched her exit with a satisfied smile still on his lips.

"Madame Mahrain." The Maloun prime minister lingered over her hand, addressing her in Arabic. "It is an honor and a great pleasure to have you visit our nation."

"The pleasure is mine, sir. What I have seen of your country so far is very impressive." Jasmine answered in the same language, that of her birth. Walker hung back circumspectly. "May I present my assistant, John Logan? I'm afraid he only speaks English."

In heavily accented English, El-Dabir turned to Walker and said, "Welcome to our country. I hope you enjoy your stay."

"Thank you, sir." Walker's tone was respectful, with a clipped British accent. He remained at Jasmine's elbow, a couple steps behind her, in a position of silent deference. She wondered if it was the first time in his life that he'd acted deferential to anyone, even if it was feigned.

She would never have believed the difference he could manage in his appearance. She'd been prepared for the lighter hair, the contacts that changed his piercing blue eyes to a nondescript hazel. Like her, he'd placed slim cotton pads inside his cheeks to alter the shape of his face. But the alteration went beyond the obvious. The black loose-fitting shirt and trousers he'd chosen were a size too big. He stood with his shoulders slightly rolled, his chin tucked. Little details taken by themselves, but together they gave him the look of a man inches shorter, many pounds lighter. His manner suggested a lowly government employee whose demeanor was light-years away from that of the confidently arrogant Walker James.

El-Dabir led them down a graciously wide hallway into a large airy room. It was furnished with a lovely piano in one corner, with chairs and couches scattered throughout the rest of the space. As Jasmine and Walker seated themselves on one of the overstuffed couches, the prime minister summoned a servant and issued an order for tea. Then he returned to his guests and sat on a chair facing them.

"I trust your trip was pleasant."

"Sheik Kamal's jet is quite comfortable. Far more luxurious than I am used to." As she spoke, Jasmine studied her host surreptitiously. Hosni El-Dabir did not look like a career politician, she mused. As most Maloun males, the prime minister wore a traditional *jellaba*. He'd donned a jacket over the hooded loose-fitting robe, and a *kaffiyeh* covered his head. His nose was flat, as though it had been misshapen in a brawl. He had the square body of a boxer, and his dark gaze had a way of sliding over her face rather than focusing on it. In contrast, his hands were well-manicured, the skin surprisingly smooth when he'd touched hers. If Maloun had an American equivalent of the syndicate, she could have easily pictured him at its helm.

"The sheik hopes you will forgive him for sending an emissary for this very important meeting. Problems at home require his attention."

El-Dabir nodded. "Please convey our regrets to Ahmed Kamal. We pray for his son's safe return."

The prime minister's tone was ingratiating. Jasmine wondered just how much, if anything, El-Dabir knew about the young sheik's disappearance. Dirk hadn't mentioned any such relationship between the two, but it seemed coincidental that Rashid would disappear around the same time that Maloun was preparing a strike against his country. Resolving to question Walker about it later, she said, "Sheik Kamal was eager to make a start in negotiating a trade agreement with your country." Falling silent as a male servant carried in a tray, Jasmine waited until the tea had been served before continuing. "It is no secret that tensions between Tamir and Montebello have increased. The sheik would like to build a relationship with Tamir's other neighbors." She paused to sip at her tea, giving the prime minister time to digest her words. He would believe Kamal anxious to gather allies, in case war broke out with Montebello. It was exactly the impression she'd hoped to give.

"A good neighbor is to be highly valued."

"Indeed. And there are many advantages for both sides

when trust is not an issue. Tamir always welcomes new trading partners, especially those countries who do not embrace the western culture.''

El-Dabir smiled, obviously pleased at the prospect. ''Talk of such an alliance is intriguing. I have acquaintances, very powerful men in our country, who share my goals for the future of Maloun. I have arranged a small dinner party in your honor for this evening, so that you may become acquainted with them and their wives.''

A leap of excitement shot through her veins, but Jasmines voice was merely polite when she answered. ''It would be a pleasure. Any avenue to further our countries' accord would be welcomed.''

El-Dabir nodded, pursing his lips. ''I feel certain Tamir and Maloun can come to an agreement. I appreciate your candor and look forward to further conversations with you on this subject.'' He smiled, resembling a crocodile showing its teeth. ''Although I must say, it is never a hardship to converse with a beautiful woman, Madame Mahrain, whatever the topic.''

Jasmine smiled, averting her gaze demurely. ''Please. You must call me Rose.''

When she was shown to her room, Jasmine unpacked leisurely, then set her purse on the small dressing table and withdrew her lipstick. Methodically she outlined her lips, colored them. A barely audible beep sounded. Without reacting, she replaced the lipstick cover, then trailed to the window, looking out at the view. There was another tiny beep. When she turned and crossed to the bed she heard yet another.

The room was bugged.

A miniscule sensor hidden in the bottom of her lipstick case was sensitive enough to pick up the presence of any security device available. Her casual trip around the room picked up a hidden camera behind the mirror, and two bugs. Her host was obviously not the trusting sort. She wondered if the devices had been planted in anticipation of her visit, or whether every guest was treated to this type of hospitality. She rather thought it was the latter.

There was a knock at her door. When she opened it she found Walker, carrying a notepad. "Would you care for a walk in the courtyard before we get ready for dinner, madame?"

With a murmur of acceptance, Jasmine preceded him down the hallway. Once downstairs they made their way to the courtyard they'd admired on the quick tour the prime minister had given them.

They didn't speak until they were outside. Walker reached for a slim gold pen in his shirt pocket, asking, "I trust your room is comfortable?"

"Yes. And yours?" During the innocuous conversation they strolled slowly through the bricked courtyard. Stone benches were situated near fountains and statues. She listened carefully, heard the telltale sounds emitted from the top of Walker's pen as they passed the center fountain. She paused as if admiring it, wondering where the detected listening device was hidden. Somewhere near the heavy marble base, she imagined.

Moving slowly, they covered the courtyard, finding other bugs located on several of the benches. Again she was struck with the paranoia the devices suggested. It wasn't until they reached the far end of the courtyard that looked out over a short wall to the busy street beyond that Walker deemed it safe to speak freely.

"Distrustful bastard, isn't he?" His voice was very nearly soundless as he appeared to study the people on the street.

"Are you certain we are out of range?"

"Planting so many of them in such a limited area suggests that each has a limited capability. Chances are they've been here for years." He looked down at the notebook he carried, as if to consult notes jotted down there. "At one time I'll bet every bench was bugged so our host could keep tabs on his guests' private conversations."

"Charming," she murmured, letting her gaze roam the area. "My room is similarly equipped."

"Mine, too. We have to figure the whole place is loaded with them."

She wished she'd remembered to retrieve the sunglasses from her purse. The afternoon sun was brutal. "We will have to be sure and not disappoint the prime minister. It would be a shame if all his eavesdropping were for nothing."

Walker didn't smile but his face lightened a fraction. "When the time comes, I'll follow your lead."

Her lips curved slightly. "That will be a welcome change, and another first for you." As soon as the words were out of her mouth she wished them back.

The mirrored lenses of his glasses made it impossible to tell what he was thinking, until his voice came, low and intimate. "Maybe you've forgotten a time when I was all too happy to let you set the pace." Memories washed over her like a warm caress, evoked by his sensual tone. "I put myself into your very capable hands then and found you to be slow, but...thorough."

Because her hands suddenly had a tendency to tremble, she clutched them together. The mental images his words elicited were vivid, graphic. There was nothing quite so sexy as a man who would lie back and let a woman explore his body, and Walker had made no secret of the pleasure he'd found when she'd done so. Venice may have been three years ago, but the memories weren't buried nearly deeply enough.

To hide their effect on her, she turned away, pretended an interest in the bustle in the street in front of them. She'd be ill-advised to let Walker think he could disconcert her with one well-placed reference to the past. "Ancient history does not interest me. I am more focused on our present assignment." It gave her a chance to change the subject, so she asked the question that had been bothering her earlier. "Do you think El-Dabir and the Brothers know anything about the young sheik's disappearance?"

Sending her a sharp look, Walker asked, "What makes you ask?"

Jasmine shrugged. "It seems odd that he would vanish around the same time the Brothers are trying to heighten the strife between the two countries."

"I thought of that, too. If the Brothers did snatch him, maybe we'll discover some trace of their actions when we get inside the compound." He sent a glance back toward the prime minister's quarters. "Actually getting us inside the Brothers' headquarters is going to be up to you. Any ideas yet about how you'll accomplish it?"

"That will depend in a large part on the events tonight, and how the talks progress with the prime minister." She paused, smiling as a pair of young children darted by, chasing a dog bigger than both of them. "El-Dabir wasn't what I expected."

"He's little more than a hired thug." Walker propped his elbows on the low wall, their shoulders brushing. "In a country as uncivilized as this one, a man doesn't hold office as long as he has without having some very interesting acquaintances."

"Acquaintances affiliated with the Brothers of Darkness."

He nodded. "I'd be surprised if some of its members weren't among the guests at the dinner tonight. If our information is correct, then leaders of the group run the country, and El-Dabir. No agreement would be made with Tamir without their involvement." As her lowly assistant, it was understood that he would excuse himself shortly after dinner, leaving the invited guests to mingle. "If you do more listening than talking this evening, you'll get a better..."

He must have seen the expression on her face, because he cut his words short. "But I don't want to tell you how to do your job."

"Yes, you do. And quite frequently." But she was finding that habit of his far less provocative than his frequent reminders of the time they'd spent together. "I will be more than willing to listen to your advice if I am allowed to tell you what you should do while the party is going on."

"Point taken," he responded dryly. "You tend to your business tonight and I'll tend to mine. We can compare notes tomorrow, unless it's urgent. Do you know where my room is?"

She nodded and looked away, feigning an interest in a nearby street vendor displaying his wares to some Malounian women. A situation would have to be urgent indeed to convince her to go to Walker's bedroom in the middle of the night. Jasmine had a strong commitment to duty, but her sense of self-preservation was equally powerful. She could imagine few scenarios so critical that she could be convinced to approach the man while he was in bed.

The color she felt rising to her cheeks could be blamed on the afternoon heat. It would be more comfortable to believe that she was indifferent to him. Until a day ago she'd almost convinced herself that she was. But an innate sense of honesty forced her to admit, at least to herself, that indifference was the last thing she felt for him.

And therein lay the real danger of this assignment.

Chapter 3

The dinner party was to be formal. Although Walker was most comfortable in the basic black worn for breaking and entering, he had packed a dark suit jacket and tie. He wore it now, as he lingered in a corner of the gathering room, observing the steady trickle of guests entering the prime minister's home. Most of the them wore traditional Maloun garb—flowing white robes for the men and brightly colored caftans for the women.

The presence of the females at the dinner gave the appearance that this was purely a social event, but Walker knew differently. Where politicians were involved, socializing *was* business. Some of his most lucrative tips had been picked up at parties much like this one.

But it would be Jasmine's job to elicit whatever interesting information was to be had tonight. After dinner, he had other matters requiring his attention.

Of its own volition, his gaze sought her out now, standing in the center of a small crowd, smiling brilliantly at a swarthy man who was bending over her hand.

The kick in the stomach he experienced at the sight was most easily blamed on the bitter tea he was drinking. In her brilliant blue caftan she resembled an exquisitely crafted Madonna he'd once stolen from the Boston home of a wealthy shipping magnate. The memory filled him with something close to nostalgia. The piece was one of the few fruits of his earlier career that he still owned. He knew he'd never look at it again without thinking of Jasmine.

She'd done something to her eyes before this trip to disguise their shape. The makeup made the upper lids look heavier, as though she'd recently climbed out of a man's bed.

The thought brought him no pleasure. He, better than anyone, knew how deceptive her looks were. They were a tool, one she wielded with skill. Right now they seemed to be working quite effectively on the man who hadn't yet released her hand as he rattled off a spate of Arabic.

Gripping his cup more tightly, he tore his gaze away. The women had gathered on one side of the room, leaving the men and Jasmine on the other. Voices, conversations mingled, broken by an occasional burst of laughter. Walker found he was able to interpret much of what was said. Jasmine had been following the script when she told El-Dabir he spoke only English. Although not fluent in Arabic, he was able to understand quite a bit of it. He'd spent a fair amount of time in one Middle Eastern trouble spot or another.

He strolled closer to the group surrounding Jasmine. Pausing in front of a rather bad portrait of the prime minister, he pretended to admire it until they were all seated for dinner. Mentally he sifted through the snippets of conversations flowing around him.

"...until he is weaned, and then I shall..."

"...perhaps we will have to let him go. He no longer..."

"...not depart from what we discussed." Instinct had Walker's inner radar honing in more closely on the last sentence. With a skill born of long practice he ignored the rest of the talk and focused on the dialogue that had caught his interest.

"I will do exactly as instructed. You will not be disappointed."

Walker recognized El-Dabir's ingratiating tones, but the other voice belonged to a stranger. Not daring to turn around at the moment, he contented himself with listening.

"There should be no problem. She is only a woman."

Inwardly amused, he wondered what Jaz would have to say about the man's assessment. There was no doubt in Walker's mind that the conversation concerned her. People drifted by, making their way into the dining room, and he shifted closer to the pair of men, as if politely making room for the guests.

"...have a hand in his own destruction." The noise from the people passing by them had covered all but the last of the sentence. Walker found himself wondering just what he'd missed. The room was clearing out and there was no longer any reason to linger. He made his way into the next room and turned, scanning the area for an empty seat. From the corner of his eye he watched the men he'd been eavesdropping on as they entered. As he'd suspected, one was the prime minister and the other a short man in his mid-sixties with a weather-beaten face. He made a mental note to ask Jasmine about him later.

Even as Walker slipped into a seat at the end of the

table, El-Dabir's companion made his way to the table head. Jasmine sat across and down the table from Walker, flanked by the prime minister and a sleekly polished man on her left. Keeping his attention trained on the dishes placed in front of him, he listened carefully as the stranger monopolized Jasmine's attention.

"You are too young and beautiful to be a widow, Madame Mahrain. How long ago did your husband die?"

"Two years," Jasmine answered with just the right amount of sorrow in her tone. "He was killed in a car accident."

"Allow me to express my regret for your loss." The stranger reached out, stroked the back of her hand for an instant. "Had you been married long?"

Walker held his breath, but he needn't have worried. Jasmine had perfected her lines before they'd left Tamir. "We had been married for ten years, and engaged for two years before that." Her smile was hauntingly sad. A man would have to be made of granite not to respond. The stranger by her side, Walker noted, did not appear to be made of stone. He stared at her with an expression all too easy for another man to recognize.

The man leaned toward her, lowered his voice. "I hope I will have the opportunity to banish some of the sorrow I see in your beautiful eyes. I would like to show you some of our country before you leave."

"That is a kind offer, Mr. Abdul."

"Please." Again he touched her hand briefly, then reached for his tea, his gaze never leaving her. "You must feel free to call me Tariq."

Jasmine hesitated, her gaze dropping to her plate. "Tariq. I do not know that I will have any free time. The business that brings me to Maloun is very serious."

"In any business, madame, there must be time for pleasure.'' The man showed his teeth in a brilliant display, clearly unwilling to give up. He appeared to be a man used to getting what he wanted, Walker thought narrowly. People acquired that kind of confidence from money, position or power. He didn't know which fit Tariq Abdul, but he'd find out.

The voices from the guests were a distant hum. Walker paused outside the only door on the lower floor that he'd found locked. It was safe to presume it was the prime minister's study.

Keeping a careful eye out for lost guests or inquisitive servants, he withdrew the pen from his pocket and checked for security devices. He exchanged the pen for a thin, flexible length of wire, which he fed into the lock. After a couple of quick twists, a click was heard. Faintly irritated, he turned the knob and slipped into the room. When people made it so easy, it took the thrill right out of it.

Gloves, he'd found, could be hard to explain if someone happened by. The container of spray he'd brought along applied a thin layer of wax to fingers and palms, while allowing for greater dexterity.

He closed the door behind him and took out a small compact machine resembling the size of a pocket organizer. A press of a button had the two halves springing open, revealing a screen on one side and command keys on the other. One of Walker's newest acquisitions, it functioned as a combination scanner and computer. He switched it on and went to the desk.

The locks on the drawers were less of a challenge than the one on the door. Swiftly he withdrew the papers he found there, then dragged the screen over each, moving it left to right until the full sheet had been copied into the mini computer. Then he moved to the next. In less than

five minutes he was done. Replacing the materials, he re-
secured the locks and surveyed the room.

Surprisingly, there was no computer in sight. Maloun
wasn't a particularly advanced country, but Walker hadn't
expected a complete lack of technology in the room where
the prime minister conducted his business. He set his mini
computer on the desk and reached for a pocket flashlight.
Playing it along the walls and floor, he studied the area.
A man like El-Dabir would have secrets. And a man with
secrets must have a place to store them, if not in encrypted
computer files, then in something a little more traditional.

He found what he was looking for a few minutes later
when he moved a painting aside. The prime minister had
made up for his lack of imagination by installing a very
decent wall safe, with numbered tumblers. In his youth
Walker would have simply drilled it or used a small
amount of plastique. But his current career often called for
a bit more finesse. He didn't want El-Dabir to know that
his security had been breached. From the pouch fastened
around his waist, he withdrew another small bag and shook
out four pieces of curved metal. The devices were fairly
new; Dirk hadn't even had a set, and Walker knew the
man prided himself on having the best.

Carefully he arranged them to surround the dial. Mag-
netized, they clung to the metal face of the safe. But these
were no ordinary magnets. The pull of the specially constructed devices would interfere with the tumbler action,
scrambling the combination until the safe simply sprang
open. He swung the dial completely around clockwise,
then reversed the action. With only a few more manipu-
lations, the door swung outward.

Reaching for his pocket flashlight again, Walker surveyed the contents. There were more papers inside, and it

didn't take a rocket scientist to guess that these would be of more interest than the ones he'd found in the prime minister's desk. He copied each of them, then set them aside. There was a .357 Magnum, complete with holster and cartridges. His brows raised. El-Dabir believed in heavy firepower.

A small black notebook was in the back, so Walker withdrew it and copied each of its pages, then replaced it. A bundle of photos revealed that the prime minister had a penchant for porn. Those were the only objects in the safe, and all of them were perched atop some stacked bundles. Examining one of them, he gave a silent whistle. Each package was full of one hundred dollar bills, U.S. currency. And there were at least fifty packages.

It was late when Jasmine entered her room. Stripping off the caftan, she hung it on a hanger. Then with a sigh of relief, she unfastened the Velcro straps of the specially designed undergarment she wore.

It covered her from breasts to hips, and completely changed the shape of her body, flattening her chest and adding pounds to her middle. It was exceedingly hot and not very comfortable, but would effectively throw off any description of her. She slipped into a short silky nightgown and went to the adjoining bathroom to brush her teeth.

And nearly had a heart attack when a hand clapped over her mouth, pulling her hard against a solid masculine chest.

''Quiet.''

The word, breathed in her ear, was accompanied by a push to the door, shutting it. Only then was the hand removed from her mouth. Her elbow came out then, slamming into Walker's ribs. She was annoyed enough with him to be pleased by his hiss of pain.

"What are you doing in my bathroom?" Her words were whispered, but didn't lack vehemence.

"Getting the hell beat out of me, apparently. Turn on the shower. Cold water."

She did so, waited until the water was beating a solid spray, then turned around. He must have found, as she had, that there was no listening device planted in the bathroom, which wasn't surprising. The moisture in the air would have interfered with its functioning. The sound of the shower running was just a precaution. Walker was nothing if not careful.

He was still dressed as he'd been at dinner, and an unwelcome shiver chased down her spine. He had seemed to arouse no undue curiosity from the men at the dinner tonight, but he'd been the object of many surreptitious glances from the ladies. Being female herself, she could appreciate their interest. On a purely objective level, of course.

The solid black he'd chosen only accentuated the aura of sexuality he exuded. Other men wouldn't pick up on such a thing, but it was certain that women did. It was something that couldn't be disguised. She wondered if he was even aware of it, and then decided in the next instant that he was. He was entirely too confident around women for it to be otherwise.

"Here." He unfolded a small handheld machine and pressed a button. Instantly a screen display on one side lit up. "I want you to skim through these, see if any of it's important. It would take me all night to decipher the Arabic."

She took the machine from him, turning it one way and then another to examine it. "What is this?" she asked, marveling at the technology. She'd never seen anything like it.

He explained how it could copy documents, storing them for later retrieval. She was impressed, and said so. Her method of taking pictures of records to be blown up for later reading was a more time-consuming process.

"If I promise to get you one of your own, would you stop playing with it and get to work?"

She looked up at him in quick delight. "You will do that?"

He stared at her silently for a minute, then cleared his throat. "Yeah, but only if you quit talking and start interpreting."

Happily, Jasmine did as he requested. She had a deep and abiding appreciation for new gadgets, secondary only to her love for clothes. He showed her how to scroll down the screen and flip to the next document.

"Correspondence only," she said after a few minutes. "The first few appear to be from city officials of Redyshah regarding a public building being constructed." A moment later she said, "Here is a letter from a man named Ali bin-Sadin." Although he didn't make a sound, she felt Walker's reaction in the sudden tenseness of his body. She glanced up. "You know of this man?"

"He's a suspected terrorist from Yanda." The rogue nation was a known haven for terrorists acting against western nations. "What's it say?"

Jasmine scrolled down on the screen. "He thanks Hosni El-Dabir for his hospitality." She was silent a moment as she read on. "He says the sympathies of his group lie with Maloun and he is certain they can do business together again in the future." She considered for a moment. "Perhaps El-Dabir introduced the man to the Brothers of Darkness."

"Maybe. The prime minister might be lining up support for the action the Brothers are planning to take against

Tamir.'' She continued to flip through copies of the pages as he spoke. ''It's believed that bin-Sadin has a training camp somewhere in Yanda. He uses it to teach terrorist techniques to new recruits.''

But she was absorbed in the information on the screen. ''After the correspondence there are bank records.''

Interest sharpening his voice, Walker said, ''Probably from the safe I found. Where are the banks?''

''The Cayman Islands,'' she said after a moment. Her brows raised. ''Our host is a wealthy man. He has more than a half a million dollars in these accounts.''

''And another hundred grand of U.S. currency in his safe.''

''Either being a public servant in Maloun is very lucrative, or he is not above bribery.''

''Since he's only a puppet of the Brothers, I'd say his personal integrity is hardly in question,'' Walker said dryly. ''What else is on there?''

''The last few pages are names, followed by dates and U.S. dollar amounts. The period of time appears to be…'' She checked back a few pages, then flipped forward. ''Over the last five years.''

''Any names you recognize?''

''The largest amounts have one of two names beside them. The first is Bonlei Marakeh. He was here tonight.''

''Which one was he?''

''He was the last to arrive.''

''The guy who wouldn't let go of your hand when you were introduced?''

There was a note she couldn't identify in his voice. ''I believe the one you are thinking of was Ari Toudan. He was…attentive.''

''Yeah, I noticed he was especially attentive to your chest. Describe this Marakeh for me.''

"Five five or six, one hundred forty pounds, sixty to sixty-five years old."

"Leathery complexion—sat at the head of the table?" At her assent, Walker gave a satisfied nod. "I'm guessing he's affiliated with the Brothers. I overheard him and El-Dabir talking, and from the little I could make out, it sounded like the prime minister was taking orders from him."

Jasmine consulted the screen again. "The other name that appears here many times is that of Tariq Abdul."

"I figured that guy for a player."

The word had her furrowing her brow. "He plays?" Although she'd begun learning English at age ten, there were still too many terms and phrases she was not familiar with. Americans especially used the same words to mean many different things.

"I figure he's someone important in Maloun," he explained.

She thought about that. All of the guests this evening must be of some importance in the country, or El-Dabir would not have invited them. But none of the other names on the screen matched those of the guests. Only Marakeh and Abdul. "Abdul is, indeed, a player. Perhaps even a member of the Brothers of Darkness."

Interest sharpening his tone, Walker asked, "Did he say something tonight?"

"He didn't mention the organization directly, but he spent this evening trying to convince me of his importance." At his look, she gave a shrug. "It is what a man does when he tries to gain the attention of a woman." Another female would understand without explanation. "Several times he mentioned a group he belongs to, without ever naming it. Once he called it the voice of Maloun."

"From the intelligence we gathered, that claim would

fit the Brothers.'' Walker fell silent for a moment. ''Did he give you any indication whether he would be coming back here?''

She managed, barely, to avoid rolling her eyes. Men could be extremely obtuse, especially when it came to the behavior of their gender. ''He will be back.''

''How can you be so sure?''

Raising a brow, she merely looked at him. Something like amusement flickered across his face. ''Of course. I didn't mean to disparage your feminine charms, Jaz. Especially since I know from personal experience just how compelling they can be.''

If he was attempting to get a reaction from her, she was determined not to give it. ''I will make it clear to El-Dabir that I have reservations about the rebel faction in the country. If he is as eager to forge a bond with Tamir as I believe he is, he will try to convince me of the organization's harmlessness. I am certain that I can lead him to suggest a visit.''

''The sooner the better.''

His distracted tone should have warned her. In the next moment he reached out, touched her hair. ''Your pins are coming loose.''

Self-consciously she reached up, meaning to resecure them. Instead she was dismayed to feel him withdraw the pin, allowing a strand of hair to escape. The instant jolt of awareness that rocketed through her veins dismayed her. ''I'll do it.''

Ignoring her, he dropped the pin in her hand and reached for the next one.

''Stop.'' She tried to push his hand away, but he was immovable. Three more pins were loosened. More hair tumbled down. She tried to move away, but he shifted with her. The pins were pressed into her palm, and he reached for more.

She made the mistake of looking at his face. His expression was intense, absorbed. The expression of a man intent on mussing the woman he planned to take to bed. She'd seen the look on his face before. Knew what it meant.

She didn't want this, didn't want the memories of Venice slipping into her mind like stealthy little thieves. He'd seemed fascinated with her hair then, too, combing his fingers through it, smoothing it back from her face when she'd lain beneath him, shattered and limp.

Her pulse tripped once, and her heart did a slow, lazy spin in her chest. He was adept at this, she reminded herself wildly. He could switch from the cool, professional agent to the all too sensual male in the flash of an instant. He was equally adept at changing back, leaving her reeling with memories and unwelcome feelings that seemed to not touch him in the slightest.

"You need to leave." With a recklessness fueled by desperation, she reached up, withdrew the last few pins, then shook her head to toss her hair back into place. His gaze never left her, his eyes following every movement.

Little tongues of flame danced through her veins. The man had to do no more than look at her, touch her, and she was a mass of quivering nerve endings. The thought filled her with despair. Her reaction was fueled by guilty snippets of memories she couldn't control. Her body recognized the source of its pleasure, even as her mind rejected him.

"It's late." Anxious to escape, she shoved past him. "And the water has been running for too long already. You need to leave before someone comes to investigate."

"Who? The prime minister? His quarters are on the

other side of the building. And there are no servants who live here that I've discovered.''

''I don't care. I want you out of here!''

''Why, Jaz?'' With his hands on her hips he pulled her back against him, and his mouth went to her shoulder. ''Are you afraid of what might happen if we're alone together too long?''

She shivered under his lips. His fingers burned through the thin silk of her nightgown, branding her flesh. ''This is a stupid risk. We know there are bugs in the other room....''

''So you'd have to be quiet this time.'' The combination of his words and his warm breath caressing her skin had a shudder working through her. She could hear the hint of humor in his voice. ''We both would.''

''No!'' She pulled away and whirled to face him. His expression abruptly shuttered. ''I think we can both agree that last time was a mistake. It is one I will not make again.''

''It doesn't have to be a mistake this time. We'd both know what to expect.''

Her lips twisted at his response. ''And what would that be, Walker? Should I expect to rise in the morning from the bed of my lover and return to an angry stranger making vicious accusations?''

''No accusations. No anger,'' he said carefully. ''We'd both go into this with our eyes wide open.''

And therein lay the heart-rending pain of it. He couldn't have said more plainly that there was nothing between them but sex, a basic physical need that he could appease with anyone. At any time.

''I do not think so.'' Her indifferent tone would have done an actress proud. ''I have grown a bit more discriminating since we parted. And it is far less complicated to

choose lovers who are not involved in our jobs, is it not?''
Without waiting for an answer, she went to her bag on the
counter, took out a hairbrush. As she pulled it through her
hair, her gaze met his in the mirror. Her hand faltered.
Banked emotion was apparent in his eyes. The new colored
contacts couldn't disguise the familiar piercing intensity.

Then, so quickly that she wondered if she'd imagined
it, the moment passed and his expression went guarded
once again. ''If you plan to stick to your new formula for
selecting lovers, you'll want to tone down your come-on
to Abdul. He doesn't strike me as a guy who needs a whole
lot of encouragement. And from what I saw tonight, you
were giving him plenty of that.''

He could elicit flash points of emotion from her, dragging her from one to the other with almost dizzying speed.
Her fingers clenched around the handle of the brush. She
longed to throw it at his arrogant head. ''You can go to
the hellfire.'' The amused lift to the corner of his mouth
at her mangled English was like throwing gasoline on a
flame. Her cursing was much more fluent in Arabic, so she
reverted to her native language. From the way his brows
skimmed upward, she knew he'd correctly interpreted at
least part of her words.

''Calm down. I'm going. Don't lock the window on the
south side while we're here.''

She pressed her lips together in an effort to regain control. ''Why?''

''Because that's how I get in.'' Before she could react,
he crooked a finger and ran a careless knuckle over the
curve of her cheek. ''Dream of me, Jaz.''

His exit stemmed any rejoinder she might have made.
Dropping the brush, she gripped the edge of the sink with
both hands, battling the welter of emotions crashing and
colliding inside her. With short, jerky movements, she

yanked off her nightgown and stepped under the shower's frigid spray.

The icy needles of water raised shivers and chills but did nothing to douse the heat that Walker had torched deep inside her. She was very much afraid that there wasn't enough cold water in the hemisphere to do that.

Chapter 4

"The talks have been progressing well." Jasmine strolled alongside Walker in the courtyard, purposefully lingering close to the listening devices. "Prime minister El-Dabir has been quite enthusiastic about forging an alliance between Tamir and Maloun. I believe Sheik Kamal will be pleased at some of the trade prospects we've discussed."

In his role as her assistant, Walker kept a respectful distance from her. But Jasmine was aware of his presence as never before. From his manner toward her in the time since, one would never suspect that he had climbed through her window two nights ago; that he'd suggested they give in to the passion that still simmered between them. No, he was firmly in character. It was a matter of pride that she appear the same.

"The development of another ally at such an uncertain time would be a relief to the sheik."

"Of course you are right. With an enemy country on

one side, Tamir must have friends surrounding its other shores. The sheik does not wish to leave his country vulnerable.''

''It sounds as though you've almost finished your negotiations here.'' Walker slipped on some sunglasses to shield himself from the blinding sun, and steered Jasmine to a bench beneath a bit of shade. ''Are you ready to return and report to Kamal?''

Jasmine settled on the bench, aware of the bug planted beneath it. She was more willing than she'd like to admit to get out of the sun. The heavy garment she wore beneath her caftan was stifling in the heat. ''I am not yet convinced that I can suggest to Kamal that he enter into an agreement with Maloun.''

''Because of the rebel faction in the country?''

''The Brothers of Darkness, yes. Each time I broach the subject, the prime minister assures me that the group is harmless. An organization more patriotic than dangerous.''

''You don't believe that?'' Walker was as good as his word on the day of their arrival. He was following her lead in the conversation; she only hoped El-Dabir acted on the misinformation.

''I do not know what to believe. But I cannot do the sheik the dishonor of suggesting an alliance, unless I can assure myself that The Brothers represent no threat. It will be my duty to voice my reservations to Kamal.''

''Of course, if you are unsure about the Brothers, there is little else you can do.''

Having laid the groundwork, Jasmine smoothly changed the subject. ''At any rate, my job here is nearly done. Did you make the changes to the car that I spoke to you about?''

Her tone had taken on a deliberately haughty note— princess to servant. Walker's mouth quirked, just a little, in recognition of the fact. "Yes, Madame Mahrain, I tuned up the engine yesterday."

Some hint of mischief seized her. She was finding that she enjoyed having him subservient to her, even in pretense. "And what about the springs in the seats? I informed you that I found them quite uncomfortable."

She couldn't read Walker's eyes behind the dark glasses, but she recognized the look that came over his face—wicked and just a little bit feral.

"Of course, madame. Your pleasure is my utmost concern, always."

Abruptly, Jasmine gave up their battle of words. In a war of double entendres, she was woefully ill-equipped. Once again he had gotten the upper hand. Because she remembered, all too well, when he had concerned himself with her pleasure. And the shattering results.

"We will have a guest joining us for dinner this evening," El-Dabir informed her. He met her in the hallway at the base of the stairs, playing the dutiful host. "I hope that meets with your approval."

"Of course, Hosni. I am not surprised you have frequent guests with the wonderful hospitality I have found here."

The man preened a bit, and Walker inwardly rolled his eyes. There was certainly a part of this farce that Jasmine was perfectly suited for—winning men over and turning them into simpleminded fools. That he had once skated too close to having the same description apply to him was a fact that still stung.

Leaving her alone in her bathroom a few nights ago had taken a great deal more control than it should have. It wasn't as though he wanted any more from her than the physical. He had strong sexual needs, and he usually didn't deny himself for as long as he had during the course of the last assignment. He was used to controlling those needs, but despite the antipathy that had developed between them, he hadn't gotten his fill of Jasmine three years ago. Hadn't steeped himself in her body deeply enough to erase this sharp-edged hunger that had flared to life the moment he'd seen her again.

Walker was a pragmatic man. The solution seemed simple enough. A few hours in Jasmine's bed would burn out the sexual frustration and stamp an end to this uncomfortable ache for her. Then, and only then, would their relationship be completely over. On his terms.

Women being the emotional creatures that they were, she was balking a bit at the sheer logic of the solution. But not for long. Whatever else she claimed, he knew when a woman was interested. As a matter of fact, knowing that Jasmine suffered from at least a shadow of the lust burning in him was equal parts comfort and frustration.

He shifted from thoughts of the physical to the professional with a long-practiced ease and followed Jasmine and El-Dabir into the drawing room. When he saw the man standing near the table there, he mentally gave credit to Jasmine's earlier prediction.

Tariq Abdul sprang to her side, displacing El-Dabir as he showered Jasmine with flowery compliments. Walker made sure the flicker of annoyance he felt didn't show on his face. Whether Abdul would prove to be connected with the Brothers remained to be seen, but some of his motives were clear enough. If ever there was a man on the make, it was this guy. And Jasmine played the part of a woman enchanted with an ease that seemed just a little too natural.

"Madame, it is the greatest pleasure to see you again."

With a sense of déjà vu, Walker sat at the large table, set for a more intimate gathering than the last time Abdul had been present, and watched, without seeming to, Jasmine's handling of the man.

"Your visit is a welcome surprise," she was telling him.

"Welcome?" Abdul's brows raised, and he inched his chair infinitesimally closer to Jasmine's. "I am glad. But it should not be a surprise. I promised that I would return. I could not have stayed away." The light in his dark eyes as they rested on the woman at his side was all too easy to read.

"I am happy we could meet one more time before I returned to Tamir." Jasmine accepted the tea the servant handed her and sipped, while Abdul exchanged a quick glance with El-Dabir.

Walker's inner radar interpreted the message passed and received between the two men. If he'd had any question that Abdul's return visit had been hastened by the conversation he and Jasmine had planted earlier that day, it was erased. He only hoped that she could pull off the rest of her task.

Issuing a sharply worded order in Arabic, El-Dabir dispatched the servant. Once the man was out of hearing, he smiled toothily. "I, too, am grateful you came by, Tariq. I believe Rose has some reservations about recommending a closer relationship between Maloun and Tamir. Perhaps you can help me convince her."

Walker watched narrowly as a delicate flush colored Jasmines cheeks. Could the woman actually blush on command? Her voice, when she spoke, was firm. "I must give the sheik the benefit of my perceptions gathered here."

"And you have concerns?" Again that quick glance exchanged between the men. Jasmine appeared to not notice. She looked for all the world like a woman out of her element, with news she was reluctant to share.

''The Brothers of Darkness continue to be something of a mystery.''

The prime minister's voice was ubiquitous. ''I have assured madame that the Brothers are not a rebel faction at all, but a nationalistic organization. It appears I have failed to allay her fears on the matter.''

Jasmine buried her face in her cup. ''One hears all sorts of rumors in my country.''

''Rumors.'' Abdul scoffed. ''There will always be gossip about such associations. One cannot put faith in rumors.''

A mulish expression settled over her face. It was one Walker was intimately acquainted with. ''I will advise Sheik Kamal of my impressions. That is my duty to my country.''

''Perhaps I can arrange for you to form a more accurate impression.'' Abdul waited for her gaze to raise questioningly to his before going on. ''The Brothers of Darkness are a discreet society, but they would not want their goals misrepresented. If I could arrange it, would you agree to stay in Maloun longer, meet with some of their spokesmen?''

Jasmine replaced her cup on the saucer with a tiny clink of china against china. ''I would welcome the opportunity to do so. I must be convinced that the entire leadership of the Brothers share Hosni's wishes for the alliance between our two countries.'' Her long lashes fluttered before her gaze fixed on Abdul's face. ''You can arrange for me to meet with the leaders?''

The man hesitated. ''That would be possible, madame, only if you would agree to meet at their compound.''

A ribbon of satisfaction curled through Walker. At last, they would get to the crucial part of their mission. Once he was on the Brothers' property, he'd lose no time searching for clues to the lab's whereabouts. And when he had its location pinpointed, he could arrange for the confiscation of the virus and destroy the threat Maloun posed to Tamir.

In the next moment his sense of satisfaction was smashed when he heard Jasmine say, ''I am afraid that will be impossible.'' It took a great deal of effort to make sure his face remained expressionless. The knot of tension forming in his stomach would be apparent to no one. Nobody appeared to be looking at him, at any rate. El-Dabir and Abdul were focused on Jasmine.

She seemed to be choosing her words with care. ''With all due respect to my esteemed companions, I must express some caution about leaving the prime minister's quarters for such a meeting. I would be most comfortable meeting each of the leaders here.''

Her meaning was clear, despite her veiled response. She didn't trust her safety to the Brothers. Grudgingly, Walker had to applaud the way she was playing the scene. Any hint of eagerness would arouse suspicion. But there was a delicate balance to be drawn between feigned unwillingness and blowing off the offer altogether. He hoped she was up to the challenge.

''I assure you, madame, that would not be feasible. It would be impossible to leave the organization headquarters deserted.''

''And it would be equally impossible for me to make such a visit.''

From Abdul's expression, it was clear he was unused to being thwarted, especially, Walker judged, by a female. El-Dabir put in, ''Perhaps it would be helpful if I could assure your safety at the compound, madame.''

''I appreciate your attempt, but I am unsure how you can do so.''

"By accompanying you to your meeting. And your assistant, of course." The nod in Walker's direction was barely an acknowledgment. All the men in the room knew in whose hands the real decision lay.

Jasmine's pause was long enough to have the Maloun men leaning forward in their chairs. "Of course, if I am to meet with the Brothers I would want you to be a part of that meeting, Hosni."

Sensing a small opening, Abdul seized on it. "So you will agree to visit the Brothers compound, in the company of the prime minister and myself?"

A natural-looking reluctance crossed Jasmine's face, and Walker's regard for her rose. With a deftness he had to admire, she'd brought the two men to exactly the point she wanted them.

"Yes. I will agree."

The massive fence surrounding the Brothers' stronghold gave the impression of heavy security, which contrasted sharply with the almost deserted air of the compound. As the lone man at the gate waved them through, Walker scanned the area. He suspected there had been some serious alterations ordered here in the hours since Jasmine had accepted the invitation yesterday. Although there were stands built atop the fence every several yards, suggesting regularly posted sentries, they were all unoccupied. It was probable that the guards who normally patrolled there, most likely armed, had been dismissed for the duration of Jasmine's visit. The Brothers would go to great lengths to convince her they were a harmless organization. He found himself awaiting the show with anticipation.

El-Dabir had ridden with Abdul, leaving Jasmine and Walker to follow in their car. They came to a stop in front of a huge home that dwarfed the prime minister's quarters both in size and opulence.

"Easy to see who controls the real money in Maloun," he muttered in an undertone.

Jasmine was studying the building. "And no real mystery as to how they acquired it."

He glanced at her. Her face was half turned away from him as she looked out the window. He wondered if she felt the same way he did on the threshold of a case—lightening bolts of adrenaline shooting through his veins; excitement layered with certain combative resolve. In the next instant she glanced at him, a hint of a smile curving her lips. Walker saw the same flare of anticipation in her eyes, and he shot her a quick unguarded grin. "Ready, Jaz?"

Their gazes met, meshed. "More than ready."

He nodded once, his narrowed gaze intent. "Let's do this."

Getting out of the car, he rounded the hood and opened the passenger door for Jasmine to disembark. Already, Abdul was striding toward them. Walker got the bags from the trunk and followed them toward the house, nerves tight and ready. If the lab was anywhere on this property he'd find it. And when he did, the Brothers of Darkness would be divested of their weapon of death and destruction. He found himself looking forward to the challenge.

"Allow me, madame." Tariq Abdul placed his hand on Jasmine's elbow. "The ground is uneven here."

Once he had steered her over the slight rockiness in the path, he failed to release her. A woman would be expected to be flattered by his attentions, especially in Maloun's patriarchal society. Rose Mahrain would be no different.

She'd given her character a great deal of thought, especially when Abdul's interest had become apparent. With his intentions focused on her as a possible conquest, he'd be less suspicious. Rose Mahrain, she imagined, would be taken aback by the man's subtly aggressive approach, but she'd be flattered, too. She was, after all, a woman. Uncertainty would war with duty. Jasmine was adept at maintaining the facade that would serve her best, while accomplishing her goals.

So she made no protest when he failed to release her arm, but let her lashes flutter like a woman bewildered yet pleased by a man's attentions. And then she went to work.

"You are very kind to take time from your busy schedule to arrange this meeting between the leaders of the Brotherhood and myself." As Jasmine spoke, she scanned the surrounding area carefully. The trip from Redyshah had taken several hours, and the scenery en route had gradually changed from the flat desert of the north to a sweep of rocky hills covered with dense vegetation. The Brothers' grounds were bordered by the hills on two sides, and it was impossible to tell how far the property extended.

"It was my pleasure. Am I right to assume this is your first trip to my country?"

They walked slowly along the narrow path outside the home, their garments brushing occasionally. Their proximity would be suggestive by Tamir's standards, Jasmine realized. Although a widow would have fewer constraints than an unmarried woman, the sheik's society was still protective of a woman's virtue. From what she had read, Maloun's culture was much the same. "It is, yes." She gave a little laugh. "Although I have traveled extensively abroad in my lifetime, I have never visited some of my neighboring countries."

"There is much to see in our world. I myself studied in America. Have you ever been there?"

If he had studied her résumé, Jasmine knew he was well aware of the answer. She gave him the one he expected. "My father was Tamir's diplomat to the United States when I was a child. I spent many years there."

"Did you study there?"

She shook her head. "I returned to my country to attend university." He'd managed, completely by accident, to touch on the one subject guaranteed to strike a chord with her. Her answer was in keeping with her guise as Rose Mahrain, but couldn't be further from the truth. There had been no mention of college in her future, but that had been the least of what had sent her fleeing from her home. She'd gotten an education of sorts on the Moroccan streets, but she was well aware that it couldn't be more dissimilar than the one the man spoke of.

"I graduated from the University of California in Los Angeles," he told her, and Jasmine felt a spark of interest.

"That is very impressive." She sounded properly awed. "The university has a wonderful reputation. Is it as beautiful in California as I have heard? We never traveled there."

"There is beauty to be found everywhere in the world, madame, but none as great as that found at my side."

The flowery compliment was meant to disconcert her, so Jasmine gave him a quick, fluttering look before glancing away. "You are too kind, but of course I was speaking of the mountains and ocean."

"Yes, I saw much splendor in the United States, but I was glad to return to my homeland. I was eager to use what I learned overseas to benefit my brothers here."

Jasmine felt a crush of excitement that she ruthlessly squashed. "What did you study while you were abroad?"

"If we pause just here…" Gently he urged her to a stop. "…we will have a perfect view of the sunset." Discreetly she inched away from him as she watched the sun drop in the sky, and waited with barely concealed impatience for his answer.

"I am a man who appreciates nature." His teeth flashed. "As a scientist, I suppose that is not surprising."

Excitement sparked and hummed in her veins. "What is surprising is your line of work." She waited for his quizzical glance before continuing. "I can not picture you in a white lab coat and thick glasses."

He laughed, amused. "That is the stereotype of scientists, is it not? Although I spent my share of time in laboratories in my college years, my interest these days is in the business side of science."

Yes, Jasmine thought grimly, she imagined that terrorism could be quite lucrative. And if Abdul was as closely affiliated with the Brothers as she suspected, his education and training would have proven invaluable to the group.

They watched the sun shatter the horizon with a glorious palette of brilliance. With seeming idleness, she asked about a building she could see in the distance, about a quarter mile from the house.

"Until this dwelling was completed, that building was the meeting place for the Brothers. It proved too small as the group enlarged." Subtly, Abdul steered her back toward the house. "Now it is rarely used. Perhaps eventually it will be torn down."

They went back to the house, Jasmine's heart pounding. Was it possible that the building housed the lab they'd come to find? Surely their task wouldn't be that easy. But no matter the lab's location, it was one thing to find out where the place was. It would be quite another to discover and destroy the virus.

After a light meal taken with Hosni and Tariq, a servant showed Jasmine to her room. Her quarters were comfortable, with a sitting room opening up to a bedroom and bath. She strode through the outer room now, eager for sleep. It had been an eventful twenty-four hours. But if she'd hoped for a quiet end to the day, her hopes were dashed when she entered her bedroom and found six-foot-two-inches of lean dangerous male lounging on her bed.

Her mouth went dry at the sight. She had no idea how long Walker had been there, but he'd made himself comfortable. His shirt was loosened, and he had his arms propped beneath his head.

When she made no effort to move, he lazily withdrew a hand and motioned for her to shut the door. She did, with just a little more force than necessary. "How is it that you seem to spend as much time in my quarters as I do?"

He lifted a brow, regarded her lazily. "Where else can we speak freely?"

Pressing her lips together, Jasmine moved farther into the room. "I take it then that you have swept our rooms."

"They're clean." His low businesslike tone shouldn't have had the power to send a frisson of awareness up her spine. "I checked the upstairs when I carried up the bags. My guess is that visitors are rarely, if ever, allowed here. I suspect the security is expended mostly on keeping intruders out of the compound altogether. Did you meet with anyone tonight?"

Shaking her head, she crossed to an uncomfortable-looking chair next to the bed. "Tariq assured me the representatives of the Brothers will greet me tomorrow. I did find out a few interesting things, however. Guess where he was educated? U.C.L.A."

Walker was silent for a moment, absorbing the news. "That's one more link in the chain. First we hear of a terrorist cell in L.A. and then a suspicious scientist from

U.C.L.A. shoots at Princess Christina. Maybe Abdul is the common thread linking the two.''

"Something tells me you are right. Did you notice the building about a quarter mile from the house?''

"I saw it. Did he say what it was?''

"Abdul claims it used to be the headquarters for the Brothers until this one was built. Do you think it is the lab?''

He gave her a wicked look. "I aim to find out. Did he tell you anything else?''

"Only that he was educated as a scientist. Which makes it even likelier that he may be the key to the virus.''

"We'll find out soon enough. From what I could tell today you're going to be on your own when the meeting is called tomorrow. I was left with the distinct impression that a lowly assistant wasn't considered important enough to be included.''

She was more than ready for her part of the assignment to begin. "How long will you need to find the lab?''

"Depends on where it's located. No more than a few days.''

"I'll need to buy us some time then.'' She fell silent for a moment, planning. "The first meeting tomorrow morning should answer some of our questions about the Brothers. I will be interested to see who takes control of the talks.''

"My bet's on Bonlei Marakeh.''

Thinking of the slightly statured man with the regal bearing, Jasmine nodded. "Perhaps I will insist on individual meetings with each of the heads. That would buy you the time you need for the search.'' She thought for a moment, already plotting strategy. "I could tell the Brothers that I must meet with each alone to be certain the leadership is all in agreement.''

''You'll have to play it by ear. I found about a dozen bedrooms upstairs, and all of them are occupied. It'll be interesting to see how many of the guests appear at the meeting tomorrow.''

When he fell silent she asked pointedly, ''And which of the rooms is yours?''

''That door will open onto a sitting area.'' Her gaze followed in the direction he gestured. ''My room is on the other side of it. They're all connected. Convenient, huh?''

Ignoring the suggestive remark, she crossed her arms. ''Since it is so close, you should have no problem finding your way back to it. It would be best to get some sleep. Tomorrow will be a long day.''

He was obviously in the mood to be irritating. At her words he merely crossed his ankles. ''I'm pretty comfortable right here.'' His grin was slow and wicked. ''Maybe I should stay.''

''You would not get much sleep.''

His brows raised. ''Promise?''

''Yes. Because I would tie you up and beat you.''

His face lightened a fraction. ''I didn't know you were into the kinky stuff, Jaz. I think I'm getting turned on.''

Somehow she managed a bored tone. ''The state is too easily accomplished to be considered much of a feat. Get out. I'll let you know when I have something to report.''

She didn't know which of them was more surprised when he did as she asked, padding lightly out of the room in his stockinged feet. Not until she heard the door closing after him did she let out a breath. She'd encountered two equally determined men tonight. But while one's touch left her repulsed, the simple thought of the other had the power to rouse sparks of excitement.

Both emotions, she thought, could be managed. It was a simple matter of control.

Releasing a breath that turned into a sigh, she closed her eyes. And wondered if she could ever make herself believe that.

Chapter 5

The moonless night was an advantage Walker was loathe to waste. The area between the mansion and the outer building was mostly free of vegetation, dotted only by the occasional tree. The cover of darkness was all that shielded his prone form from detection.

Using his elbows against the ground, he inched forward infinitesimally. The night-vision goggles he wore allowed him to watch the guards patrolling the building. Regular three-hour intervals, he calculated, and the two-man shift had changed twice in the time he'd been watching. Rather than each man taking one side, they rotated approximately every ten minutes. He'd examined all sides of the building from a distance, and decided on his point of entry. His best bet was one of the windows. He'd have about seven minutes to get inside, eight at the most.

Continuing to move a fraction at a time, he didn't pause again until he was about four hundred yards from the site. Then he shrugged out of the bag he had rigged to his back, unzipped it, and began going through his tools, choosing the ones he'd need.

The length of thin resilient rope was looped around his shoulder. The short slender wire that he'd tucked into his shirt pocket could serve effectively and silently as a garrote. Taking out one of the guards though, would be a last resort. A dead body appearing on the compound would raise some uncomfortable questions.

He shielded his wrist and tapped his watch, studying the numbers revealed in its glow. The last guard had rounded the corner of the building forty seconds earlier. It was time to make his move.

In a crouch, he ran to the building, a swift shadow with surprising speed. Uncoiling the rope he carried, he reached for the heavy hook in his bag, attached it and tossed it up to the top of the window frame. He caught it on the second attempt, pulling firm to assure himself of its secureness. Then, nimbly as a spider ascending its web, he climbed up the side of the building, and found a pleasant surprise. The window had been left open.

He supposed that with the guards posted outside and the distance of the window from the ground, a breach of security wouldn't seem plausible. The searing heat in the daytime made opening windows to the much cooler night air a logical attempt at air-conditioning. He tucked his glass cutter and tube of adhesive into his backpack, swung his feet over the windowsill and, while maintaining his hold on the rope, slid down the wall on the other side. Jumping with near soundlessness to the floor, he turned his attention to the contents of the room.

Shadowy stacks of crates formed narrow aisles. Walker stopped in front of one pile, lifted a crate from the stack, and set it on the floor. He shrugged out of the bag and let it drop next to the crate, reached into it and took out a small crowbar. With a few quick levers he had the top loosened and lifted, setting it aside. Reaching for his pocket flashlight, he shielded it with his hand and turned it on.

Anticipation quickly turned to grimness. The contents were unassembled, but he'd been in the business long enough to recognize automatic assault rifles.

Replacing the lid, he put the crate back in place and wandered the aisles, making random checks on crates. In addition to the weapons, he found heat-detecting scopes, hand grenades, and enough ammunition to keep a small army equipped for months.

Which was, he supposed, exactly what the Brothers of Darkness had planned.

The building was cavernous, the endless row of crates its only contents. When Walker had satisfied himself with the interior, he replaced the bag on his back, retraced his steps and grasped the rope he'd left dangling from the upper window. A few steps had him even with the windowsill again, where he hesitated until the guard went by. Then, with quick, efficient movements, he switched the rope to hang outside the building, and began his descent.

He was halfway down when a sudden movement caught his eye. A figure rounded the corner and then lounged against the building. Walker hung there in frozen suspension as the guard furtively shook out a cigarette, lit it. He kept his breathing shallow as he willed the man to not look up. The guard dragged deeply on the cigarette, blew out a stream of smoke.

His options limited, Walker remained still. If he made a motion back toward the window, some slight sound might alert the man. Hanging the way he was in plain sight, Walker was a sitting duck if the guard should happen to look up. He reached inside his shirt carefully, withdrawing the small pistol he had strapped across his chest.

The silent deadly tableau stretched until the guard straightened, stubbed out his cigarette, picked up the butt and put it in his pocket. Then he ambled around the corner again. Walker waited another minute, then continued down to the ground, and retrieved his rope.

Making his way back to the house, it wasn't his narrow escape that filled his mind, but the plans of the Brotherhood. It was impossible to know for sure whether the supply of weapons corresponded to the number of forces the Brothers could summon. But one thing was certain.

The Brothers of Darkness were armed for war.

Jasmine extended her hand regally to the newcomer, her serene air giving no indication of her inner thoughts. Ridah Nulam. The stranger's name was filed away with the names of the eleven others who filled the room. Hours later, she would be able to recall with intricate detail the name of each and a succinct description. She'd have to arrange a meeting with Walker. She hadn't seen him since the previous evening, and she was eager to hear what he'd uncovered.

It was the present, however, that required her utmost concentration. There wasn't a doubt in her mind that she was in the presence of twelve of the most dangerous men in the Middle East.

They were assembled in a room that appeared to serve as an office. One long table held no fewer than eight computers, and several desks were scattered around the room. The guests, however, were gathered at the far side of the room, seated on low couches and chairs. Jasmine assumed that it was no accident she'd been shown to a chair flanked by Tariq Abdul and Prime Minister Hosni El-Dabir.

''Madame Mahrain, it is an honor to have you visit our compound.'' Bonlei Marakeh spoke, his midnight gaze fixed on hers. Although she'd met him only a few days earlier at the prime minister's, he seemed to have grown in stature in the time since. From the respect tendered the man from the others in the room, it was easy to discern that he was a power in the Brothers. Walker's prediction was likely correct. The man probably served as the head of the organization.

''Despite my best efforts, Madame Mahrain retained doubts about the pure intentions of the Brothers.'' El-Dabir's ingratiating tone was cut short by a sharp look from Marakeh.

''Madame is diligent in her obligation to Sheik Kamal.'' His obsidian gaze shifted back to Jasmine's. ''He is fortunate, indeed, to have an emissary of your loyalty.''

Inclining her head slightly, Jasmine returned, ''It is kind of you to meet with me. Tariq has given me a little information about your organization, but as you are aware, rumors are often accepted as truth. Sheik Kamal depends on my report to make a decision regarding the development of trade between our two countries. I want very much to be able to tell him he should have no reservations on that score.''

Marakeh smiled, although his eyes remained watchful. ''Rest assured, madame, that would suit us, as well. Perhaps we should start with what you know, or have heard about the Brothers of Darkness.''

Sensing the minefield ahead, she sidestepped nimbly. ''As I am sure you are aware, little besides speculation is known about your organization. I suppose any group that operates clandestinely is prone to be the target of rumors.''

''Our group would not seem clandestine to anyone in our country. We have been visionaries for economic growth and prosperity, while working to bring updated technology and health care to our people. It is our goal to modernize our country, without the corrupting influence of the western society.''

Jasmine recognized the party line he was spouting. She'd read some of their doctrine, provided by El-Dabir. ''I am sure you are aware that Sheik Kamal has similar goals.''

The man nodded. ''As you say. We have been very fortunate that our fine prime minister shares our agenda, but change is a slow, laborious process. Gaining the sheik's trust by opening trade relations will be mutually advantageous for both of our countries. We will not have to rely on the shakier relationships with some of our Middle Eastern neighbors for our oil needs. And Tamir will have a new and eager market for its goods.'' He spread his hands. ''Both of our countries win.''

Pretending to hesitate, Jasmine gave every pretense of a woman reluctant to be candid. ''If I may be frank, sir…the goals you express are admirable. But what of those who say that the Brothers are little more than state-sponsored terrorists?''

She pretended not to hear El-Dabir's indrawn breath, nor to notice the sudden tension that emanated from Abdul. Her focus remained on Marakeh. He remained every bit as composed as a moment ago. She supposed most would never recognize the flare of anger that flickered in his eyes. Certainly it wasn't reflected in his voice.

''Yes, we have heard these ridiculous accusations, as well. But always we ask, where is the proof? Our organization exists only in our own country. Who would we terrorize? Our own people?'' He shook his head, as if baffled by such talk. ''Our name, perhaps, causes such speculation. But are not our countrymen our brothers? And is our goal not to lift our country out of the darkness of poverty and despair by bringing a new prosperity to our people?''

Jasmine hadn't expected the man to admit to anything, but his assurances rang hollow. Given their intelligence regarding the group's objective, and the Brothers' terrorist cell near L.A., the group's true ambition was all too obvious. For the first time she wondered if the L.A. cell was the organization's only one in the States. Given their hostility to western influences, it stood to reason they would have more than one.

''The goals you state are admirable,'' she said. ''Are they representative of your viewpoint, or that of the entire leadership of the Brothers?''

''An excellent question. But I can assure you that should anything happen to me, the next in line to take control would be subject to the same laws and powers designated by our constitution.''

The information was both valuable and chilling. Terrorist cells tended to be concentric. Remove the person at its helm and the cell would cease to exist. Each operated separately from the other, with only loose common goals to connect them. But according to Marakeh, the Brothers' power didn't rest with individuals, but with a group. If something happened to the leader, there was another waiting to take over the goals. Such a setup represented much more of a threat.

She slid a look to the the man seated beside her. It appeared that most of the men collected in the room shared equal status in the group. But she thought that Abdul must hold some sort of second in command position. He had been entrusted with the decision to invite her to the compound, and she thought that was significant.

Twelve pairs of eyes were trained on her. Smoothly she

asked, "And where does Prime Minister El-Dabir enter your plan? As leader of Maloun, is it not his job to make the decisions regarding the future of the country?"

"Of course. And we are fortunate that the people of our country have the wisdom to elect a man of Hosni's stature."

Jasmine turned her head a bit to smile at El-Dabir, who looked flushed and pathetically proud at the man's compliment. "Indeed," she said. "I have been very impressed with his vision for Maloun." She turned back to Marakeh as he continued to speak.

"We are simple men." He gestured to the men in the room. "Businessmen, all of us, with similar goals for our country. Part of our function is to raise the money our prime minister needs for his ideas. We are what Americans would refer to as philanthropists."

There were smiles and murmurs of agreement from the men around the room. A chill skated over Jasmine's skin, despite the heat in the room. *Philanthropists.* If the word's definition included men intent on destroying some of their closest neighbors, it just might fit.

In the still hours after midnight Walker roamed freely through the house, his stockinged feet soundless. The only security he'd found was on the door leading to the office, and a fairly intricate alarm system at the house entrance that he'd love to try his hand at. He figured he could have it disconnected in under ten minutes. He'd found no reason to amend his original impression that the compound had few visitors. Its surrounding walls and the sentries that came back on duty at night would be enough to dissuade most intruders.

But Walker wasn't most intruders.

There was no doubt that investigating from the inside

had its advantages, but there was a downside, as well. He could leave no traces of attempts to breach security, which tended to limit his options. Which just meant he'd have to be creative.

He paused in the downstairs hallway, studying a pre-Raphaelite sculpture. With reverent hands, he lifted it from its pedestal and turned it over to examine it. Most would assume the piece was a reproduction, but then most didn't have Walker's experience, or his sources. A statue very much like this one had been stolen from a private collection in London just two years ago. After only the most cursory examinations, Walker set it back in its place, convinced the lost item had somehow managed to find its way to the Brothers of Darkness compound.

Moving on, he shone his flashlight on an excruciatingly ugly painting from the Renaissance. There was no denying the value of the piece, but Walker wouldn't have stolen it even in his younger years. A thief had to maintain some standards.

No expense had been spared in decorating the huge home, and he was struck again by the wealth amassed here. How had the Brothers managed to finance the artwork, the small arsenal, the as-yet-undiscovered lab? If he could answer those questions before they left here, he'd be in the position to destroy the strength of the Brothers for a very long time. Maybe forever.

He was a man who believed in tying up loose ends.

Making his way stealthily to the office, he played the beam of the flashlight over the door without touching it. He'd already ascertained there was no lock. No, the security protecting it was less obvious. The door had been rigged to be heat and motion sensitive, and a fine job done of it, too. The tiny conduit that would hold the wires were almost hidden beside the woodwork. The first time someone so much as brushed against the door without first disconnecting the silent alarm, it would sound, alerting... who? Someone in the house or a guard outside? Unlike the front gate and the building he'd explored out back, there were no guards in the vicinity of the home. It really didn't matter, in any case. He didn't intend to trip the alarm.

Holding the flashlight in his teeth, he squatted beside the door and went to work. In a couple of minutes he was easing the conduit away to reveal the wires beneath. He studied them intently for several moments, then traced the woven colored wires to the first joint in the system. A smile broke over his face. To the careless eye it appeared a simple cross-right-cross variation, if one didn't comprehend the significance of the tiny dip switches. No doubt inside the door there was a panel to turn off the alarm. Disconnecting the wires alone would trigger it. It was a seemingly foolproof system, if the intruder lacked Walker's knowledge. The key was the combination of up and down positions to these switches.

He shone the flashlight on his watch, wondered if he should press his luck. He'd already spent several hours searching for signs of security, and he'd have at least another couple nights before they left.

The challenge, though, was too great to ignore. Withdrawing a slim tool with a fine point from a small pouch at his waist, he went to work on the dip switches. He was halfway done when an almost inaudible whisper sounded behind him.

"As I believe they say in America, you are busted."

In a blur of motion he was up, spun and had a hard arm against the figure's throat. When logic caught up with instinct, he relaxed his arm, but his whisper was furious. "That's a good way to get yourself killed, Jaz."

She turned, their position still close. ''You overestimate your skills.''

Despite her disparaging words, his gaze arrowed to her delicate throat. He reached out a hand to touch her there, as if to assure himself he hadn't injured her. He hadn't tempered his strength, he'd responded as he would to any threat, immediately and savagely. He could have really hurt her, and the knowledge sent a fresh burst of fury through his veins.

''What the hell are you doing down here?'' His words didn't lack ferocity, despite their near soundlessness. ''This part is my job, remember?''

''You leave me very little room to forget.'' She stepped away from his touch with a nonchalance that fired his temper all over again. ''Someone is moving around upstairs. I knew you were not in your room, so I came out in case I was needed.''

Her meaning was clear. She'd come out to offer herself as a diversion, should one be necessary. That shouldn't have had the power to infuriate him, but somehow it did. Especially coupled as it was with the fact that she'd managed to take him by surprise a moment ago. He'd have to credit her skills or his carelessness for that, and both burned equally. ''I can take care of myself. What I can't do is worry about my job and you, as well. So go back upstairs before you alert anyone.''

She tossed her head and glared at him, the movement sending her cloud of dark hair tumbling into disarray. His attention was distracted by the movement. She'd taken care to remain in character, he noted, even in the middle of the night. She wore her bulky undergarment under her robe, and her hair was long and loose. She looked as though she'd just crawled out of a man's bed, and memory hit him like a vicious right jab. She hadn't looked so different in *his* bed. Eyes heavy and slumberous, hair tangled by his hands. The image was too sharp, too immediate, to be ignored.

And because she seemed to be having no trouble ignoring it, he scowled at her again. "I told you..."

"I am not hard of hearing." Her barely audible voice held a snap. "You are taking a risk coming down here by yourself. Try to set your feelings for me aside, Walker, and treat me like you would any of your other partners."

Her words had just enough truth in them to nick his conscience. He couldn't deny the accompanying twinge of discomfort they brought. Unfamiliar with the emotion, he lifted a careless shoulder. "Suit yourself." Turning away, he crouched and went back to work. "Stay away from the door. The slightest movement will set off the alarm."

"The windows in the office are not wired. Perhaps that would be a less risky way to enter."

"You'd risk having the guards at the front gate spot you. The office's proximity to the front of the house is probably no accident."

"Guards? How many?"

Walker wielded his pick on the dip switches, working swiftly to avoid setting the alarm. "I counted half a dozen. They come on duty after everyone's..."

There was a small sound at the top of the stairs and they both froze, staring for a split second into each other's eyes. Then before he could hiss out a command, Jasmine whirled away from him, strode down the darkened hallway, and around the corner.

Cursing mentally, Walker swiftly retraced the steps he'd taken on the switches, then replaced the conduit. His ears strained for the sound of voices.

"Madame." There was no mistaking Abdul's voice, or

its slight hint of underlying suspicion. "This is an odd time for you to be roaming about."

"I am sorry if I awakened you."

Walker's hand, usually as steady as a surgeon's, stilled. Even from a distance he could note the tremble in her voice, the slight catch in her words.

"I have trouble sleeping sometimes. Ever since..."

Working swiftly, Walker had the conduit replaced and fastened. He flattened himself against the wall, waited for Jasmine to play out her scene.

"Have you ever been haunted by memories of a loved one, Tariq?" Jasmine's voice was a wistful sound, thick with unshed tears.

"I am saddened by your loss." Abdul spoke again, sounding a bit further away. Jasmine was leading him toward the dining room, in the opposite direction from Walker. He felt a grudging measure of respect. Her instincts were flawless. After a few more moments he moved a bit closer to the stairway. When he was convinced that she had Abdul completely occupied, Walker could slip upstairs.

"You are far too young to be left a widow, Madame Mahrain. Rose."

Walker froze. The man's familiarity was unmistakable. In her attempt to give Walker escape time, she may well have landed herself in a precarious position.

"I loved my husband very much. Enough to wish it had been me instead of him in that car, my body pulled from the wreckage."

"You must not speak that way."

"It is true." Her insistence sounded a little wild, a woman full of grief and despair. "For two years I have been alone now, and for what purpose? Better that we had died together."

"No, Rose, not better. You have been slumbering in grief for so long, you forget the beauty of life. The pleasures it holds." Walker had only to bend his body backward an inch to peer around the corner into the dining room, see Abdul place his hands on Jasmine's shoulders. Walker's fingers curled into his palms.

Abdul's voice went on, low and soothing. A man seeing an opportunity to prey on what he thought was a vulnerable, helpless woman and turn the situation to his own advantage. "Two years is a long time to grieve. Your husband would not expect you to shut yourself off forever. If he loved you..." His voice tapered off suggestively.

"He did. We were devoted to each other."

"Then he would wish you happiness."

Walker bared his teeth at the neat way Abdul sprung the trap. Because, of course, the man was intimating that a widow should find that happiness in his arms. He remained where he was, torn. Duty demanded that he avoid detection at all costs. He should slip up the stairs right now and wait for another night to raid the office.

But duty was battling emotion. He was loathe to leave Jasmine down here with Abdul. The situation could take an ugly turn—could demand more from her than any agent should be expected to give.

"You are right." Her voice held just the right touch of sadness and wistfulness. "It has been a long time since I've felt anything at all. Sometimes I wonder if I ever shall again."

Damn the woman! She couldn't have said anything more guaranteed to egg Abdul on. A man would construe her words as a personal challenge. He'd fantasize about reawakening such a woman, of being the one to reintroduce her to the pleasures of life. Walker didn't doubt that Tariq Abdul would fancy himself that man.

And he couldn't figure out why the hell he should care.

She was his colleague. He excused his concern with a tinge of discomfort. He had a responsibility for the outcome of this assignment, and for her. Any partner of his would elicit similar feelings of concern. He thought the words, and tried desperately to believe them.

Walker focused on the murmur of voices again.

"A woman of your sensitivity, your loveliness, should not be without a man in her life to care for her. To make her remember what it is to be a woman."

"You flatter me, I think."

"Not at all. Please give me permission to speak freely, Rose. I have not made my admiration for you a secret, after all."

Jasmine ducked her head demurely. Encouraged, Abdul moved closer. "You need a man who appreciates your courage, your strength, your fine mind." His arms came around, reached around her gently, pulled her to him. Walker's muscles bunched.

"I appreciate all those things about you, my dear."

It was the perfect time to make his escape. Jasmine had diverted Abdul all too well. The liberties the man was taking would be frowned on in this society. But it occurred to Walker that he was probably wasting his concern for Jasmine's handling of the situation.

Three years ago she'd handled him just as adroitly, hadn't she? And he'd been just as gullible as Abdul. Their time together had been aside from the mission, and had ended up sabotaging his assignment altogether. Because Jasmine LeBarr had proved she'd use any means at her disposal to accomplish her mission.

Bitterly, he tore his gaze away from the embracing couple. Taking the stairs silently, he headed toward his room, where he was already certain he'd get very little sleep.

Chapter 6

Less than an hour later Jasmine took a deep breath to quell rising nerves, and slipped into Walker's bedroom. She paused, allowing her eyes time to adjust to the darkness, before noting that his bed was empty. In the next instant her gaze found him, leaning a shoulder against the window on the opposite wall.

The sight of him sent her already shaky nerves scrambling. He'd divested himself of his shirt, and she could see the pale outline of his body in the darkness. His features were shadowed, but there was no mistaking that wide-shouldered torso, the muscled body. Nor her reaction to both.

He made no movement, so she forced herself to approach him on limbs that seemed suddenly wooden. "I thought you might be sleeping. I am sure you have not gotten much rest lately."

"Worried about me, Jaz? I'm touched."

His sardonic tone had the nerves in her stomach knotting. "I thought we should take the opportunity to share findings. Or have you forgotten why we are here?"

"*I* haven't forgotten." He didn't bother to explain the inflection he'd given the word, and she was quite certain that was for the best. She was beginning to think that the two of them were incapable of reacting to each other in any civilized manner.

The response they *were* capable of slipped stealthily into her memory, and was firmly pushed aside. "This can wait," she said bluntly, half turning away. Approaching Walker in his current mood wasn't going to accomplish anything.

"I got into the building out back last night."

"Already?" She faced him again, saw his nod. "Was there any trouble?"

"Please." His tone was insulted. "There were only two guards. I'm sure the Brothers figure the number is more than adequate given the security maintained at the perimeter of the compound."

She frowned. "You mentioned they'd reinstated the security."

He made a gesture toward the window and she moved next to him to peer out. Accepting the night vision binoculars he handed her, she held them up to her eyes. "They've gone to great lengths to make it appear as though this compound is unprotected. I suppose that helps them make their point that their organization is harmless."

He grunted. "Yeah, about as harmless as a country of terrorists can be. That building is full of assault weapons, all kinds, and enough ammunition to equip a small army."

She lowered the binoculars to stare at him. "You believe they have that many troops at their command?"

"I can't be sure. That's something else I need to find out. That stockpile suggests they have a number of men they hope to equip. The only suggestion of that presence is the guards that patrol when we're supposed to be sleeping. They have to live somewhere, and I haven't noticed anyone in the house other than guests or servants, have you?''

Jasmine shook her head, and he went on. ''That means there has to be a place nearby to house them. See if you can find out just how much area the Brothers have on the compound.''

''What do you intend to do?''

He lifted a bare shoulder in a negligible shrug. ''The guards patrolling that building are on a three-hour rotation. I heard a vehicle start up when they switched. I'll follow one of the Jeeps, see where I end up.''

She wanted to protest. What he was suggesting was dangerous, far more dangerous than anything he'd done so far. He might well find himself thrust amid the stronghold of the Brothers' army, and the chance of discovery would be calculated. With effort, she stemmed her protest. He wouldn't welcome an attempt to tell him how to do his job. She understood the sentiment, having felt the same way on numerous occasions.

So she said simply, ''I will see what I can discover tomorrow and let you know. If, as you suggest, the compound is big enough to house a large number of troops, then surely it encompasses enough area on which to hide a lab, as well.''

''Exactly.''

Pushing away from the wall, Walker began to prowl the room. His edginess fostered her own, and her muscles went tense. ''The Brothers appear to have a well-organized setup.'' She told him about her guess regarding the concentric cells. ''I am beginning to wonder if they have a broader base than we believed scattered across the United

States and perhaps Europe. It would be helpful if we could find out how many cells there are, and where they are located. This job won't be finished until we cripple the Brothers completely.''

There was an odd note of approval in his tone. "I agree. And our best bet for finding that information, along with the location of the lab, is going to be in the office."

"It is a shame Abdul interrupted your efforts tonight." Some quiver of awareness had her turning to keep Walker in her sight. His pacing seemed less like restlessness than like a big cat's stealthy stalking. She shook off the fanciful thought. Because if he was to be likened to an animal of prey, Jasmine was all too aware how the analogy would define her.

He remained silent, circling the room slowly. Circling *her.* Nerves bumped in her stomach. To distract him, and herself, she began to tell him about the events of the meeting earlier that day. "The twelve men brought here to meet with me represent the powers in the Brothers of Darkness. From what I can gather, each man controls one facet of the organization. I think you were right—Bonlei Marakeh is at the helm. I will begin meeting with each of the individuals tomorrow, to get a better understanding of their place in the structure."

She'd managed to distract him with her words. He stilled. "You're meeting with all twelve of them? That'll give us plenty of time to find the information we need and get out of here. Have you learned where each of these men is stationed? Whether they're within the country or outside it?"

"I'll find out," she promised. "It remains to be seen how much real information they intend to share with me. My best source remains Abdul. Although he is a careful man, he is liable to let something slip in his efforts to impress me.''

''Yeah, I caught a glimpse of his *efforts* a while ago. Looked like they were working, too.''

The edge was back to his voice, and after delivering the stinging remark he was on the move again. This time, however, it wasn't awareness shaking Jasmine, it was anger. It seemed far safer than the latter. ''You are lucky I was there to divert his attention from you. Your presence downstairs at that hour would have been difficult to explain.''

His tone was the caustic one she recognized too well. ''Certainly I wouldn't have had the advantage in that area that you do, but I think I could have managed. Seemed like the least you could do, at any rate. It was probably your movements that alerted him in the first place.''

Jasmine's fingers curled into her palms at the unfairness of his accusation. ''I didn't come downstairs until I heard noises. Either they were yours or Abdul heard you and was coming to investigate. Perhaps you are slipping, *Ghost*.''

''Don't worry about me. Just be sure that you don't get tripped up in the little game you're playing with Abdul. You may end up paying a lot more for that information than you're planning on.''

The insult in his words was impossible to miss. Fury shook her words. ''Do you honestly believe that I would sleep with Abdul for an *assignment?*''

There was just enough moonlight spilling through the window for her to make out the twist of his lips as he came to a halt in front of her. Catching her chin in his fingers, he leaned down and drawled, ''Well, it's not like you haven't done it before, is it, sweetheart?''

Quick reflexes and well-honed instincts were all that prevented his eye from being blackened. With Jasmine's

fist grasped in his hand, he pulled her closer, close enough
for her to feel the heat emanating from his body. He shook
his head in mock reproach. "Control yourself, Jaz. I'm just
giving you a friendly warning. Abdul might not be as for-
giving of your tactics as I was."

Her foot shot out, her intent to lay him flat. He moved
to deflect the kick. He lost his balance, retaining his hold
on her, and she landed hard on him. She lay there for an
instant, dazed, her breath sawing out of her lungs. Then
his arms snaked around her and in an instant he had her
flipped to her back, his body stretched out on top of hers.

"Did I hit a nerve, Jaz?" That he could croon the hate-
ful words in such a soft voice was almost as wounding as
his meaning. "I think in our line of work it's best to have
no illusions about ourselves, don't you?"

She made no attempt to quell the bitterness in her voice.
"Believe me, I hold no illusions about myself. And I have
none whatsoever about you."

His arm was banded across her back, sealing her to him.
She could think of a dozen moves that would incapacitate
him, and free herself, but couldn't gather the strength to
try any of them.

There was an odd spear of pain in her chest that owed
nothing to her oxygen-starved lungs and everything to his
words. On a wave of desolation she realized that the most
powerful tool she could hand the man was her reaction to
him. His ability to hurt her hadn't faded over the years, it
had just honed a keener edge. And if she had a hint of
self-preservation left, she'd be running from him, from this
situation, as fast as she could.

She raised her knee sharply, intending to dislodge him.
He shifted his hips before she could inflict any damage,
then clamped one of his legs over both of her own. His

teeth flashed briefly before doing a gradual fade as awareness filled his eyes.

Their position was far too suggestive; far too intimate.
Breaths mingled, gazes held. She could feel every hard
inch of him; bone, sinew and muscle. And the feel of his
familiar form pressed against hers was leeching the
strength from her limbs.

Moistening her lips, she tried to ignore the way his gaze
followed her movement. "This will not solve the problems
in our working relationship."

His gaze was still arrowed on her mouth. "Maybe not.
But it would solve a couple of problems of mine." He
lowered his head slowly, giving her time to divine his intention. But it wasn't until the last moment that she could
find the strength to turn her face away.

His lips brushed her cheek, his mouth cruising over her
jawline, before he investigated the hollow at her throat.
When his teeth closed delicately over the sensitive cord
there, she shivered.

"This is not helping." The words were difficult to summon. Impossible to mean.

"Ignoring it isn't helping, either." She could feel her
own pulse, the blood beating a rapid tattoo in her veins.
The rigid length of him was pressed against her hip, hard
and ready. "No illusions, remember?" The words were
rasped, low and rough against her ear. "And I'm through
pretending that I can ignore this, Jaz. Or you." The stinging kiss he pressed to the corner of her mouth had her
breath tangling with his. "The question is, when are you
going to stop pretending?"

His mouth closed over hers before she could make a
response, although she doubted she would have been able
to fashion one. The dark magic of his flavor still worked
its spell, depleting her lungs of oxygen, her limbs of

strength. His mouth sealed against hers and he came more fully atop her body, his weight partially supported by his elbows on the floor on either side of her.

The robe and undergarment she wore failed to insulate her from his heat, from the weight of his body. As their mouths twisted together, he didn't wrestle with her clothes at all. He merely bunched up her robe in one hand, and swept his palm beneath it, sliding it up her thigh in a long silken stroke.

His touch torched a flame that flickered in its wake, and her hands reached up to clasp his shoulders. Instead of pushing him away, her fingers immediately recognized his form, turned caressing. His hair-roughened chest was explored, on a journey that was tantalizingly familiar. Reason faded to a distant protest as his mouth pressed hers wider, allowing him access. His tongue swept in, hot and urgent and she met it with her own.

His finger traced the slim band holding the stiletto strapped to her thigh, and she shivered helplessly. His mouth grew hungrier and he devoured her, with lips, tongue and teeth. And then, in the next instant his palm moved just as boldly, cupping her, rubbing rhythmically at the damp fabric that separated him from her moist warmth.

The pleasure, the bone-numbing anticipation brought a shock of memory. Of Walker above her, beneath her. Of his hips hammering against hers as they both strained to get closer. And closer. And how far away they had been the next day.

She tore her mouth from his, but couldn't prevent her shudder when he sent one finger skating beneath the elastic of her panties. "We must stop."

"Why?" His lips were as determined as his words. Her earlobe was caught between his teeth and scored lightly.

She despaired of finding the courage, or the strength, to push him away. But words could be a weapon of another kind, and she wielded them desperately. "What kind of man are you, Walker, to accuse me of whoring myself for this assignment, and then try to use me as the same?"

Her biting words were as effective as a dash of cold water. She could feel his body go still against hers, one inch of muscle at a time. His head raised an inch, and his eyes glittered into hers. Had she not been so angry herself, she might have quailed beneath the look in his eyes. "I never called you a whore."

She didn't know where the sheath of ice came from. She suspected from somewhere deep inside her. Because she was cold now, glacial, from the certainty of the truth she spoke. "Perhaps you did not use the word. But your meaning was clear. I have no *illusions* about that."

She made no attempt to veil the mockery of the word, and it had the desired effect. He rolled off her and rose to his feet. Jasmine ignored the hand he extended and stood without help. She was loathe to touch him again. She didn't trust herself to do so.

Slowly, with a great deal more attention than the act required, she gathered her robe around herself, smoothed the garment.

"Jaz."

When he would have taken her arm, she sidestepped. "There is nothing more to say, Walker. Nothing that has not been said before."

He jammed his hands into his pockets, stared at her steadily. "Not even I'm sorry?"

The words had her gaze flying to his. He couldn't have said anything more guaranteed to shock her. "What are you sorry for, Walker? For saying the words? Or for thinking them?" His gaze slid from hers and she pressed on, the anguish in her heart sounding in her voice. "Tell me that you didn't believe it three years ago. Look me in the eyes and admit that you don't think I used you in exactly that way."

His silence sprouted fangs and sank deep. It took all the dignity she could muster to force a humorless smile. "Your silence speaks much more loudly than your apology ever could." She turned and walked toward the door leading to the sitting room linking their quarters. She forced her posture ramrod-straight, because to bend, to relax at all, would bring total collapse.

As she walked out the door there was still a forlorn part of her wishing that he'd call her back.

And an even more certain part knowing that he wouldn't.

The tiny click of the door signaling Jasmine's exit resounded over and over again in Walker's brain. Jamming a hand through his hair he turned to the window again, stared sightlessly out into the darkness. It would be dawn in a few hours. If he had any sense at all he'd try to get some sleep.

But if that recent scene was any indication, good sense was something he had in all too short supply. God knew if he'd been thinking clearly at all he wouldn't have touched Jasmine. Wouldn't still want her. Wouldn't still hate her for it.

She'd come damn close to knocking him on his ass a while ago, and he was honest enough to admit that he would have deserved it. He didn't know what demon caused him to ride her about the night they'd spent together. About the way they'd parted.

He could still see the hurt in her exquisite dark eyes, and the memory twisted his gut. He could have handled her anger, but knowing he'd caused her pain made him feel like a bastard. Emotions were a messy, sticky affair, and he usually did a better job avoiding them altogether. The fact that they surfaced around Jaz was profoundly disturbing.

Women didn't get to him—or at least they hadn't in the last decade or so. Sure, he'd been burned once, but he'd only been seventeen and more susceptible to being led around by his hormones. The memory brought a dart of deprecation. Sweet, beautiful Laura. He'd been no match for her either in age or experience. He'd taken her into his bed and then into his confidence. His reward for both was to come home from a job one night to find her gone. She'd cleaned out his apartment, and, even more devastating, the items he'd held to be fenced later had been systematically picked over. He'd always thought it telling that he'd missed that little Renoir she'd stolen from him far more fiercely than he'd missed the woman.

He leaned one shoulder against the wall and willed his muscles to relax. He'd been lucky then, damn lucky, that Laura had merely plotted to rob him and not turn him over to the cops. His present would have been very much different if she had. But he'd only had to learn that particular lesson once. Women, especially beautiful ones, were lethal if not kept at a distance. An emotional one, at least.

He turned into the room to pace. The experience hadn't inflicted any lasting damage, although it had hardened him. And he'd never forgotten the lesson she'd taught him until that night with Jasmine three years ago.

He could still remember seeing her standing across that crowded ballroom in Venice. He'd never been one to allow himself to be distracted from the assignment at hand, but she'd been exquisite and he hadn't been able to take his eyes off of her.

He'd known who she was, of course. Dirk had mentioned her several times, and he knew she'd been another of the man's protégés, picked up off the streets of Morocco to be molded by Dirk's hand. Walker hadn't known what had been different about Venice, why his purely male admiration for her had flickered into a much deeper interest.

The memory lingered, refusing to be banished. He'd walked across the ballroom and taken her hand, led her to the dance floor. But it hadn't been long before the crush of people, the noise, had them searching for a more private spot.

They'd danced together on one of the balconies under the stars, and the seclusion had fostered intimacy, then flamed it. And when the evening had called for greater privacy, he'd taken her to his room, and focused on nothing but her.

The next morning she'd been gone. And hours later he'd discovered the Star of Benzia had vanished, as well. It was the first time he'd had to tell a client that he'd failed his assignment. The first time he'd had to admit to himself that a woman had managed to distract him from the job at hand, and then beat him at his own game.

His gaze trailed to the door linking their rooms. He wished he could go to her now. He wished that he could tell her it didn't matter anymore.

He wished like hell that it didn't.

"Oh, excuse me."

Jasmine hovered in the doorway of the office, an apologetic smile on her lips. Tariq Abdul covered the mouthpiece on the phone. "May I help you, madame?"

There was no familiar smile on his lips. His eyes were watchful. But with the sound of someone fast approaching in the hallway, Jasmine hadn't dared linger there any longer attempting to listen to Abdul's one-sided conversation.

She made a pretense of backing out the doorway. "I am sorry. I did not realize this room was occupied."

"Please, stay." His words, though couched as a request, sounded like a command. "What it is that you needed here?"

It was telling how easily the man's suspicions were aroused. She was accustomed, however, to calming such suspicions. Even trivializing them.

"I lost a bracelet. I met with the assembled representatives in this room, and thought I would check here first."

As she continued to hover uncertainly in the doorway, he made a motion for her to remain, and finished speaking to the other party on the phone. His words, however, gave very little information about the identity of the caller. Reaching for a pad of paper and a pencil, he kept his gaze on Jasmine as he wrote down some information before signing off on the call.

His eyes remained cool as he tore off the paper and continued to watch her. Nerves reared in her stomach. It would be a challenge to wipe the wariness from his face. "I am sorry to interrupt your call. I could have returned."

"Not at all." He creased the paper and slipped it into a pocket in his *jellaba.* "Perhaps I can help you."

Giving him a casual smile, Jasmine walked into the room and past him. "I hope so. I would hate to think my carelessness would cost me such a valued keepsake."

She sank to her knees in front of the couch and, using her body as a shield, loosened the clasp on the bracelet she wore on her wrist.

"Was it a gift from your late husband, Rose?" Tariq moved closer and tension spiked. Pulling off the pretense with him so close would be risky.

And surely it was indicative of some flaw in her makeup that she found herself relishing the prospect so completely.

"No, I received it from my father on my eighteenth birthday." She tucked her fingertips into the seam of the cushions, allowed the loosened jewelry to slip down her arm. The wide sleeves of her caftan would mask the movement, if she could manage to distract Abdul from watching her too closely. "It matches the necklace I am wearing." She lifted her other hand to her throat, and, as she'd hoped, his gaze lingered there for a moment. It was long enough to divest herself of the bracelet and tuck it out of sight in the couch cushions.

"Indeed, it is lovely, and would be a shame to lose. Allow me."

She moved aside as she pretended to continue her search on the other end of the couch, leaving Abdul to the area where she'd planted the piece. "If I am not able to find it here, I think I must check outside where we walked. I have already looked all over my bedroom."

From the corner of her eye she saw him hesitate, dive deeper into the couch cushion, and withdraw the bracelet she'd so recently planted. "Your worries are over, madame."

She assumed an expression of pleasure. "Oh, how wonderful! Thank you. I do not know what I would have done if I'd lost the piece for good." She allowed him to help her rise, noting that his earlier suspicions seemed allayed.

"May I?" Submitting to his ministrations, Jasmine watched as he fastened the bracelet back on her wrist, but she wasn't congratulating herself on a narrow escape. Instead, she was wondering how she could get her hands on the scrap of paper so tantalizingly close in the man's pocket.

When his fingers would have stayed to caress the skin

of her wrist, she cast her gaze downward and stepped away. "I must be getting back."

"So quickly, Rose? We have not had a chance to talk much today." A note of intimacy crept into the man's voice. "Were you able to sleep well, after we parted last night?"

Her hands went to her cheeks, as if to cover a flush. "I owe you an apology. I do not usually indulge in emotion in front of people I barely know."

"You must not feel uncomfortable." Abdul stepped in front of her, effectively blocking any escape a distressed woman would be tempted to make. "I would be very happy to hear that I had some small part in soothing your feelings last night."

Jasmine looked at the man from beneath her lashes. This was one of those times in an agent's career when split-second decisions needed to be made about the course of action to take. Normally she wouldn't think twice, but Walker, damn him, had made her hesitate.

She couldn't allow his opinion of her to alter what she knew she had to do. But it was maddening that the scene with him was responsible for doubts surfacing, even for a moment. Pushing them from her mind, she widened her eyes, noting by the man's arrested look that she had his attention. And when he pulled her into his arms, she went willingly, her body softening against his.

His lips met hers at approximately the same time her fingers slipped into the pocket of his *jellaba*.

After only a few moments she tore her mouth from his, tucked her head against his shoulder. The man's lips went to the side of her throat and she used the moment to glance down at the paper she'd unfolded.

Omer X435 7:00.

By the time Abdul had raised his head and opened his

eyes to contemplate the woman in his arms, the note had been refolded and placed back in his pocket. She pulled away from him, and immediately his hands went to her shoulders.

"You will forgive my liberty, Rose. But I find myself overcome with feelings for you and have from the first time we met."

The delivery was low and smooth, a well-rehearsed line. Jasmine wondered derisively about the intelligence of women who fell for it. "This is not proper, Mr. Abdul. I fear I have given you the wrong idea."

"What idea, Rose? That you are a beautiful woman whose outward strength masks an abiding vulnerability?"

"My role in Maloun is one as emissary. It does not leave me free to follow my feelings…only my duty."

He seized on her words. "Dare I hope that these feelings you speak of might have something to do with me? I can assure you, they are returned." He dared to press a kiss to her forehead. "Very warmly."

She made her voice sound determined—but torn. "I must get back to the duties. I only took advantage of a small break to search for my bracelet." She slipped away from him and started for the door.

"We will talk later, Rose." The promise in his voice was ominous. It slid over her skin and left a chill in its wake.

Chapter 7

"How are the meetings going?" Walker walked alongside Jasmine. Their leisurely stroll suggested nothing more devious than a couple in search of the slightly cooler air afforded by early evening.

"Slowly," she answered, blowing out a breath. She would have preferred avoiding Walker until the memory of last night was a little less vivid, and her feelings a little less raw. But she'd be hard-pressed to determine just how long a time that would take. Longer, she was certain, than this assignment allowed them.

With a calm she was proud of, she continued, "Interestingly enough, Marakeh is present at each of them—I believe to control the exchange of information. When I ask a question that might draw the person out, he jumps in and steers the conversation back to the designated topic." It was, she'd found, profoundly frustrating. "I did manage to find out that the compound is over a hundred square kilometers. Ample space to house any troops they may have, as well as the lab itself. I also discovered that the Brothers will be hosting another visitor soon."

Interest sharpened Walker's voice. "Who?"

"Do you know anyone by the name of Omer?"

"Dr. Sinan Omer?" While Jasmine shrugged, Walker gave a tuneless whistle. "Well, well. This is gonna get interesting."

Her brows raised. "Why? Who is this man?"

"Remember when I told you about the biologist from U.C.L.A. suspected of being linked to the Brothers' cell there?"

Jasmine immediately made the connection. "He is arriving soon. I have the flight number and time, but not the date. Do you think he is affiliated with the lab?"

"I wouldn't be surprised if he's taken to visit it. Makes me wonder just how close the virus is to being finished." Walker slid a glance at her, and then, totally surprising her, said, "Nice job, Jaz. How'd you happen to pick that up?"

"Abdul was on the phone. I could not make out much from his side of the conversation, but I was able to look at the note he scribbled."

"How'd you manage that?"

Without missing a beat she replied coolly, "Well, I slept with him, of course. You, of all people, should know how powerful a tool sex can be when it comes to getting what I want."

The look on his face told her that he failed to find the humor in her remark. She was dismayed herself at the bitter edge to the words. It indicated the depth to which he'd hurt her, and she'd learned long ago not to give Walker such a weapon.

Reaching up a hand, she smoothed back a strand of hair that had worked loose from the knot she'd fixed it in. And at the same time fought to tuck back the emotions that still throbbed. "Actually I did not have to have sex with the man to get the information, despite your opinions about my morals. I merely allowed him to kiss me and used the opportunity to pick his pocket."

Walker's face was a study of emotion, a contrast of anger and disbelief. "You did what?"

"Picked his pocket," she repeated deliberately. "I am sure you are familiar with the concept."

"Of all the harebrained, dim-witted stunts to pull!"

Although the insults themselves were foreign to her, their meanings were clear enough. Answering temper snapped through her, and it was a welcome emotion. Anger was an effective shield against the continued hurt inflicted by his low opinion of her. "It was a calculated risk."

His gaze abruptly narrowed. "Need I ask how you managed to get close enough to the guy to pull this off?"

Her chin tilted and she met his gaze unwaveringly. She refused to let him make her feel ashamed. In her training she'd been taught to use every advantage open to her in the course of her job, and that naturally meant using her looks. She doubted very much that Walker hadn't done the same when the occasion demanded it.

"I needed an excuse to be there at all. I could tell from Abdul's demeanor that he was unhappy to have me happen into the study during his phone call. He was also a little suspicious of my timing. I used the opportunity that presented itself. I thought the call might be important to us."

She could read the effort it took for him to keep his stance, his stride relaxed, as if their casual conversation was about nothing more important than the weather. His tone was a blistering contrast to his casual posture. "It was a risk all right, and a stupid one at that. There would have been easier ways to get that information, if it actually turns out that we need it at all.''

She stopped and turned to him, his body blocking her from view of the house. His words were a dare, and they had a predictable effect on her. ''Do you really think it was a risk, Walker?''

''Damn right I do. Get it through your head, Jaz, you're here as window dressing. I'll do the investigating, I'll take the chances.''

''Of course. I suppose you will be wanting this back.''

His gaze dropped to the car keys she pressed into his palm, and he stared at them for a moment in disbelief. ''I hope you'll forgive the 'risk' I took in relieving you of them a moment ago.''

''How the hell...''

Her brows skimmed upward, pleasantly surprised for once to have the upper hand. ''You have your talents, Ghost, and I have mine. Now if you'll excuse me...I really need to get back to my meetings.''

She brushed by him, making her way back toward the house. Leaving Walker staring after her, stunned and out of sorts, filled her with a satisfaction that was impossible to deny.

Walker had managed a couple hours of sleep before awakening and stealing out of the house for some more late-night reconnoitering. From what Jasmine had told him that day, it appeared that the compound was far larger than he'd feared. The Brothers had ample space in which to tuck away the lab. He may not find it that night, but he was determined to discover the answers to at least some of his questions.

He spent an hour studying the security at the front gate. Once darkness fell, there was no longer any attempt to hide the lengths taken to keep the compound impenetrable. The night-vision binoculars gave him a means to observe the activity.

He counted a full dozen men stationed at any given time. As had the guards at the outbuilding, the men arrived by Jeep, and each was heavily armed. The distance from the house enabled the comings and goings to be accomplished circumspectly.

Once he'd satisfied himself with what he'd learned there, Walker melted into the shadows and made his way to the outside building once again. Tonight he was determined to find just how far away the troops for the Brothers were kept. And how many they numbered.

Remembering the direction the Jeeps had arrived from, he moved away, gauging his distance carefully. And then, hunched behind a small boulder, he settled in to wait.

He'd never be considered a patient man, but waiting was something often called for in his line of work. He did it with the effortless stillness that came from practice. Years of experience had given him absolute control over his body.

Unfortunately that control didn't seem to extend to his brain.

His mind stubbornly insisted on conjuring up images of Jasmine—smiling, although usually not at him; her beautiful face composed, serious or even angry. But none of the mental pictures had the power to slice at him as had the hurt that had flashed across her face on a couple of occasions. Hurt for which he'd been responsible.

He shifted uncomfortably in the small area and a night creature, startled by his movement, scurried away. No one would accuse him a being a particularly gentle man, but he'd never been one given to hurting women, to insulting them. He liked to believe he was above that, but it was probably closer to the truth that he'd just never given a damn before, either way.

Which didn't explain why it was different with Jasmine. Why *she* was different.

The noise of an approaching vehicle sounded, saving Walker from the uncomfortable path his thoughts were taking. He pulled the binoculars from his pack and trained them in the direction of the vehicle. It was descending from the hills, its journey slow and rough. He waited for it to roll by, within a hundred feet of his hiding place. Once it passed, Walker lost no time. In a crouch he began making his way up the hill, retracing the path the Jeep had taken. The scrub brush gradually turned to shallow-rooted evergreens, but the soil remained rocky and sandy. He took cover where he could and continued to make his way up the increasingly steeper hills.

He took cover once more when he heard a Jeep approach with the off-duty guards. He watched it through the binoculars, gauging its direction. Adjusting his, he continued his journey. The higher he climbed, the thicker the vegetation grew, allowing him to jog upright, and he used his night-vision goggles to find his way. He'd come about three miles already, he estimated, and there was no telling how much farther he had to go. If he didn't find the camp in a couple more hours he'd have to turn back, in order to return to the house before dawn.

At the top of a rocky knoll he stopped and rested, pulling a canteen from his pack and drinking sparingly. Then he started over the hill, finding his way down carefully, searching for footholds.

He was only halfway down the hill when the rock he'd braced his weight against gave way. When he felt it slip, he moved, but not quickly enough. The rock rolled down the hill and, off balance, he followed it, scrabbling wildly for something to break his fall. He rolled, protecting his head with his arms, so when he came up hard against yet another large rock, it was his wrist that took the brunt of the blow. Pain exploded, and Walker cursed silently and creatively.

Rising, he gingerly took stock of his injuries, and was relieved to discover he likely hadn't broken anything. His wrist was already throbbing like a bitch, but he still had some mobility in it. He retrieved the backpack he'd lost during his crashing descent, and shrugged into it again.

It was with greater care this time that he made his way down the rest of the hill and through the dense trees before coming to a stop again. He reached for the binoculars and released a breath of satisfaction. Another thousand yards below was a clearing filled with large tents and Jeeps.

He'd found the Brothers' troops.

Moving as close to the camp as he dared, he then circled it completely. He counted two dozen large tents in all, but there was no way from his distance to estimate which were filled with people, and how many were lodged in each. There was only one way to find out.

Soundlessly, he moved down into the clearing to investigate more closely.

Dreams whispered through Jasmine's sleep, veiled images that could drift freely through her subconscious. She dreamed of Walker, could all but feel his heat, his weight. She shifted restlessly, her movements a faint whisper of silk against cotton. His face hazed in her mind, his mouth faintly twisted in a mocking smile. The image made her restless, and she turned away, her eyes coming open. Then she blinked uncomprehendingly in the dark. The man had stepped out of her unconscious and into her bedroom.

His face was close to hers, and he had one finger poised

lightly against her lips. He needn't have bothered. It was a moment before Jasmine could disentangle the dream from the reality, and when she did she came up in bed in one smooth movement.

This wasn't the man from her dream, his face masked in sardonic amusement. No, this man was dressed for the night, a black watch cap covering his dark hair, his face and hands darkened to help avoid detection. Jasmine took this all in with one quick glance. But it was the shadow of pain in his eyes that had concern sharpening her voice.

"What's wrong?"

"Nothing. Just need your help with something." The near soundless words were breathed in her ear, and she obeyed immediately. They rose and she followed him into the bathroom. It wasn't until she turned on the light that she saw that one of the sleeves of his dark shirt was soaked in blood.

Her stomach jittered oddly, but her voice remained even enough. "What happened?"

"Don't worry, I wasn't discovered." He leaned heavily against the sink. "I followed the Jeeps back and found a camp of sorts in the hills. Lost my footing and rolled a ways. I need some help getting out of this shirt."

The fact that he'd awakened her, that he'd sought her out for help at all, alerted her that he was purposefully downplaying the injury. "Let me do it." Her fingers brushed against his as she pulled the tight-fitting black shirt from the waistband of his pants. Perhaps it was the remnants of the dreams that had so recently been chased away, but she found herself all too aware of his muscled body as it was bared, inches at a time, by her ministrations.

They freed one arm and he used it to yank the shirt over his head. Stopping him before he peeled it down his injured arm, she pushed his hand away and eased the shirt off slowly. She sucked in a deep breath when she saw the puffiness already forming around his wrist bone, and the long ugly gash on the underside of the same arm.

"It would have been simpler, I believe, had you chosen to walk down that hill." She masked her concern with a casual tone as she turned on the taps and pushed his hands into the water.

"Dammit, Jaz, I can wash myself. I just needed…"

"You need to clean your hands, and while we are at it, your face. Then the wound must be sanitized."

He twisted his arm to study the injury. "Think you can stitch it up for me?"

A giant fist clenched in her stomach and refused to release. "We will cleanse it before we decide what is needed. What did you discover this evening?"

"Approximately one hundred men are situated in a makeshift camp in the hills directly east of here, about four miles. My guess is that it's temporary quarters, moved there for the duration of our stay. I couldn't find a well or source of water, and the cooking is being done over fires."

Reaching for a hand towel, she glanced up at him as she dried his hands. "They went to a lot of trouble."

"It's in their best interest to convince you of their harmlessness. Having armed troops around wouldn't further that cause." When she gently began to clean the cut he made no sound of pain, but she saw the way his mouth thinned.

"So there was no sign of the lab?"

He shook his head, then thwarted her efforts by twisting his arm around to examine the injury. "The lab would have to have electricity and running water. That's why I figure it must be fairly close by. The Brothers would want to keep an eye on it, and their troops are here. I'll have to keep looking."

His words were almost too precise. She gave him a

quick look and noted the white lines around his mouth. Tearing her gaze away, she reached for a bottle and shook out some pills. He reacted just as she'd expected.

"Forget it, I don't want my thinking clouded."

"It is just an antibiotic. With as much dirt as you got in that cut, you have to be careful about infection."

He was still shaking his head. "I've got some back in my room."

She let a measure of the exasperation she felt sound in her voice. "Just take them, Walker."

He eyed her for a moment before taking the pills from her and swallowing them dry. She returned his gaze unblinkingly, the lie she'd just uttered not weighing at all on her conscience. He needed sleep and he wasn't going to get it with his wrist throbbing all night. If she had to deceive him to get him to take pain pills, it was, she reasoned, for a good cause. It certainly wouldn't damage his opinion of her. He already believed her capable of far worse.

She handed him the washcloth so he could wash his face using his uninjured arm. She wet another cloth and wiped at the cut. "I think butterfly bandages will work just as well on your arm, and leave less of a scar."

One corner of his mouth lifted. "Yeah, I'm concerned about the scar. Don't want to ruin my Adonis-like physique, do I?"

Adonis-like was an all too apt description, but she certainly wouldn't give him the satisfaction of saying so. While he scrubbed at his face she turned away to dig in her makeup case. Withdrawing a tube, she squeezed out some ointment and gently worked it over the wound. Then she fixed some bandages to hold it together.

"You really need some ice to control the swelling of your wrist," she told him.

Walker flexed his fingers testingly, scowling when the stiffness there prevented him from making a fist. "It's not worth chancing going downstairs for. Do you have anything to wrap it with?"

There was just a hint of a slur to his words and she looked at him consideringly. Maybe she should have cut down on the number of pills, but he was a big man and she'd thought he'd require twice the dosage that she would.

"I think I can find something." She turned and walked back into the bedroom, acutely aware of his presence behind her. Motioning for him to sit on the bed, she went to the dresser.

When she returned to his side he'd toed off his shoes and lain back on the pillow that she had, all too recently, been sleeping on. She read his thoughts as easily as if they'd been written on a billboard. "Not one word, Walker."

He gave a sleepy smile that lacked innocence. "I have to admit that I've given a lot of thought about getting into your bed, but none of them played out quite like this."

It was best, she decided, to ignore his ribald remark. With the pair of nail scissors she'd taken out, she clipped off one leg of a pair of pantyhose, and used the nylon to wrap his wrist. She was all too aware of his partial nudity while she worked, all too aware of his nearness. Of his breathing, soft and even.

"Tell me you've worn these before and I'll die a happy man, Jaz."

"I am still holding the scissors," she pointed out as she snipped at one end and tied the makeshift bandage in a neat knot. "Do not tempt me."

"Seems only fair." His voice was thick with exhaustion. The drug was doing its work. His free hand reached up, caught in the hair that swung beside her face. She stiffened, and he cupped the back of her head, kneaded gently. ''You've tempted me for three years. Three years, Jaz.'' The words were coming slower now, and his eyelids were heavy. ''Did you ever think of me?''

Her heart was hammering so fast that she wondered if he could hear it. ''No.''

His low laugh was a seductive glide down her spine, and called her a liar. ''I don't believe you.''

''If your wrist swells too much, I will have to loosen the bandage, and rewrap it.'' Her voice was just a little wild, her words too clearly an attempt to divert his attention. It failed miserably. His hand was still wrapped in her hair, his intent gaze still held her captive.

''I've thought of you, Jaz. Thought of us. Remember how it was that night? I think you do. It's burned on my brain, baby, did you know that?'' He was exerting pressure, one infinitesimal fraction at a time, bringing her face closer to his. ''I've hated you ever since. And I've wanted you. I can't help wanting you.''

The words were formed against her lips and her eyes fluttered closed for an instant as she allowed all the heat, all the magic, to flow between them again. Her mouth softened against his and she returned his kiss, which was unlike any other they'd shared. Maybe it was his tiredness, combined with the drugs she'd slipped him, but this kiss lacked the urgency she was used to from him. Instead it was slow, wet, and deep. Infinitely carnal. He seduced her with his mouth, wooed her with his tongue. She was urged closer, and her body went boneless.

While the kiss was different, her reaction to it was the same. Liquid fire licked through her veins and everything inside her focused on one man. One need. With Walker's experience he'd know he hadn't been her first. She was determined he never learn that he'd been her last.

Memory sliced through the haze of desire with clean brutal strokes and gave her the strength to tear her mouth away. Pressing her hands against his chest, she rose, her breathing ragged. She didn't look at him, couldn't. Instead she walked on unsteady legs to the bathroom, rested both hands on the sink and stared sightlessly into the mirror. Jasmine didn't recognize her reflection. The woman looking back at her had hair mussed and wild, lips swollen and wet, a pulse hammering wildly at the base of her throat. Closing her eyes allowed her to shut out the reflection, but there was no denying the need that still hammered inside her body. Emotion was battling logic and pride. Emotion was winning.

To give herself time to turn the tide of that battle, she took some hand towels and ran the cold water over them. She brought one to her face, wishing the cool pressure would quench the fires that flickered through her veins.

After long minutes passed Jasmine took a deep breath and fought through the fog of desire. Grabbing the towels and a couple of dry ones, she went back into the bedroom, and found Walker asleep.

She stared down at him for an instant. The combination of the painkillers and exhaustion had conquered his considerable will. And it had also saved her from a decision she still wasn't sure she'd had the strength to make. Quickly, with innate gentleness, she wrapped his wrist in the icy towels, rested them on the dry ones, and slipped a pillow beneath as support. Then she paused, uncertain what to do next.

Sleep didn't soften Walker's stubborn jaw, but she thought the pain she'd seen tightening his mouth had lessened. Whether that was due to the medication or their kiss, she didn't want to consider.

Oddly enough, although he'd woken her from a sound slumber earlier, she no longer felt the slightest bit sleepy. He tended to have that effect on her; tying her emotions in knots that would be much too complicated to easily disentangle.

Sinking down onto the bed beside him, she had a sudden, fervent wish that she'd never taken the assignment that had brought her and Walker together three years ago. That she'd never heard of the Star of Benzia. It was an odd wish, as that mission had made her career.

The Star. She could still recall the golden lights that had shot out of the huge pink diamond. Still feel the warm vibrations it had given off. One priceless gem. Three who claimed ownership. Her loyalty had been to her clients, the family who had lost it to the Nazis in the Second World War. Their ancestors had found it; had fought for it; had died for it. And there had been so little left of the family's memories when they'd been forced to flee Germany.

She'd done her research. The story had checked out and she'd agreed that the stone belonged with the Endelman family, rather than in the private collection it had ended up in. The wealthy collector had acquired it through questionable means. Jasmine had no doubts about what had needed to be done. It had seemed such a simple way to right one of the wrongs that had been visited on a family so long ago.

The recollections drew a sigh from her. Because, of course, nothing was ever as simple as it seemed. Her sources hadn't informed her that there was another claimant to the stone, one just as committed to its return. When she'd met Walker in Venice she'd never even considered that they were at cross purposes on the same assignment.

No, it hadn't been the mission, or any mission, that she'd considered once he'd approached her. And she thought, she was sure, that the job hadn't been on Walker's mind then, either. For the first time since she'd fled her home for the Moroccan streets, she'd been driven by pure, unadulterated emotion.

She'd been haunted by the repercussions ever since.

Starting, she glanced down to find Walker's hand on her leg. The action was reminiscent of the one night they'd spent together, when he'd reached for her, even during the time they dozed. The connection had contrasted sharply to the distance that had yawned between them when she'd returned to his quarters the following evening. That was when she'd learned that her success in procuring the Star had dealt his mission a death blow. It had also marked the end of their relationship before it had really begun.

Her throat closed. The old saying was wrong. Time didn't heal all wounds. Shrugging off the memories, she dimmed the lamp and crawled into bed. And as the minutes ticked away into hours she tried to convince herself that lying in bed next to this man didn't feel natural. Didn't feel right.

But she didn't quite manage to believe it.

Chapter 8

"And where are you off to so early this morning, Tariq?"

At Jasmine's purposefully flirtatious tone, the man paused. Instead of walking through the open front door, he turned and watched her descend the stairs, a flicker of male appreciation on his face. "You are an early riser yourself, madame. And the fairest thing I have laid eyes on yet this day."

Her lips curved and, reaching the bottom of the stairway, she waited for him to make his way toward her, to take her hand in his. When he pressed his mouth to her palm, her stomach clutched with revulsion, but she kept the smile fixed on her face. "I will not consider the earliness of the hour in your compliment, sir, but I will give you a chance to repeat it later in the day."

Her words elicited the answer she'd been hoping for. His face shadowed. "I am afraid that pleasure will be denied me until tomorrow. My driver has the car waiting. I have some...business to take care of today in Redyshah. But I will return tomorrow." He still had not released her hand, and used his grasp on it to tug her a bit closer. "Perhaps then you will grant me some private time. I think it is time we got to know one another better."

Despite the warm air in the home, Jasmine could feel a chill work over her skin. "Your business must be important, indeed, for you to make such a long trip and back overnight."

He gave a shrug. Clearly his mind was more focused on the conquest he had planned for Jasmine than on her words. "Not so important, as necessary. Just an acquaintance who demands my attention."

"I see."

The deliberate frost on her words had his handsome face frowning, and when she freed her hand to walk by him, puzzlement sounded in his voice. "Rose? Will you promise to save some time for me tomorrow evening?"

"This acquaintance of yours," Jasmine said, keeping the back of her head to him and the ice sheathing her words, "is she very demanding?"

There was a moment of silence before Abdul reached for her and turned her to face him. The stamp of male amusement on his face spoke clearer than words that her pretense had worked. "Dare I hope that is jealousy I hear in your voice, Rose?"

Jasmine kept her voice chilly, and her expression distant. "Not at all. Please excuse my prying. Your personal life is your own concern, of course." Deliberately she lifted her shoulder, the image of a woman in a fit of pique.

Instead of releasing her, his hand on her arm grew caressing. "I am man enough to appreciate your jealousy, my dear, even if there is no cause for it. I merely go to the airport to pick up a friend who is arriving, that is all.

An old college acquaintance of mine.'' His head dipped and he pressed a kiss to her temple. "And the last time I saw him, he was definitely not female."

He was going to pick up Omer. A measure of anticipation flickered to life. Jasmine was eager to discover just what connection the scientist had with the Brothers of Darkness. She found the lack of enthusiasm with which Abdul spoke of his old friend a bit odd. If, as she and Walker suspected, Omer was coming to help with the virus, she would think Abdul would be more eager for the scientist's arrival. In an attempt to draw him out a bit more on the subject, and to divert him from running his hand up her back, she stepped away, forcing an abashed expression to her face. "You misunderstood my interest, Tariq, I assure you."

Voice laced with indulgence, the man responded, "I hope not. And you can be certain that there will be no pleasure mixed with the business I have with Sinan."

"Your college friend? Oh, but you certainly must be excited to see him again. How long has it been since you have seen him?"

"We…keep in touch. But if his arrival here causes you to be cross with me, I shall send him back to the States immediately."

The smile she aimed at him then was as brilliant as it was false. "Do not be silly. I look forward to seeing you again tomorrow evening. You and your guest."

He'd started to draw her into his arms, but her words arrested him. "My guest?"

Daringly, Jasmine ran a hand over the lapel of the jacket he wore over his suit. "Of course. You would not deny me the opportunity to draw your friend out about your days as a wild college student."

His smile grew predatory and intimate. "Of course, you

shall meet Sinan. But I warn you, madame...I shall be quite selfish about sharing you tomorrow evening...with anybody.''

She forced herself to soften against him when he brought her closer, pressing his mouth to hers. And when she doubted her ability to pretend any longer, she slipped from his arms.

With visible reluctance he went to the door and picked up the bag he'd set there. When his hand was on the doorknob, she said, ''Tariq?''

She waited for him to look back before she smiled, slow and secretively. ''Until tomorrow.''

Satisfaction coursed through her when he threw her one last look, filled with mingled desire and frustration, before going through the door.

Jasmine had no doubt that she would have to come up with a way to deal with Abdul tomorrow evening. Something that would put him off, without antagonizing him too deeply. She knew she'd have to tread carefully. The more intent Abdul grew on her, the more determined he'd be. And despite Walker's less than admirable opinion of her morals, sex was not something she'd use to accomplish their mission, no matter how noble the cause may be.

She turned then and he was there. His approach had been silent, and he stood at the top of the stairs surveying her. Although his face was expressionless, she knew he'd witnessed the entire exchange between her and Abdul. Her stomach pitched. It would only solidify his already black opinion of her. She wondered what he thought that said about him, that he was still attracted to her in spite of it.

He'd made no attempt to keep that attraction secret from her. Not three years ago. Not a week ago. Not last night.

She'd gotten very little sleep, lying next to him, listening to his breathing. Memory was a sneaky thing, and past and present had entwined through the hours last night, weaving a bittersweet trap. When she'd awakened this morning it was to find Walker's arm keeping her tucked against his side. The will to move had been hard to summon, but eventually she'd done just that. She had far too much pride to get involved with a man who held her in such low esteem. It was surely due to some internal weakness that his opinion of her mattered at all.

And because it did matter, too much, she kept her voice casual. "Good morning. I am afraid we are too early for breakfast. No one else seems to be around."

"I can wait, I suppose. I was about to take a walk outside before it grows too warm. Would you like to join me?"

Senses screaming in the negative, Jasmine preceded him out the door and down the steps. The car that had taken Abdul was already out of sight as they made their way slowly around the corner of the large home.

She stole a glance at Walker, assessing. He'd showered and shaved, dressing in all white today. The shirt he'd chosen was long-sleeved, and she supposed it did an adequate job covering the wound she'd bandaged last night. His wrist, she noted, was no longer wrapped, and was puffy enough to obscure the bone.

"It's still swollen."

He flexed his fingers, managing to restrain most of a wince. "Stiff as hell, too."

"You could have used more rest." The moment the words were out of her mouth she wished them back. They showed a concern she wished she didn't feel, and hinted at an emotion she was determined to keep buried.

The look on his face told her that neither had escaped him. "I'm sure you're surprised I didn't get more sleep.

But the next time you try to slip me a mickey, Jaz, you'll have to use something that packs a bit more punch.''

He noted the slight frown on her forehead, so he explained. "You drugged me. Those weren't antibiotics you gave me last night. What the hell were they?''

"Painkillers." He caught the wide sleeve of her caftan, halting her movement. She turned to face him defiantly. "I knew you would be too stubborn to take anything, and it does our assignment no good if you allow yourself to get run-down."

Instead of slipping into combat mode as she'd expected, he continued to study her. To divert him, she repeated the conversation she'd had with Abdul earlier. "He will return with Omer tomorrow," she concluded. "Their relationship puzzles me. Abdul did not speak of the man with much affection. Perhaps I can learn more about their connection once they return."

"It's what we can learn from the computers in the office that I'm most concerned with right now. Tonight's the night, and I'm going to need your help."

She masked her surprise with a raised brow. "Two nights in a row? You should be careful, Walker. I will begin to believe I am more than window dressing on this trip."

If he recognized his own words turned against him, he gave no indication of it. "With Abdul gone until tomorrow it'll be a good opportunity to get into the office and break the encryption on the computers."

"I do not know much about computers."

"That's okay. I do. What I need help with isn't the computers, anyway. It's getting into the office. With this sprain, I can't rely on enough dexterity to dismantle the alarm without setting it off. That's where you come in."

The possibility of working together with him that evening filled her with trepidation. And far more pleasure than it should have. "Alarm systems are an area I have some expertise in."

He shot her a pointed look. "I just need you to be my hands, Jaz. I'll tell you every move to make, and you'll get us into the office. Who knows? Once we crack the computer security, we just might nail down the location of the lab. That would set all our plans on the fast track."

The possibility elicited a smile from her. "That would certainly answer our biggest problem."

"One of them." She didn't know what to make of his cryptic response, and her eyes widened as he moved closer. "We have some unfinished business that needs to be cleared up between us, first."

Warily, she tried to retreat. Walker kept step with her, keeping their proximity intact. "I think we have already agreed that business between us...should remain strictly that."

"Have we?" He reached out a hand, smoothed a finger along the tight knot she'd contained her hair in. "I'm not sure I agree with that, but I do have one thing I need to tell you."

He was standing much too close. Her eyes darted beyond him, but his shoulders blocked her view. She was prepared to have him make a suggestive remark about their sleeping arrangements last night. Perhaps even to hear a cutting barb about the scene he'd surely witnessed between her and Abdul. What she wasn't prepared for was to have him move closer, whisper a kiss over her lips. "Thanks for last night, Jaz. I owe you one."

Stunned, she could only stare at him. It took more effort than it should have to manage a steady voice. "That is what partners are for, are they not? You watch my back, and I watch yours?"

She couldn't identify the expression that flickered across his face. "Yeah. That's what partners are for."

The tiny beam of light speared through the blanketing darkness of the hallway. Walker held the pocket flashlight steady as he mouthed instructions into Jasmine's ear. "That's it. Slow and steady. You've got it, baby. Lift it off." The narrow conduit was lifted away from the wall and set on the floor. He swept the beam along the woodwork until he found the tiny set of dip switches he'd discovered the last time. "See those? There's a combination to their positions that will deactivate the alarm. You should have about fifteen seconds to make all the adjustments, before it trips. Think you can handle it?"

She turned her face to his. They were close enough that he could feel the softness of her cheek as it brushed his. "It will take me no more than ten."

He considered her in the darkness for a moment, wondering for an instant if *he* could handle *her*. To say that he usually worked alone would be a lie. Some jobs he did solitary, but others called for working with a team. Nor was this the first time he'd worked with a woman. But it was different working with Jasmine.

Everything was different with Jasmine.

She was as comfortable working under the cover of night as he was. He'd sensed the adrenaline coursing through her veins as soon as she'd joined him this evening, dressed in formfitting black for this task. He wondered what kind of defect in his character made him a sucker for a woman whose sense of adventure affected him like the most seductive of perfumes.

Turning his attention to the switches, he studied them carefully. One false move on her part, one whispered mistake from him, and this thing would be all over. Even if they got back to their rooms without being discovered, there would be no time to replace the plastic first. It would be apparent that the security had been breached, and it wouldn't take Marakeh much time to figure out who the chief suspects were. If that happened, Walker knew he and Jasmine would never leave the compound alive.

The danger of the situation didn't bother him, but it did help focus his attention. He could take care of himself, but there was no way he was going to place Jasmine at risk. So he spent an extra few moments studying the switches. When he was certain, he breathed, ''You're going to position them to up-up-up-down-down-up-down. Got that?''

''Wouldn't we just reverse the positions they are in now?''

He shook his head. ''Not in this kind of system. Repeat the placements back to me.'' He waited until she did so, before saying, ''Once you start, don't stop until you're done. Ready?''

Her hair brushed his face as she nodded, shifted closer. Time crawled to a stop as she poised the pick above the set of switches. Then she bent closer, and he shifted the light to give her a better view. The fingers on his injured hand curled, and he cursed the stiffness there. He'd much rather be in the driver's seat himself. He didn't relish trusting such a delicate operation to anyone else, not even when circumstances dictated it.

He stopped breathing as she began to move, not with enough swiftness to be careless, but quickly enough. He watched as she flipped each switch, with precise movements until she'd reached the end of the line.

His breath released in a near silent sound. Eight seconds. She had a sure hand.

''Anything else I can help you with?''

He heard the smugness in her tone, and bit back a grin.

She was entitled to it. She had a deft touch. "Don't get cocky. We're not inside yet. Put the conduit back on. We don't want to take any chances in case someone happens by."

He held the light until she had the plastic fastened and then they both rose and moved to the door. Walker eased it open, glanced immediately at the alarm box mounted next to it inside the room and saw that the telltale red light was dark. Jaz was right. They made a good team.

He crossed to the bank of computers, scanning them with the light, while he considered where to start. Jaz nudged him, and when he looked up she pointed to the one at the far end of the table.

He followed her. "Are you sure?"

"It's the one I've seen Marakeh sit at. And Abdul stood before that desk when he spoke with Omer on the phone."

That was good enough for Walker, so he handed her the flashlight and reached inside the pack he had strapped around his waist. Extracting the encryption CD, he turned on the computer and placed the software in the carousel.

There were quicker, more discreet programs on the market that could be planted to record the password the next time the computer was used. All that remained to do in that case was to retrieve the information later. But time was of the essence in this case. He was starting to get an itchy feeling, and they needed more answers, fast. He refused to believe that the restlessness had anything to do with the moves Abdul was putting on Jasmine.

It had taken far more effort than it should have to keep from reacting to the scene she'd played out with the man that morning. And although he was certain he'd kept his expression impassive, there had been no denying the burning in his gut. It was useless to try to convince himself that the sensation had anything to do with the normal responsibility he'd feel for any team member. He couldn't ever before recall wanting to put his fist in someone's face for kissing one of his partners.

No, the difference in this situation was Jaz. He was ready to admit that. He just wasn't sure what he was going to do about it.

Handing a small pad and pencil to her, he said, "Keep track of the keys we get hits on." He booted up the program and meticulously began to press each key on the keyboard. When a key was pressed that matched one of the characters in the password, a tiny sound was elicited from the computer. When he'd finished, Jasmine showed him the pad. The password was nine characters.

Methodically, Walker entered stage two in the software program, entering each of the nine characters again. An answering sound came only after he'd entered the character that should be first in the sequence. It took half an hour to work out the password, but without the encryption software it would have been nearly impossible.

Glancing at his watch, Walker extracted the CD and restarted the computer. When the message box on screen demanded his password, he was certain he heard Jasmine hiss in a breath. He tapped in the mixture of letters and symbols that made up Marakeh's password and in another moment the screen cleared, allowing him access to the files.

"We're in, sweetheart." His whisper was near soundless, but Jasmine was close enough to hear it. She gave him a quick delighted smile. The files were numbered rather than named, so Walker began to open them in order. "Skim these and tell me if you find anything we can use."

Kneeling beside him, Jasmine leaned forward for a better view of the screen. Obligingly, he shifted a bit. "It appears to be a list of names. Marakeh's name is here. So is Abdul's. El-Dabir's.'' She scanned the page before announcing, ''Every man I have spoken with here, each individual who is a leader of the Brothers is listed, along with almost two hundred others.''

''Membership roster for the Brothers of Darkness?''

She nodded. ''Probably. Not a very large list for a group intending to take over a country.''

Walker didn't answer. It depended, he supposed, on how the group decided to take it over. The number came close to matching the troops he'd found in the encampment, but neither jibed with the amount of arms he'd seen in the outbuilding. Two files later, he pieced that puzzle together when Jasmine found a ledger.

''They're selling arms. Dammit, those guns aren't to supply his own troops, at least not completely.'' In disgust, Walker hit his palm lightly on the desk.

''Bin Sadin has been a very good customer of theirs.'' Jasmine's voice interrupted his thoughts. ''So has the government of Yanda.''

The U.S. government would be interested in that, Walker mused. When they returned to Tamir he'd make sure to get word to the proper places. Destruction of the lab would only partially defuse Maloun's threat. The entire building of weapons needed to be confiscated to cut off the Brothers' source of income. They wanted to destroy the organization completely, not just cripple it.

''Look.'' Jasmine's finger reached out, stopping short of touching the screen. Distracted by something in her voice, he gave her a sharp look before directing his attention to where she was pointing. As he struggled with the Arabic, she continued, ''The plan is detailed here. They will send fifty men to Tamir to put the virus in the drinking water. Each man has ten to fifteen targets. Every city and town in the country is listed here, with water treatment plants, water towers, lakes, rivers..." She swallowed hard. "It says the virus is expected to take effect in the first twelve hours after the hit. Within two days, eighty percent of the population is expected to be dead."

Walker stared at her, his thoughts grim. He saw the sick realization in her face, knew it was reflected on his own. The coup would be near bloodless, but no less deadly. Most of the people would be too sick, or grieving from the deaths of loved ones to put up a fight. And when the population had been decimated, the Brothers would move in a small well-equipped army to take over the country. And shift the control of the oil supply to their own needs.

She continued reading, her voice a near whisper. "Apparently there was some discussion initially about which method of contamination would be the most...effective. It was decided that turning the anthrax agents airborne would not provide a guarantee of widespread deaths in a quick enough fashion." Pausing, she swallowed once before going on. "It says that poisoning the water supply, although more labor-intensive, would provide the surest means of mass destruction."

A chill worked through him. He'd already been aware of the group's ambition, but it was peculiarly gruesome to find it articulated in such dispassionate detail. He listened while Jasmine interpreted reports from scientists, doctors, detailing the effects the virus would have on the nervous system.

He stopped her as she reported on a file that contained information from a Center of Disease Control report, detailing survival techniques in contaminated areas. Walker's brows rose as she read parts of it.

"How the hell did they get their hands on that information?" he asked grimly. "The CDC doesn't broadcast those kinds of details."

Absorbed in her reading, Jasmine didn't look up. "The heading on the report indicates it was written to the Pentagon, with copies forwarded to congress. The Brothers must have bought this information. From the looks of things, they don't lack for *financing*."

And anything was for sale, it seemed, if the price was right.

The fingers on Walker's good hand curled into a fist. It would be a waste of energy to rage against traitors who put their own greed ahead of the deaths of innocents. He'd focus his energy on stopping the Brothers before they could put their plan in operation.

Jasmine bumped his fingers from the mouse as she clicked out the file and opened the next. They found more reports on the virus, and a list of precautions for the Brothers' troops to take while they spread the virus. For the first time it occurred to Walker that the group was taking a chance themselves using biological terrorism to take over a country. After they released the virus, the nation would be a risk to anyone who would live there.

His attention shifted as Jasmine opened a file containing a map of the sheik's palace, a schedule of his routine, and detailed accounts of his family's activities and whereabouts. "Anything in there about Rashid?" he asked.

Skimming quickly, Jasmine shook her head, and he frowned. He was getting a hunch that the Brothers knew nothing about the young sheik, which made his disappearance all the more mysterious.

The next file contained similar data on the Sebastiani family. There was no doubt that the information had been compiled to assist the Brothers in the efforts to cause havoc between the two royal families.

Checking his watch, Walker said, "You finish up here while I search the rest of the room." Jasmine didn't look up, engrossed in the computer. The locks on the desk drawers were picked with ease, even though he had to work left-handed. Whatever papers he found were copied on his mini-computer to be interpreted later. They worked in silence until he'd gone through all desks and file cabinets, before approaching Jaz again.

"Are you about done?"

Stifling a yawn, she nodded.

"Shut it down, then, and let's get out of here. We still have to reactivate the alarm before we go upstairs."

Obediently, she clicked out of the file she had open and tapped in the command to log out. Walker made one more quick scan of the room, ensuring they'd left nothing out of place. Then he followed her through the door.

It took only a few minutes to lift the conduit, replace the switches to their former positions, and then screw the plastic back into place. Jasmine worked with silent efficiency, and Walker found himself enjoying watching her. Of course, he should have figured that she was not without skills. She had, somehow, managed to circumvent some of the tightest security in Europe to lift the Star right from beneath everyone's noses—the owner...the guards...and Walker himself.

The memory still provided a kick in the ego. He'd give a lot to know how she'd managed it. But it was doubtful he'd ever shove pride aside to ask her for details.

He followed her back upstairs and into her room. She moved through the shadows unerringly until she reached her bedside table and turned on a small lamp. Then she pulled the band from her hair, and let it fall loose around her shoulders.

A fist of desire exploded in his gut. And because it annoyed him, he scowled. He didn't appreciate feeling like one of those damn dogs in a Pavlovian laboratory, conditioned to respond to certain stimulus.

But Jaz made for one hell of a stimulus.

He watched her through narrowed eyes as she paced the room, pulling the curtain aside, letting it fall. She moved with a smooth, lithe grace that hinted at the supple power encased in that sleek skin of hers. The black leggings she wore with the close-fitting black shirt showcased her willow-slim body, hugged those generous curves. He'd never seen a more feminine woman, nor one more certain of her own charms.

And right now, one so obviously troubled.

Still watching her, he crossed to the bed, dropped down on it. "I found what looks like a dossier on Sinan Omer in that locked cabinet. Think you can translate it for me?"

"Of course."

Despite her agreement, she made no move to join him. Instead she crossed to the dresser, opened a drawer, pushed it shut again.

"Did you find anything more of interest in the computer files?" Walker could think of no other reason for her restlessness.

"I did discover more details about what the Brothers intended to do with Tamir once the virus has been released. Apparently the troops will be sent in to establish martial law, as well as enough workers to keep the country's oil production running smoothly. I do not think that any of the Brothers' leaders will spend much time there." There was a note of irony in her voice. "It has been decided the climate would be too dangerous to chance the health of any of the leaders. Because of Tamir's isolation, they actually think they can keep reports of their actions from filtering out for several weeks. And since the country has no ties with the west, the Brothers do not feel they need fear interference from the world's superpowers.''

''And none of Tamir's allies could mount a decent defense even if they were willing.'' Walker couldn't argue with the Brothers' logic. The country was fiercely independent and so secluded from its neighbors that it was particularly vulnerable to just this sort of an attack.

In the silence that followed, Walker realized Jaz still hadn't completely shared what was troubling her. ''And?''

''And there was yet another file containing maps. It listed locations all over the country.''

Interest sharpening, he straightened. ''Locations for what?''

She met his gaze, eyes wide and haunted. ''For graveyards. It appears the Brothers have thought of everything. They have already determined how to dispose of the hundreds of thousands of bodies. Every fifty kilometers all over the country they've marked a place to dig holes for mass burials.''

Chapter 9

"It doesn't matter what the bastards plan, Jaz. We're going to stop them."

Jasmine fingered the lace on the curtain, her stomach still knotted. It should get easier, she thought. She'd come a long way from the naive girl she'd been when she'd first fled from her father's house to the Moroccan streets. But no matter what she'd seen in the course of her missions, she never failed to be appalled at the antipathy people could have for one another. She thought if there was a principle driving the destruction, perhaps it could be more easily understood. Hatred, however despicable, was at least an explanation. But avarice, greed, thirst for power…the motivations were so devoid of emotion that their acts seemed more sinister, somehow. More evil.

"I just wished I had found something in the files to suggest how close the Brothers are to enacting their plans." Despite the warm air, a chill broke out over her skin. She rubbed her arms as she spoke. "And I found nothing to suggest where the lab is located."

A shrug sounded in Walker's voice. "We're not done yet. We have to sift through this information I copied. And I still don't think we'd have been allowed here if they were as close to finishing the virus as they'd like. Why would the Brothers care about alleviating Tamir's suspicions if they had the capability to make their bioterrorist hit immediately? It takes a hell of a lot of technology, a hell of a lot of money to buy the people and equipment to make this whole thing happen."

She nodded, and hoped he was right. "Perhaps I should be encouraged that there was nothing else in the computer files about the virus itself. That must mean all the information is held at the lab." The look she sent him then was direct, determined. "Which is all the more reason to make sure nothing of the lab is left remaining."

He gave her a faint, hard smile. "We'll arrange it. But first things first. Come over here and let's get started on this information."

Jasmine sat down next to him on the edge of the bed while he opened the tiny computer, flipped it on. Moments later the screen was filled with Arabic and she leaned closer for a look. Scanning the documents, however, quickly filled her with dismay. "This is correspondence only, and reports from each of the leaders on their areas of expertise."

He blew out a breath. "Okay. We'll find the lab another way." For some reason she found the certainty in his voice oddly soothing. "Take a look at the last several pages I copied. They've got Omer's name all over them."

"You are right. It is a dossier on Sinan Omer." Frowning, she took the computer from him to study the screen more closely. "His education, background, his work of the last few years is all documented."

It was Walker's turn to frown as he leaned over to look at the screen more closely. He made an annoyed sound, as she was scrolling much more quickly that he could interpret the Arabic. "Is there a date on it?"

She checked, then shook her head. "No, but the last item in it happened shortly before Princess Christina was shot at in San Diego. You said he was questioned in regard to that."

"He was." His index finger beat a rapid tattoo against the side of the computer while he thought. "But they didn't have the proof to hold him, and right after he was arrested as a suspect in Princess Christina's shooting he skipped bail and disappeared. With his sudden appearance in Maloun, there's no doubt in my mind that he was the shooter."

"If we are correct and the Brothers invited him here to help with the virus, perhaps they completed a background investigation on him first to ensure that they could trust him. I will be very interested in what he has to say tomorrow."

He lifted his gaze from the screen and studied her profile instead. "What makes you think you'll learn anything from him?"

She didn't notice the shift in his interest. "Perhaps he will not tell me anything directly," she admitted. "But he will surely speak to someone, will he not? To Abdul or Marakeh? Their conversation could shed some light on the questions we still have about his role here."

"If we have to, we'll plant a listening device to discover the lab's location. It's risky—I'll only try it as a last resort."

She remained silent. With a tug of conscience she recognized he was correct about the hazards associated with a bug. They had no idea whether daily sweeps were conducted on the grounds, and if the device were found, there would be no suspects besides the outsiders from Tamir. But there would be ways around those risks. Ways that called for a bit more creativity. She didn't bother sharing the thought with Walker. He could be amazingly close-minded about some of her ideas.

Instead, she just handed the computer back to him. He took it, but his attention was focused on her. "I don't know what you're plotting in that beautiful head of yours, but you'd better rethink it." The angling of her chin was its own response, one he apparently didn't care for. He crooked his finger, turned her face to his. "We're about to get to the most delicate part of the assignment, and any misstep will blow us out of the water."

Jerking her chin loose from his grip, she rose from the bed. "I will do what is necessary to do my job, Walker. You would expect no less from a partner, would you?"

Partner. Less than an hour ago they'd worked together like a well-oiled team. He hadn't wanted to use her, but his injury had forced him. She thought, without conceit, that he would have to acknowledge now how well they complemented each other, in a way other than the physical. It appeared she'd been wrong.

An odd hurt welled up inside her, one she was becoming all too used to. He was just as determined as ever to cast her help aside, to carry out the mission as much as possible on his own. Theirs was a small world, one where news traveled, and she'd never heard that Walker James had a problem working with women.

Which meant, of course, that the only woman he had a problem with was *her.*

She sensed him behind her, though his big body hadn't

made a sound in his approach. Turning to face him, she gave an involuntary swallow, took a step backward.

His face stamped with grim purpose, he lowered it close to hers. Gazes met, battled. "Whatever you're planning, forget it. We're almost there. No more chances. It's not worth it at this point."

"The Ghost is recommending playing it safe?" Jasmine didn't recognize the impulse that fueled her words, but she recognized the moment they hit their mark.

Walker's eyes narrowed. "Not necessarily safe, just smart."

Coolly, she asked, "Were you playing it safe—excuse me, *smart*—when I beat you to the Star of Benzia?" A muscle in his jaw clenched and a surge of exhilaration rocketed through her. There was a dim distant part of her that was whispering caution, but it was silenced by an overwhelming urge to provoke the man to a reaction. *Any* reaction.

His hands slapped against the wall on either side of her, but it wasn't her caged position that made her shiver. It was the dark and dangerous light in his eyes. They seemed to burn into her own, igniting a heat that was all too familiar.

"You have the nerve to bring up the Star? After what you did?"

There was heat in her veins, a feverish flame. It was fueling a recklessness that was as perilous as it was unusual.

"What did I do, exactly, Walker? You never really said." Her head tilted back, she dared him with the angle of her chin, the edge to her words. "Oh, there were lots of accusations.... Wait, I remember. I supposedly slept with you to steal your plans for getting the Star." She pretended to consider that thought, then threw it back at him. "Were you careless enough to leave them lying around your motel room for me to snoop through while you slept? You did sleep that night, did you not? For a few minutes, at least."

There was dangerous gleam in his eyes and a decided clip to his tone. "Drop it, Jaz."

"Did you ever check to see exactly how the Star's disappearance was managed? I think you would have found our techniques vary to a large degree. Not the least in which was, I was successful. You were not."

His mouth was a thin hard line, his jaw was like granite. Yet still she pressed on, fueled by some self-destructive impulse she'd never been aware of. "Perhaps, you should have learned then that too much caution can be its own kind of risk. He who waits too long…loses."

He moved closer, and her heart lodged in her throat. His elbows bent, and he let his forearms take his weight. "Do you want to know what I learned from that little lesson, Jaz?" He turned his head, and his stubbled jaw scraped her skin. A shudder worked through her. He raised his head, and she saw the satisfied glint in his eye. Her reaction hadn't been lost on him. "I discovered, again, that the most beautiful women are the most treacherous. That sex—" he dropped a string of stinging kisses from jawbone to earlobe "—is a distraction that I can't afford when I'm planning a job." His fingers threaded through her hair and he used them to tilt her face up to his. "And I found that exotic Moroccan beauties were the biggest risk of all."

His kiss was heady. She'd been walking a tightrope, she thought fuzzily, her lips softening against his clever mouth. She'd deliberately pushed and prodded to get a response from him. And she'd brought him to this one, with words fueled by hurt and clouded by emotion.

And he was teaching her, right now, all about taking risks.

His flavor traced through her senses, dark and dangerous. It mingled with the desire rushing through her veins, and stifled the warning that was sounding alarms in her mind.

Because this changed nothing. It never had, with Walker. Afterward there would be complications, trampled feelings. He was a man who believed in planning and forethought, and for him this would be an unusually reckless course of action. For her it would be devastating.

She was still living with the regrets from the last mistake she'd made with him. To compound them now, to give in to the quicksand of temptation yet again would be an action guaranteed to haunt her.

It was that certainty that had her dragging her mouth from his, and then shivering when his lips found a sensitive area below her ear. "This is stupid."

If she'd thought to dissuade him with her blunt observation, she'd failed. Miserably. Perhaps if her voice had been a little less breathless. A little more steady. Instead, a rich, masculine chuckle sounded in her ear and Walker skimmed his lips over her forehead. "A moment ago you were trying to convince me that sometimes chances have to be taken. That playing it safe can be costly."

She opened her mouth to answer, then shuddered when his uninjured hand closed over her breast. She wanted to point out that she feared she would be the only one paying the costs. He'd left her easily enough after their one night together. Had harbored stubbornly fixed opinions of her ever since. And she knew without asking that he hadn't been plagued by the memories, as she'd been.

"So what kind of costs will we pay for this, Jasmine?" His voice was as low and smooth as rumpled velvet, and sent a shiver skating down her spine. "Will we be left with images that lurk in the corners of our minds, coloring everything else we touch? Everyone we meet?"

His words stilled something in her, and she tried to look at him to discern his meaning. But his tongue was working behind her ear, languid strokes that seduced and excited. "Will this be the time that will build the memories stronger? Or the time that will burn them away for good?" Her hands clenched on his shoulders when he nipped at her throat, before soothing it with his tongue.

He lifted his head then, and his smile was pure wicked invitation, beckoning her to plunge into the flames of perdition with him. "The question is, how big a price would be too high to pay?"

Her hands went to his chest to wedge a bit more space between them. She desperately needed that distance to think. To gather her defenses, which he so easily could turn to shambles. But she didn't move him—couldn't. And her desire to do so was rapidly vanishing. "This is not a game. Sex is not casual to me."

Something in his gaze changed then, softened. "Nothing between us could ever be casual, Jaz. It would be far easier if it were." His hand went beneath her shirt, skimming over bare skin, leaving a wake of sensitized nerves. She struggled to interpret his cryptic words, but sensation was bumping through her veins, making thought difficult to summon.

His touch brought a jumble of memories, all of them erotic, all of them unwelcome. He had swift, sure fingers, and he knew just how to touch her. Just what made her moan, and gasp and shudder. It was a powerful weapon to arm him with, and one he showed little mercy in wielding.

Fingers flexing over her waist, he moved his touch upward, inch by infinitesimal inch, his gaze never releasing hers. Her breath was coming in short ragged spurts, and his eyes were heavy-lidded, intent. He reached into her bra, cupped her breast, flicking his thumb across her tight nipple.

The long anticipated touch had her breath shuddering out of her and she arched against him. This time it was he who stepped back, and she used the opportunity to pull his shirt from his waistband and slide her hands inside along his smooth sides. He went rigid for a moment, his nostrils flaring, and she surveyed him from beneath eyelids that wanted to droop.

There was no mistaking the desire stamped on his face, and it called to something inside her. Her fingers changed direction of their own accord, skated up his rib cage, flexing on his solid pectorals and she felt the shudder work through him.

The blood in her veins went molten and her head lolled. Perhaps she could have withstood the call to her own sexuality, but the temptation to uncage his was irresistible. Walker had a hard muscular body that hinted at raw power, tightly leashed. But she well remembered what happened when his control was battered and he lost the battle for restraint. Remembered the sheen on his slick skin, the ferocity of his mouth, and the wildness of his touch.

And she wanted it. She wanted to feel that power as his body moved against hers, over hers. She wanted to feel his control snap, feel again his untamed response when she teased him beyond all bearing. This time she knew what she was asking for, she promised herself, as she pushed his shirt up his chest. This time, she would be the one who walked away.

Deliberately, she scraped one of her nails over his nipple, and was rewarded by one hard jerk of his body against hers. Satisfied, she skated her hands over his chest, tangled her fingers in his chest hair, fiercely glad that he hadn't elected to shave it off. A pleased sound rumbled in his chest and he moved his shoulders.

"Help me get it off."

She obeyed, taking her time with the task, letting her fingers stroke and tease along the way. By the time she pushed it over his head, he had to release her to yank it off his arms, and she smiled at the impatience suggested in his actions. But instead of closing the distance between them again immediately, he remained where he was, face carved with arousal. He reached out, hooked a finger in the neckline of her shirt. "Now this."

Jasmine hesitated, her fingers faltering as her gaze lifted to his. The hint of the dare in his voice was reflected in his expression. As if to soothe her nerves, his finger turned caressing, stroking her breastbone lightly above the neckline of her shirt. "I want to see you, Jaz. All of you." His voice glided over her as sensuously as his caress. "No darkness between us this time. The light stays on. I want to touch every inch of you. And I want you to do the same to me."

His husky voice was rough with arousal, rife with promise. And because she found herself wanting the same, she did as he requested. She pulled off the shirt, to let it drop from nerveless fingers when she met his gaze again. Her skin was painted with liquid fire from his look alone and she doubted her ability to strip in front of him completely. Her limbs were no longer taking orders from her mind.

Reaching out, he traced the tip of his index finger along the lacy border of her bra, caressing the skin that threatened to spill over the top. Her weakness for clothes was reflected in the fancy lingerie. The sheer lace hid very little. Walker reached behind her, released the catch with one sure flick, and the bra loosened.

Jasmine swallowed hard. His hot, ardent regard was impossible to deny, impossible to resist. He hooked the straps in his fingers, and tugged lightly, urging the bra down her arms. He followed the journey with his gaze, intent. The garment clung to her curves for a moment longer, before loosening, falling completely away.

Even then he didn't move toward her. Not right away. He watched her with the air of a man intent on stamping her image on his brain. Which was ridiculous, of course. She struggled to shake the fog of desire from her brain. This was Walker. She'd had no doubts about how easily he'd forgotten her after their last time together.

"So beautiful." His whisper seemed dragged out of him, his fingertips barely skimming her skin. "You're so damn perfect, Jaz." Finally he reached for her, stroked and squeezed her softness lightly. She had a moment to appreciate the picture his lighter skin made against her dusky tones before pleasure eddied again, threatened to pull her under.

Leaning forward, he took her nipple into his mouth and suckled strongly from her, drawing her gasp. Her hands went to his shoulders, fingers clutching on to the corded strength she found there. Her shoulders went back, farther and farther, until they met with the wall, and still she couldn't press close enough. Her hands slid to his head, and she pressed him nearer.

His teeth scraped at her delicate skin, and scalded her senses. She lifted a leg mindlessly, stroked it along his and felt his big body shudder and quake. He released her and straightened. His touch impatient, he stripped her of the close-fitting leggings and stockings, leaving them tangled on the floor.

She was exposed to him, in a way that left a woman feeling beautiful yet vulnerable. Cherished, but exposed.

Walker sank to his knees, his hands stroking her from thigh to calf to the arch of her feet and back. She jerked helplessly, his breath close, so close, to where she was damp and aching. He continued caressing her, his heavy-lidded eyes on hers and when she went boneless, pliant, when her grasp on his shoulders was all that kept her from sliding down the wall, he put his mouth on her.

The wild cry clawing in her throat went unheard. Jasmine clamped her teeth down hard on her bottom lip while her sight blurred, her senses raged. His hands went to her bottom and he arched her to him, allowing him to steep himself in her. The tip of his tongue slid along her sensitive folds, swirled around that sensitive bundle of nerves, causing a response she was helpless to deny. Her release was immediate and explosive, shock waves of pleasure spinning out in endless circles of gold.

She would have slid to the floor if he'd released her, would have pooled at his feet in a liquid mass of pleasure. But Walker didn't release her, nor did he give her time to recover. He made his way back up her body with short stinging kisses, sampling every curve, every indentation, every inch of flesh along the way. Her senses began to haze again.

The ridge of muscles in his back were tense, and her fingers soothed, stroked, as feeling began to return to the rest of her body. She forced her weighted eyelids to open, and Walker filled her sight. Features etched with arousal, sharpened by need. There was a rigid control about him, though desire all but seeped from the edges. She wondered just how long it would take him to lose that restraint.

She wanted that, she discovered, quite desperately. To that end, she brought one hand skimming around to his chest, flexed her fingers so her nails scored his skin ever so slightly. She felt his quick hiss of breath, and smiled, slow and surely. With a long, wandering sweep of her hand she found his hip, lingered, brushing his sex, before her fingers danced away again. All the while her gaze held his. She wanted to watch him when he lost control. Wanted to see what touches made him swallow hard, what places made him groan.

But most of all she wanted to see his face when she closed her hand around his hot, hard shaft. There was a slash of color over his cheekbones and arousal had tightened his features. Made them look intent and just a little cruel. Her fingers curled around him and he thrust into her touch, an involuntary demanding movement that stole her breath, had desire glazing her insides again. She stroked the length of him, felt the turgid heat, velvet over steel. Her other hand joined the first and she began to tease him in earnest, flickering touches designed to please them both.

She all but heard his control snap. One moment she was stroking him with a movement designed to drive him crazy, and in the next he had her pinned between the wall and his equally hard body. With a grunt he lifted her off her feet, his arms under her bottom. At his urging, she wrapped her legs around his hips, leaving her open to him. Vulnerable. He tested her readiness by slipping one large finger inside her, swallowing her moan with his mouth covering hers. She was damp from her earlier release, and she caught her lip in her teeth as he explored her. Her arms twisted around his neck. In the next instant he removed his finger, replacing it with the velvety blunt tip of his sex.

He eased his way inside, halting when his entry provoked her muffled cry. He paused, sweat forming on his brow. Jasmine shifted but there was no place to move. They were as close as two people could be. Closer. Her head tossed as he pressed deeper, another inch, before stopping again.

He whispered words in her ears, his voice raw and harsh. Sex words, hot, explicit. What he wanted to do to her, how he wanted her to touch him.

He felt huge inside her, even now while he was still and pulsing. It had been a long time for her, and although his finger had felt wonderful, his sex was much much bigger than his finger had been. Her breath felt as if it were being torn from her lungs. ''More,'' he rasped, his mouth at her ear. ''Give me more.'' She was helpless to deny him. He pulled one of her legs higher, so her ankle clasped around his lower back, and used the position to seat himself, deeply, fully, impaling her with his hard length.

She muffled her whimpers against his throat. It was too much. He was too much. He filled her so completely she wondered how she would stand it when he began thrusting.

He held there, still but for the locomotive pounding in his chest. It kept time with the hammering in her own. ''Look at me.'' His low voice was a demand, a plea. ''Give me all. I want it all.''

He reached down, opened her soft folds so that his movements would stimulate the sensitive bundle of nerves there. He pressed against her more tightly, his torso rasping her sensitive nipples. Then he began to move.

Slowly at first. A long, velvet glide that almost removed his sex from her completely, before pushing back inside her. Deeper. Hotter. Harder.

''Walker.'' She couldn't bear it, the sensations were coming so hard and fast they were impossible to sort. She was exquisitely sensitized from his earlier ministrations, and each of his thrusts rasped against swollen tissue. The sensation bordered between pleasure and pain, then only pleasure again when he increased the rhythm of his movements.

The dim light in the room was all but blocked out by his wide shoulders. Jasmine clung helplessly to him, her eyes wide and nearly sightless as he pounded into her, each movement stronger than the next. She had wanted this. She'd wanted to see his control slip its leash and be set free in all its savage hunger. Had wanted to feel the uncontrollable hammering of his hips against hers, feel the heat and sweat of him, hear the low groans that escaped him as he took pleasure in her body. This at least was uncomplicated. This was inescapable.

The urgency of his desire sparked her own. The wild pounding of his body against hers called to everything primal inside her. His eyes had gone blank, but it was her name on his lips as he lunged into her. And when she reached down to cup his heavy masculinity he shivered and reared back, slamming against her more strongly. She felt herself tumbling over the edge even as she heard the low, harsh moan torn from him, felt the last wild thrust he gave.

And the last thing she heard was her name.

Walker held Jasmine close in bed, her body spooned to his. He stroked his hand over her lazily, giving them both time to relax. There would be little opportunity for that later. Already, spent desire was recircling, building anew. His fingers paused on the curve of her hip, flexing gently. There was a whisper of caution sounding now, not like the prickle of nerves he felt when a situation was about to become deadly, but a warning, nonetheless.

He was a man who'd courted danger nearly all his life. If truth be told, he welcomed it, sought it out. His wasn't a character to accept boredom willingly.

But in his arms lay danger of a far different sort. He'd thought—he'd hoped—that getting his fill of her would burn this passion out. Would quench the hunger she'd fired in him three years ago that still burned, unabated. That possibility was seeming increasingly unlikely. The hunger still flickered, and it was getting stronger by the moment. He was beginning to doubt he had enough time, enough strength, to satiate it completely.

Uneasily he moved, and she shifted with him. She said his name, only that one word, her voice an exotic whisper in the night. Leaning forward he pressed a kiss to her neck, brought one of her legs up over his and slipped inside her again, began to move.

Pleasure shimmered in his veins as he felt the delicate pulsations of adjustment she made around his intrusion. Jasmine had spoken of risks. He knew now just how true her words had been. The biggest risk he'd ever taken was lying in his arms right now.

Chapter 10

It was shortly past dawn when Walker slipped from Jasmine's bed. He'd meant to escape quietly, without another thought of the night they'd spent, or of her. And of course he failed miserably.

He stood by the bed, half hoping she'd waken, just so he could watch the sleep chase from her eyes and see what would take its place. He wanted to know if there would be welcome or regrets in her expression. If her hand would go in search of him even before she woke, already missing the heat of his body.

The admission was as shocking as it was terrifying. Women had always been much too easy to leave for him to be comfortable with this unfamiliar urge to linger now. And this woman especially was one to be wary of. His mind knew that.

But still he hesitated. Without his conscious permission his hand crept out, tucked one errant strand back over her bare shoulder, touching nothing but the silken hair. But when that was done he found he still couldn't move away.

All that glorious hair had been tumbled by his own hand during the night, and it was a lush tangle now around her bare shoulders. He felt desire stir, again, and felt a baffled kind of amusement. As little time as they'd spent sleeping last night he'd have thought wanting her again impossible. Time after time he'd been proven wrong.

It wasn't until after the second time he'd made love to her that the thought of protection had even occurred to him. The oversight had stunned him. He hadn't had unprotected sex since he was fifteen and too stupid to know any better. When he'd approached it with Jasmine she reminded him that she was on the Pill, as most female agents were. Too many things could go wrong on a mission to take those kinds of risks.

But he was hit anew with the kind of chance he'd taken. Not only hadn't he used protection, he hadn't thought of it. And even once the thought had occurred and he'd gone to his room and gotten some condoms, he had resented it. Fiercely.

There'd been nothing between them those first times, just skin against skin, and the sensation had driven him wild. He hadn't been able to get enough of her, taking her over and over during the night, as if through sheer repetition he'd take the edge off the hunger that had showed no signs of abating. He wondered now if it would.

Her lips parted then, she gave a little sigh, and he found himself held rapt, studying her. He wondered for a moment what language she dreamed in. It was a personal question, one he had no right to ask, but he wanted to, anyway. And it occurred to him then, that although he knew what made her shudder, what sent her hurtling to release, he had very little knowledge of what was inside her. How she thought. Where she came from, and where she was going.

The thought was so foreign that he took a step back. Where the hell had it come from? He couldn't remember a time when it had mattered to him. He'd always had little interest about what went on inside a woman. It was their attractive packaging that caught his eye, and that had always been enough for him. Frowning a bit, he tore his gaze away from her and made his way soundlessly back to his room, stepped into the shower.

Setting the water to lukewarm, he stood there for long minutes, his good hand braced on the wall, head bent under the punishing spray. His injured wrist still throbbed a bit, but the bandages Jaz had placed on the cut were still in place. With the injury it was going to take him twice as long to do what he needed to do today. He hoped he wouldn't have to call on her to help him again. He wasn't sure that more time in her company was in either of their best interests.

Turning off the shower, he grabbed a towel and wiped it over his body. Dropping it, he raked a careless hand through his hair and went to pull on some clothes. There was an urge, one far too powerful for comfort, to go back to Jaz's room, to slip into bed with her again. To slide into her, watch her come awake as pleasure built to a shattering release for both of them. It took more effort than it should have to force his mind on the matters at hand. There was nothing to be gained by allowing either of them to be distracted from the assignment. And the fact that he needed reminding was proof of the woman's danger.

Twenty minutes later Walker made his way into the building that served as a garage. Since their arrival, he'd been checking the car daily, in what he hoped had looked like routine maintenance by a driver/assistant who had very little else to do.

Opening the car door, he reached in and took a mirror from the glove box. With a quick glance to assure his privacy, he unscrewed the end of it and unfolded the flexible handle coiled inside. When it was a full two-feet long he locked the handle into place and passed the mirror under the edges of the car. Turning it one way, then another, he checked every inch of the chassis. Slowly he made his way around the car, until he'd assured himself that there were no foreign devices planted beneath it.

It had been an action he'd taken daily, and it was borne more from habit than logic. He tended to think that planting any sort of mechanism beneath their car was a little too subtle for the leaders of the group. If either he or Jaz triggered their distrust, he rather thought the group would react more directly.

He replaced the handle and mirror in the glove box, and opened the hood of the car. Since they hadn't discovered the location of the lab last night when they'd broken into the computers he had to be ready with the next plan. He hoped like hell that the conclusions he and Jaz had drawn about Omer were correct. They were going to have a hell of a lot riding on them.

He was banking on the fact that the Brothers wouldn't be bring a scientist here of Omer's reputation if they weren't going to use him to help finish the virus. And it would stand to figure, then, that someone would have to take the man to the lab at some point.

And therein lay their best chance of locating the building.

Loosening the parts he would need from the engine, Walker tucked them away in his pocket and went to the dash. Taking off the compass mounted there, he put it in the bag and crawled out of the car, closing the door. Planting a tracking device on the car that would travel to the lab would pinpoint its location almost exactly. He had no way to follow the car, however, so a traditional mechanism would prove useless. Instead he was going to have to improvise. The pocket-size computer would come in handy again. He gave silent thanks for the wonders of technology.

The sound of an approaching vehicle had him pretending a renewed interest in the car's engine. A Jeep slowly rolled into the garage. He recognized one of the two men as the guard who'd stolen a smoke the night Walker had entered the weapons storeroom.

The other man said something to Walker in Arabic. Giving a shrug, he replied, "Sorry. Only English."

One man continued to regard him warily, but the other, the guard from the building, nudged his companion, rattling off rapid-fire orders. Walker couldn't decipher all of the words, but he caught the gist of the message. The Jeep was to be checked over while it was kept here for Tariq Abdul's use later that day.

Giving a mental grin, Walker slammed the hood of the car shut. Once he got the device constructed he wouldn't have far to go to find the vehicle to plant it on.

From the sunlight pouring through her window, Jasmine knew she'd slept far later than normal. She woke slowly, pushing her mass of hair back from her face, sitting up in bed. And discovered that she was nude. Her gaze was drawn immediately, inexorably, to the pillow next to hers.

There was no indentation there. Walker had risen long ago. Memories of the night assaulted her, and an edgy blade of panic ran side by side with a warm ribbon of satisfaction. She'd had the chance to back away last night, and instead she'd stepped into his arms. It had been her decision, and one she wasn't going to waste regrets on now.

She was under no illusions about their relationship. When the mission was over they'd go their separate ways. And this time she'd be the one, she promised herself, who walked away without a backward glance.

But until then…until then… For the first time in her life Jasmine was going to reach out with both hands and take what she wanted. And damn the consequences.

There would be no physical consequences, at least. Walker had seemed relieved when she reminded him she took birth control, and she should feel relieved, too. Becoming a single parent would mean living a totally different kind of life from the one she'd made for herself, and the thought both terrified and entranced her. If the time ever came that she did have a child, she thought with a tinge of bitterness, she wouldn't raise it with the demand for perfection. She wouldn't expect it to be an extension of herself, to be used as a pawn to further her own ends.

She wouldn't, she thought as she strode to the closet for her robe, treat it the way her father had treated her.

As always, thoughts of the family she'd left behind had her chest clutching with mingled regret and anger. Regret for the time she'd lost with her siblings, and her mother. And still simmering anger for the father who had forced her to choose between family and independence.

There was a shiver working down her spine, and she grabbed for her robe, holding it in front of her as she whirled around to find Walker standing in her room.

His entry had been silent, as usual, but she seemed to have developed a sixth sense about his presence. It was something more than instinct, something innately female responding to male. She'd felt it the first time Dirk had introduced the two of them, and then again when she'd looked across the crowded ballroom in Venice to meet his gaze.

There was a slight smile playing around his mouth, and he leaned against the doorjamb as he studied her. "You don't need the robe on my account, Jaz."

She wished—oh, how she wished—that she could be as casual as he. As it was, her movements were jerky as she gave him her back and yanked the robe on, tying it tightly around her waist. "There is a custom in polite society called knocking. Perhaps you have heard of it."

It was clear when she turned around that her sarcasm had had no effect. His expression was still amused, but his eyes were hot, avid, as they wandered over her figure, her legs, bared by the robe.

The look was disconcerting, and worse, ignited flickers of heat that would be better ignored. "I need to get dressed and downstairs."

"It's only seven," he replied, pushing away from the door and ambling toward her. "Nobody's going to miss you yet. I need your help with something."

An absurd sense of disappointment bloomed, to be ruthlessly shoved aside. On one level, this was actually progress. Twice now Walker had come asking for her assistance, twice they'd acted as the team they were supposed to be. She should be pleased that he was beginning to accept her professionally, especially since she'd already promised herself that she was in control of the more personal side of their relationship.

But in a war between logic and emotion, logic wasn't always the winner. It was all Jasmine could do to remain expressionless while she followed him back to his bedroom. She stopped short in the doorway, stared from his bed to him. "What is this?"

"This—" he strode to the bed and sat on its edge

"—is going to be a tracking device. I figure our quickest chance of finding the lab is to plant this on the vehicle Abdul uses to take Omer to see it."

She sent him a quick glance. "I hope our assumptions about Omer's appearance prove correct."

"I think it's a good guess. Two of the guards brought in a Jeep for Abdul's use later today." He reached down, pulled on some latex gloves, and picked up a piece of the partially constructed device. "Once planted on the chassis, it'll record the direction and mileage of the vehicle. I can monitor it with the computer, pinpoint the distance and direction it drives."

Nodding, Jasmine sat beside the scattered parts on the bed. "Abdul is due to arrive with Omer today. I would imagine they would go to the lab later this afternoon or tomorrow at the latest."

"If that proves to be the case, you'll need to start laying the groundwork for your departure. As soon as I nail down the location, we'll be heading out. Where are you in your talks with the leaders?"

She made a face. "I am half done." The appointments had become excruciatingly boring, each of them following the same format. She was introduced to a leader, given a description of his humanitarian intent, and then bombarded for several hours with rhetoric. Marakeh still presided over each one, interjecting something occasionally, or steering the conversation in another direction when Jasmine's questions became too pointed. "I can always tell Marakeh at any given time that I am convinced, and there is no need to carry on with the rest of the meetings." If truth be known, she would welcome the chance to escape early. It was all she could do in the afternoons to keep from yawning. And after the little sleep she'd been allowed last night, she would have a most difficult time today.

Because she could feel the flush working up through her cheeks, she lowered her head, the curtain of her hair shielding her features from him. Other than that quick, lusty look he'd painted her with earlier, Walker gave no indication that his mind was on anything other than the business at hand. She would do well to follow his lead.

Without being told, she picked up the spare pair of gloves on the bed, snapped them on. ''Tell me what to do.''

She kept her attention trained on his instructions, and immediately understood why he'd needed her help. His fingers still lacked dexterity from the sprain, and he wasn't able to easily manipulate the tiny pieces that needed to be hooked together and placed in the device.

They worked silently for several minutes, the only sound in the room Walker's directions. ''See that wire...here? He tapped the miniscule blue strand disappearing into the device. ''Wrap it three times around that screw...no, the other way. That's right. Now put those two parts together...push until you hear the click. Okay.'' He reached over, took it from her, and put the entire device in a hard plastic shell. ''I'll get this in place this morning. What time is your first meeting?''

She stifled a sigh. Not all an agent's work was flash and excitement. For that matter, not nearly enough of it was. But when it came to jobs, she much preferred the high-intensity snatch of a valuable gem to the plodding pretense she was engaged in with the Brothers. ''Nine. I need to get ready.'' She prepared to rise, caught Walker's eyes on her, and glanced down. Her robe had parted to reveal one long line of thigh, and there was no mistaking his interest.

Jasmine went to yank her robe closed, was thwarted by his hand. His fingers closed on her thigh, his gaze never wavered from hers, and a shudder worked through her. A familiar light was in his eyes, one that warmed even as it devoured. His fingers splayed, his thumb caressing her skin as it moved, inch by excruciating inch, closer to her center.

She grabbed his hand to still his journey, but he didn't release her. Not yet.

"We haven't talked about last night."

It was the last thing she'd thought he'd say, the last thing she was prepared for. Her mind scrambled through the haze of desire, reached for the resolution she'd made earlier that morning. "There's…there's nothing to talk about."

"Isn't there?"

It would be easier, far easier, to have this conversation if the warmth of his touch wasn't fractions of an inch away from where she was beginning to ache, if she didn't have the memories from last night to tantalize her. "We are both adults, Walker." Her voice was just steady enough to sound convincing. "Both of us know exactly what we want, do we not?"

A slight frown worked between his brows. "Yeah." He stopped, cleared his throat. "I guess."

Her brisk nod was at odds with the nerves twisting in her stomach. "The job is our first responsibility. Whatever happens between us… I mean…it cannot distract from our assignment."

"It won't." His brow was still furrowed, and his eyes narrowed as he studied her. "But last night had nothing to do with the job, Jaz. For me, or for you."

Swallowing hard, she risked a glance at him before looking away again. That hard, slightly predatory look on his face was too blatantly sexual to ignore.

"I'm not willing to waste any more of the time that we have. If you don't want last night to happen again, you'd better say it now."

She stared helplessly at him, drowning in the sensuality of his words, on his face. It would be best to briskly dismiss last night as an aberration, one not to be repeated. But she doubted her ability to deliver the lie convincingly. And whatever else there was between them, she was determined there wouldn't be dishonesty.

"There is not much time left on this assignment. I agree. We will not waste what is left."

As if her words relieved him, he let out a breath, and his hand became caressing again. The soothing, subtly sensual movements heated her skin, melted the muscle beneath to warm wax. His action stilled once more when she continued. "As you said before, we both know what we want. We will part ways after the mission is completed without regrets, will we not?"

His eyes slitted, and his answer was slow in coming. "Yeah. Of course."

She nodded. His answer was exactly as she'd expected, so there was no reason for the word to feel as if it had serrated edges. It took more strength than she'd known she possessed to rise, head for the door. "I must get ready. If you need me, I will be in the study at nine."

Although her legs were a bit unsteady, they carried her regally to the doorway. She didn't look back, couldn't. She had played the scene according to his rules. And whatever it took, she'd carry it through to the end.

Jasmine gave very serious consideration to Walker's warning about a listening device before she decided to disregard it. While the tracking mechanism might be all they needed to lead them to the lab, there was no need to ignore other avenues of information, was there? Especially if the information could be gotten with only minimal risk.

So it was with that thought in mind that she had planted

the miniscule bug in the center of the case in which she kept her sunglasses. Without a sweep conducted in her presence, the device would only be discovered upon the closest of examinations. She thought the risk calculated enough to appeal to even Walker.

The glasses were tucked safely away in her purse, sitting neatly next to her open briefcase. She looked over the pad she was taking notes on and smiled politely at Kobi al-Rosnan, her current appointment and the eighth of the twelve leaders of the Brothers. She wondered for a moment if the men were being introduced in order of importance, or if the schedule was random. Certainly this man looked more like a bookkeeper than an internationally known geologist. Tall, thin, bespectacled, al-Rosnan had gone on for over an hour about the importance of his work for Maloun, and had put Jasmine's tenuous thread of patience to the test. Until he brought up a topic guaranteed to snare her interest.

"How fascinating." She seized the first opening she could when the man paused to take a breath. "Your work on decreasing the time it takes to refine crude oil could surely be of value to our part of the world. Have you had the chance to put your work into practice other than in clinical trials?" She looked from Marakeh to al-Rosnan. "I was under the impression that Maloun was not an oil rich nation."

There was a smile on Marakeh's lips, but his eyes remained watchful. "You are correct, of course. Dr. al-Rosnan has done most of his work for foreign nations, and is eager to shift his talents to benefit the people of Maloun. We have some oil production in the northern part of our country. It is there he concentrates most of his research."

Jasmine smiled and nodded her understanding, filled with a grim realization. She had no doubt that it was

Tamir's oil that the Brothers were focused on. By perfecting a technique to speed up the refining process, they could get the oil to market that much quicker once they took over the country.

"Lunch will be served soon," Marakeh announced. "If you have no more questions for Dr. al-Rosnan..."

Capping her pen, Jasmine replaced it in her briefcase. "No, he has been quite thorough. I will admit, however, that I have only the most general idea about his work." She smiled abashedly. "Science was never my best subject at university."

Abdul would have made a flattering remark about a beautiful woman not needing to know such things, but Marakeh merely nodded, made a small sign of dismissal to al-Rosnan. "I am certain you have proved your value to Sheik Kamal in many ways, regardless."

Her smile intact, she examined the remark for any hidden meanings. The man was maddeningly enigmatic. This one, she had long been certain, was the true power behind the Brothers of Darkness.

Which meant, of course, that he was primarily responsible for the plans she'd read through last night, detailing in dry objective detail how they planned to kill hundreds of thousands of people, get rid of their bodies to avoid contamination, and take over Tamir and its oil supply.

She'd thought, when she was young and still naive, that her own father had been cruel. And while it was true he'd been single-minded and committed to his own path, she'd come to realize that far worse evil lurked in the world. Over the years she'd met men like Marakeh, to whom human life had no more value than a grain of sand. To whom money, power, meant everything. She'd long since revised her estimation of her father, even if she hadn't yet forgiven him.

Her smile was brilliant, and the lie fell easily from her lips. "I can not tell you how impressed I am with the scope of your vision for Maloun. From the leaders I've spoken with, it appears you have thought of every avenue possible to help your country."

"I assure you, Madame Mahrain, that there is nothing the Brothers would not do to further the goals of the people of Maloun."

That, she thought darkly, was becoming increasingly apparent.

Marakeh and al-Rosnan were excusing themselves when the front door opened and voices sounded in the hallway. Jasmine felt a leap of excitement. Abdul had returned. She could feel the adrenaline pumping in her veins. The juncture it would take remained to be seen, but the outcome wasn't in doubt.

She never once contemplated the possibility of failure.

There was a welcoming smile on her lips when the men entered the study. "Tariq. I trust your trip went well." The warm tone was its own message, one the man responded to as expected.

"It was uneventful." He crossed the room, took her hand in his and brought it to his lips. Was that a hint of tongue touching her palm? She hid her distaste behind a blinding smile, and forced herself to not yank away from him.

"And this must be your college friend." Discreetly tugging at her hand, she looked beyond Abdul to the slightly built man following him. She hid her interest behind a pleasant tone. "I have quite looked forward to meeting you, sir."

The men were a study in contrasts. Where Abdul was tall, strongly built, Dr. Sinan Omer was nearly six inches shorter, and small-framed. With his neatly trimmed beard and small, gold-wire-rimmed glasses, he wasn't a man who would stand out in a crowd. She had no doubt that he'd melted into the mob quite effectively after shooting at Princess Christina. The miracle was that someone had managed to identify him as the culprit.

"May I introduce Madame Rose Mahrain." Abdul had released her, but hadn't left her side. "As an emissary from Tamir, she has graciously conceded to meet with the leadership of the Brothers to discuss improving national relations."

Omer wore a suit, without the signature *kaffiyeh* that most of the men on the compound affected. He approached her, took the hand that Abdul had finally released, and shook it. The gesture was purely that of the western culture, and Abdul's reaction to it was telling. She thought she saw something approaching contempt cross his face, then it was gone.

"I am hoping to get all sorts of information from you, Doctor." Jasmine kept her voice light, noting the slightly panicked look Omer shot at Abdul. "Tariq has declined to enlighten me about any of his less scholarly pastimes while at university. You were his roommate, were you not? No doubt you can tell all sorts of tales about him."

The man's smile was stiff. "I am afraid there is nothing exciting to tell. Tariq and I were quite serious about our studies."

Her brows skimmed upward and she made a small moue of disappointment. "Then perhaps I did not miss out on as much as I feared by choosing to study in my own country. Although I still think the two of you may be holding back."

Moving to the table, she shut the briefcase and turned to face them again. "Perhaps you can find the time, Tariq, for a walk before lunch. I would like to hear about your trip. You are most welcome, as well, Dr. Omer.''

Abdul followed her, leaning just a little closer than would be considered proper as she picked up the briefcase. ''I would be delighted, of course, madame. I must admit, thoughts of…seeing you again filled my mind the entire trip.''

Tilting her head flirtatiously, she gripped her briefcase more firmly, and deliberately left her bag sitting on the table. ''If you would not mind giving me a few minutes to freshen up?''

''It is totally unnecessary, for your beauty needs no enhancement.'' Jasmine managed, barely, to avoid rolling her eyes at the flowery compliment. ''But I will await your return eagerly.''

He was no more eager, she thought, than she was to get upstairs and listen to whatever the two men had to say to each other.

Chapter 11

Jasmine slipped into her room and went to the bedside table. The small wireless receiver she'd set on top was programmed to pick up the messages relayed by the transmitter she'd secreted downstairs. Putting the earphones on, she manipulated the volume and heard Omer's voice. A satisfied smile crossed her face. Walker wasn't the only one who could acquire the latest in intelligence gadgetry.

"...will I speak with Bonlei Marakeh?" She walked to the bathroom and closed the door, in case one of the servants picked that time to enter her room to clean it.

"You will speak to him when he deems it suitable. Consider yourself fortunate you were allowed here at all."

Frowning, she puzzled over the Abdul's terse tone. He didn't sound as though he were addressing an old friend and colleague. She remembered again his lack of enthusiasm prior to his trip to the airport. Either she and Walker had misinterpreted Omer's sudden arrival in Maloun, or there was far more to the men's relationship than they'd suspected.

"Where else would I have gone, Tariq?" An obvious element of anxiety threaded through the scientist's voice. "Had I stayed any longer in the States, I would have gone to prison. They know it was I who shot at the Princess Christina at the symposium in San Diego."

There was a rattle of ice against crystal. Jasmine could picture Abdul pouring some ice water from the decanter that sat on the table in front of the couch. "Ah, but it was your own stupidity that got you into such a situation. I must warn you, my friend, Marakeh was quite angry when he'd heard what you had done."

"But I acted for the good of the cause! Surely you told him that!"

There was a small sound, as if Abdul had set down his glass. "Your exploits were your own, and cost us some international scrutiny that we would rather avoid. No one here will thank you for that."

Silence reigned for several moments. Unconsciously, Jasmine leaned closer to the listening device, anxious for other disclosures from the two men. The next voice was Omer's. "From what you said about the Sebastianis, I thought the Brothers would welcome such a strike." The words were uttered stiffly. "Had I been more fully apprised of the Brothers' goals, perhaps I would have acted differently."

The low laugh Abdul gave sounded contemptuous. "Our goals are for natives of our country, not for outsiders already corrupted by the west."

There was scuffle of movement heard, then Omer said, "How dare you question my patriotism!"

Unconsciously, Jasmine sucked in a breath, held it. But Abdul's voice was mild enough when he answered. "How could I not? You are completely westernized, Sinan. You cannot help that you have an American mother, but it was your own decision to make your career in the empire of the imperialists. Tell me, why would I believe you worthy to share in our vision for the future of Maloun?''

"Do you forget my father is a native of this country? Do you forget what he endured at the hands of the Sebastianis?''

"If not for those facts, my friend, you might not be here. But if you are to stay, you must convince Marakeh of your loyalty.''

Eagerly Omer said, "But that is exactly what I want to do, Tariq. I am willing to be of any help possible for the Brothers' cause.''

"Good. Perhaps your fervor will be put to the test. We are engaged in an...experiment that you may be able to assist us with.''

"I would be happy to help however possible. The one thing I will miss leaving in America, besides my family, is the work I was doing there. My team had spent quite a bit of time engaged in a confidential study regarding the makeup of various infectious diseases.''

"Really? That sounds intriguing.'' But of course, Abdul already had that information. It had been included, Jasmine recalled, in the dossier collected on Omer. Abdul didn't appear to fully trust his old college friend, much less respect him. But there was no doubt that he'd use him to further the Brothers' goals.

Abdul went on. "Perhaps Bonlei will grant you permission to use your talents on a more worthy cause after the two of you speak.''

"I am at his service. And yours.''

Silence stretched, then Sinan switched subjects. "Tell me about the woman.''

"Oh…" A shrug sounded in Abdul's voice. "There is nothing to tell. She is of no consequence."

A wicked smile tilted Jasmine's lips. Of no consequence, was she? Hopefully Abdul would continue to believe that. It was to her advantage to keep him, and the rest of his group, unsuspecting. Clear up to the time when they destroyed the organization, and its threat, for good.

"Perhaps you have not changed so much from when we were in college together. Is she another of your conquests, then?"

The arrogance in Abdul's reply wiped the smile off her lips. "Not yet. But she will be, my friend." There was companionable laughter at his words. "She will be very soon."

That's another surprise in store for you, Abdul, Jasmine thought. It was difficult to choose which of them would give her the greater satisfaction.

"I was not expecting to find that you were entertaining a Tamir emissary. Have relations with our neighboring countries changed so much then, that Tamir is now an ally?"

"An ally?" Tariq gave an amused laugh. "If all goes according to plan, our two countries will be as one." The irony of the man's words escaped Omer, but it wasn't lost on Jasmine. She'd always relished matching wits with a worthy adversary, but the stakes in this particular mission were higher than most. A country's entire population depended on her and Walker's success.

When their conversation turned to people they had known while attending U.C.L.A., Jasmine took off the earphones and hit the key to erase the tiny disc's recording. Then she took a quick look in the mirror, repaired her lipstick and hurried back downstairs.

She entered the office with a soft knock, wearing a dazzling smile. "I hope I have not been keeping you too long."

Abdul crossed to her, bent over her hand indulgently. "I can assure you, Rose, a woman like you is worth the wait."

"Let me just get my sunglasses." She went to the table where the case lay, and while she slipped the glasses out, her thumbnail flipped the tiny switch, turning off the miniscule transmitter. Facing the men again, she said, "Dr. Omer, would you care to join us in our walk?"

Before he could answer Abdul said smoothly, "Sinan wishes to speak to Marakeh before we dine. I hope you will be satisfied with only me as a companion."

"Of course, Tariq." Taking the arm he extended, Jasmine slipped on her glasses and allowed him to lead her outside. They remained in the shade, where they could find it, and soon the heat had added a sheen of perspiration to the man's face.

"Your friend seems very nice. Has he changed much since you last saw him?"

Abdul shrugged. "Sinan would like me to believe he has changed. How much remains to be seen."

His cryptic response fired her interest. Shooting him a sidelong glance, she inquired, "Was there something about him, then, that you objected to before?"

He stopped her, directing her to a small bench near the house. The overhang of the roof shielded them from the worst of the sun's rays. "Like your country, Maloun has a healthy distrust of western influences. Sinan has spent all of his life in America, with the exception of occasional visits to his motherland. That is enough sometimes to make me question his true loyalties."

All of which explained the dossier on the scientist, Jasmine concluded. The Brothers must be desperate for

Omer's services if they were willing to solicit his help despite their subtle distrust.

She was distracted from her thoughts by the heavy hand placed much too familiarly on her thigh. With effort, she tempered the strength with which she'd dearly love to throw it off, and merely covered his hand with hers, moved it away primly. "Tariq, you embarrass me."

He leaned closer, his gaze fixed on hers. It was all too easy to read the emotion in their dark depths. "Rose, surely I have not kept my intentions a secret. My feelings for you are of the most serious nature. Dare I hope that you missed me at all last night?"

Playing the coquette was a bore, but in each of her jobs she was called on to serve in whatever way necessary. She imagined it was due to some flaw in her makeup that she much preferred circumventing security and acquiring state secrets to engaging in a false tête-à-tête.

Giving Abdul an arch look, Jasmine discreetly took his hand from her thigh and held it tightly in hers to avoid having him touch her again. "Of course, I did. I was hoping that perhaps we could spend some time together later today. This afternoon perhaps?"

A shadow crossed the man's face. "I am afraid that may not be possible. I may...there is another errand I may have to take care of."

She gave him a deliberate pout and watched the way his gaze lingered on her lips. "Another errand, Tariq?"

"My duties are varied, Rose." There was a hint of rebuke in his tone. He was a man unused to being questioned by a woman. His domineering nature was more than a product of his culture. She felt a shudder work down her spine. She didn't doubt that Abdul had a cruel streak, an evil side that he resisted showing her. She could well imagine his reaction when he found that she and Walker had outwitted him.

"I promise…" His hand turned in her own and caressed her palm warmly. "We will have some time together this evening. I intend to have you all to myself." The words had nerves spiking in her stomach, which were sharpened when he picked up her hand, brought it to his lips. "You will see then just how intense my feelings for you are."

Putting the tracking device together had been a hell of a lot less complicated than planting it proved to be. Walker hadn't yet found an uninterrupted five minutes of time when at least one other man wasn't hovering over the Jeep. Waiting for his chance, he purposefully lingered in the garage, finding one excuse after another that would keep him there.

The man tinkering with the Jeep must be a mechanic. He was checking the tires, changing spark plugs. Walker was willing to wait until he'd finished. The last thing he needed was for someone to decide to slide under the vehicle to do more work once the device had been wired into place.

Deciding there was one task that could conceivably keep him in the garage for hours, Walker went to the house and managed to make the kitchen help understand his request for a bucket of water and some rags. Then he returned to the car, and took his time scrubbing it down.

If his activities seemed less than exciting, it wasn't the first time he'd spent his time waiting. At least he'd have something to show for that time in this case, he thought amusedly. If Jaz decided to give her driver/assistant a bad time about the car again, he'd be able to present her with a gleaming vehicle as an answer.

Jaz. The thought of her quickly had his humor fading.

She'd managed to surprise him with the casual way she'd mentioned enjoying each other before going their separate ways. He didn't particularly care for having his own words turned on him, even if they did sum up his own feelings. Which, of course, they did.

He shoved a rag into the soapy water and began soaping the vehicle with quick vicious movements. It was a relief to have an arrangement left so uncomplicated. There'd be no scene between them this time when they parted. No whispers of anger and regret to linger. No, when the assignment was over they'd part as…if not friends, at least on friendly terms. It was best that way, better, if he was truthful, than he'd dared hope for.

Which didn't explain this nagging sense of disappointment he felt. A sense that something very valuable was about to slip through his fingers.

Baffled, he shoved the rag into the pail and squeezed out the excess water. He'd never thought of himself as a contrary sort. So it was hard to figure why he wasn't completely satisfied with getting exactly what he wanted.

A string of Arabic curses filled the air. His eyebrows climbing, Walker looked over at the man working on the Jeep. Apparently the work wasn't going particularly well. The cussing lacked Jasmine's inventiveness, but made up for that in volume. Whistling tunelessly, he squatted and gave his full attention to shining the wheels, prepared to be patient.

An hour and countless buckets of water later, Walker was considering the distinct possibility that he was going to have to wax the car, as well. How long could a simple tune-up take? he wondered balefully. His movements slow, he glanced sideways at the hapless mechanic. He didn't doubt he could have performed the task for the man in half the time, using only his uninjured hand.

It was another half hour before the mechanic began gathering up his tools. He slammed down the hood of the Jeep, then got in it and turned the ignition. Apparently satisfied with the sound of the engine, he turned it off again, got out of the vehicle and strode from the garage.

Walker gave the man five minutes, then ten. When it seemed likely he wouldn't return, he lost no time. Reaching into his own vehicle, he unwrapped the tracking device and uncoiled the length of wire at each of the four corners of the casing. He took the time to go to the entrance, take a quick glance outside. There was no one in sight. Quickly, he grabbed some pliers and dropped to the floor, crawling beneath the car near the front tire. Holding the mechanism with his injured hand, he attached the device to the axle with the wires, and wrapped them tightly. The beauty of the device was that it worked independently of the vehicle; it didn't have to be attached through the steering mechanism or speedometer, because a computer would do the tracking. All he had to do was remove it discreetly when he was finished with it, which should be easy enough to do after nightfall.

Moments later he dumped his bucket of dirty water outside the garage, and laid out the rags he'd used to wash the car to dry in the sun. The trap had been set; everything was in place. All that remained was for someone from the compound to drive to the lab. And Walker had a lot riding on his assumption that Omer would be given a tour of the laboratory facilities soon.

Although the familiar adrenaline was present, there was another more unusual sensation layering it. The end of the assignment was near, as was his remaining time with Jasmine. He was willing to admit that he wasn't going to have his fill of her before they parted.

He just wasn't willing to identify why the realization burned.

"You were late for dinner, John." Jasmine made a point of going over to address Walker after the meal, all too aware that Tariq's gaze rarely left her.

"I washed the sand and dust from the car, madame. I know how insistent you are on a clean vehicle."

Her lips wanted to curve, badly. His deferential tone didn't suit him. He was far too self-assured and confident...at times bordering on arrogant. But no one here would know that about him. Nobody would realize, at least not until long after they'd left, the enormity of the charade the two of them had been engaged in.

"That must have been a tiring job on such a hot day." The others had moved from the dining room, and Omer was conversing with Tariq. Her voice dropped to a whisper. "I believe Abdul is planning to take Omer to the lab sometime this afternoon."

"It did leave me feeling a bit flushed." His next words were delivered sotto voce. "Everything's set." Tone returning to normal volume, he continued. "I intended to wax the car, as well, but I'm afraid the heat exhausted me. I believe I'll go to my room, have a bit of a nap." The fussiness of his voice, coupled with the precise British accent, had Jasmine fighting to keep her composure.

"Of course. I hope you will feel better afterward." She moved away from him and toward the door. The near silent exchange had been brief, but it was clear that everything was in place. The next few hours would tell them whether the assignment was nearing its culmination, or if they'd have to find yet another way to discover the location of the lab.

In either case, Jasmine thought as she made her way

back to the office for the afternoon's appointment, the course of their investigation had just come to a critical juncture.

Five hours later Jasmine gratefully slipped into the shower to cool off before the evening meal. Other than bed, it was the only place she was free of the stifling undergarment, which grew more uncomfortable by the hour. The first thing she would do after this assignment was over, she determined, would be to toss the thing in the nearest incinerator. A fitting end for a device that kept her body temperature at least two degrees higher than normal.

Wiping the water from her face, Jasmine caught a glint of movement from the corner of her eye. She froze, eyes watchful even as the spray continued beating down. Again there was a slight shadow against the glass.

Moving slowly, she reached for the stiletto she'd unstrapped from around her thigh, wielding it with the ease of long familiarity. The water was left running. Her gaze was trained on the door. Then, in a blur of motion, she kicked it open, spun, and placed the tip of the knife against warm masculine skin.

Walker glanced down at the stiletto pressed tightly against his throat before raising his gaze to her face. He held up his hand, which was clutching a towel. "I guess you won't need help drying off."

Resisting the urge to shove him, hard, she merely lowered the knife and whipped the towel from his hand. "Idiot! I could have killed you."

Carefully studying her expression, he replied, "Something tells me you're still considering it."

She wrapped the towel around herself and fastened it securely, belatedly aware that she'd just attacked the man while she was totally naked. The fact that he seemed to have enjoyed it only made the experience more humiliating.

She made a scathing remark disparaging his parentage. Uttering it in Arabic didn't detract from its obvious message. He smiled, slow and wide and devastating. "I'll assume you mean me to interpret that figuratively and not literally. And I'll admit I should have waited for you in your bedroom. Although—" he painted her with an appreciative look "—I'd be lying if I denied the pleasure just now was all mine."

She stalked by him into the next room. "Perhaps you would not be so quick to say so if you knew just what I can do with that stiletto."

He glanced back toward the bathroom where she'd blessedly left the knife. "I don't doubt your prowess, Jaz, but something tells me you're lethal enough without the knife. Come to my room. I want to show you something."

Her tone was snappish. "I will be there when I get dressed." Crossing to the closet, she looked over her shoulder to find him waiting, hands tucked into his pockets.

"A little privacy, please?"

Her ice-edged words had little effect on him, other than to make his grin wider. "No problem." When he took his time closing the door behind him, it took all her composure to not hurl something after him.

Instead of the temper she wanted to vent, she focused on getting dressed in record time, redonning the hated undergarment, then going back to the bathroom to retrieve the stiletto. She hadn't been exaggerating her prowess with the weapon. She'd discovered in the first week on the Moroccan streets that she'd learn to protect herself, or die. She'd acquired the skill with the knife quickly, but it wouldn't have been enough to save her life one steamy night six years ago.

The years couldn't dispel the chill from the memory. Dirk Longfield had rescued her that night, and her life had never been the same. She'd never had reason to regret it.

She pulled her hair back into an intricate knot and secured it with a jeweled comb that had been the gift of a grateful government two years ago. Only then did she cross through the sitting room that connected their bedrooms to enter the one where Walker waited.

He was hunched over the small desk in the corner, and he looked up at her entrance. "I think we might have hit a bull's-eye."

"Abdul left?"

"At about oh-three-hundred." She hurried over to join him as he returned his attention to the computer. "The computer shows that they traveled forty-two point seven kilometers, mainly southwest before stopping. The Jeep hasn't moved since."

"Southwest..." Jasmine shut her eyes, attempting to recall the topography of the country. "The terrain gets even rockier with more hills and vegetation toward the south."

"Yeah, look at this." Walker pointed to the map he'd brought with him. With Maloun's main roads and highways depicted, it should arouse no suspicion since they'd arrived by car. But the map clearly illustrated how few roads were actually built into the southern part of the nation. "We're approximately here. Forty-three miles would put the lab somewhere in this region." He indicated the area with his index finger. "Probably only another forty miles or so from there is the ocean, and our escape once we finish this job." When she raised her gaze questioningly, he told her, "When we pinpoint the lab's location, I'll send a transmission to the ship I've arranged to have pick us up. I figured we'd have a better chance of getting away undetected if we were out of Maloun's airspace.''

"You are sure Abdul would not have taken Omer anywhere else?"

Walker shook his head. "The encampment is only ten miles or so to the west. The building storing the weapons can be seen from the house. Where else could he have taken him? There aren't any towns in the area. It's the lab, all right. And if it isn't…'' His shrug sounded in his voice. "Then we start searching the area. It's around there someplace. I doubt it would be any farther away from the house. It has to be close enough for Marakeh to keep fairly close tabs on its progress."

She took a deep breath, satisfaction filling her. "You cannot imagine how I look forward to destroying the Brothers' plans."

"You and me both. You can start winding things up here. All I need to do to is wait for the Jeep to return to retrieve the tracking device. We'll leave tomorrow."

Jasmine nodded. "It appears that our assumptions were correct about the way the Brothers want to use Omer. He and Abdul spoke about Omer's attempt on Princess Christina's life, but it appeared that he acted on his own. Abdul was quite put out by his action."

Walker considered the information. "Seems mighty coincidental that he'd just happen to take a potshot at the princess at the same time the Brothers were striking at the Sebastianis, intent on making it look like Kamal."

"I think Abdul stays in touch with Omer, but he doesn't fully entrust him with the organization's goals. Omer knew enough to think he was being helpful, but complained about not being in the inner circle of the Brothers. It appears that Abdul still doesn't quite trust him, but he is willing to use him."

''Which makes it even more likely that the virus isn't completed. They must be banking on Omer's expertise to help finish it for them.'' He frowned then, looked at her. ''How'd you happen to come up with this information?''

Maintaining an innocent expression, she moved away. ''That is not important, is it?'' Seeing the argument on his face, she went on hastily, ''What is important is that we both have strings that are loose.''

It was easy to tell from his quizzical look that she hadn't gotten the slang term exactly right. ''We have some loose ends, right. But this should be the easy part. You tell Marakeh we're ready to go, I'll get the tracking device, and then we're out of here.'' He caught her hand when she would have moved away. ''We'll compare notes again after the house is quiet. Don't take any unnecessary risks before then, Jaz.'' His thumb skimmed over her knuckles absently, the gesture oddly lover-like.

She allowed herself to cling, just for a moment, to the caressing tone in his voice, in his touch. She didn't bother to tell him that for her, the most dangerous part of the assignment was at hand. For she didn't doubt that when Abdul returned she was going to be faced with a man determined to make their relationship a physical one.

And disengaging herself from that situation was going to require skills that no amount of experience as a spy could adequately prepare her for.

Chapter 12

"Forgive me for interrupting you." Finding Marakeh and El-Dabir in the office, Jasmine made a production of backing out of the doorway. "I thought to find Tariq here."

"Please come in, Madame Mahrain." Despite the growing familiarity of El-Dabir and Abdul, Marakeh continued to address her in a more formal manner. It could most likely be attributed to his age, Jasmine thought as she obeyed his request and entered the office. Decades older than Abdul or the prime minister, Marakeh was a product of a far more formal generation, even given Maloun's patriarchal culture.

"I expect Tariq and Sinan back shortly." Both men waited for her to sit before reseating themselves, Marakeh behind the desk and Hosni in a chair beside hers.

"I imagine they had much to catch up on. I know how I enjoy spending time with some of my old classmates."

Not a flicker of expression crossed the man's face. "They have much to discuss."

She was glad the success of the assignment hadn't depended on her ability to pry information out of Marakeh. Certainly she would have been doomed to failure. He was as closemouthed an individual as she'd ever met. "How long is Sinan planning to visit?"

El-Dabir answered. "I believe Sinan has returned to Maloun permanently."

Papers on the desk rustled as Marakeh straightened them. "It remains to be seen how long he will stay." There was the slightest hint of rebuke in his tone, but it was too subtle for the prime minister.

"Dr. Omer has set aside his career in the United States to put his considerable knowledge to work for the Brothers of Darkness." El-Dabir paused dramatically as he dispensed that piece of propaganda for Jasmine's benefit. "He is not the first to disregard personal wealth for the good of Maloun." His smile reminded her of a shark's—all white sharp teeth below lifeless eyes. "Our altruistic reputation is becoming well known."

Sensing the disapproval emanating from Marakeh at the other man's verbosity, Jasmine said only, "From what I have seen, he will join a number of very committed individuals, each with their own area of expertise. Your organization is fortunate indeed to have the dedication of such experts."

"It is our goals, rather than the organization itself, that attracts such commitment, madame." Marakeh surveyed her unblinkingly. "Maloun stands to gain a great deal with the individual knowledge and skills of the Brothers."

"And Tamir stands to gain a great deal by aligning itself more closely with your country." Aware that she had the complete attention of both of the men, she crossed her ankles primly beneath her caftan. "I intend to tell Sheik Kamal just how impressed I have been by all I have learned here."

El-Dabir sent a quick look to Marakeh before switching his attention back to Jasmine. "You sound like you have made a decision, Rose."

She inclined her head. "Indeed I have, gentlemen." Addressing Marakeh, she added, "I realize I have not yet met with each leader of the Brothers, but I do not believe I have been precipitous in my decision. Everything I have learned has only emphasized my initial opinion. Hosni's vision for Maloun is in line with the sheik's goals for Tamir. And with the dedication and knowledge of the Brothers of Darkness behind him, I have no doubt that your country will be successful in your endeavors to bring prosperity to your nation."

A rare smile crossed Marakeh's lips. "That is good news indeed, madame. I am pleased we have managed to lay your reservations about our organization to rest."

She gave a decisive nod. "I would be willing to meet with the rest of your representatives, of course, but it would be unnecessary. I am prepared to report to Sheik Kamal that an alliance with Maloun will be advantageous to both countries. And that any fears about the Brothers of Darkness are unfounded."

It would be difficult to miss the triumph in the glance the two men exchanged. Pretending to be unaware of it, Jasmine continued, "Would you be available to meet with the sheik after I have had time to brief him, Hosni?"

"You can be assured—" El-Dabir's eyes glittered darkly "—that I will put myself at Sheik Kamal's disposal."

"I see no reason to delay my return to Tamir. I am eager to deliver my findings. I think we can agree, gentleman—"

Jasmine folded her hands in her lap ''——that our meeting has proved fruitful for all involved.''

The meal that evening was something in the order of a celebration. Although Marakeh proclaimed it as a goodwill gesture in light of Jasmine's announced imminent departure, she was certain that it was the decision she'd arrived at that was the reason for her host's high spirits.

She'd succeeded in convincing the leaders that she was gullible enough to believe their relentless propaganda; that she was willing to be an unwitting tool in their mission to destroy Sheik Kamal and his country. There was more than a little regret in knowing she wouldn't be around to observe their reaction when they found themselves the ones destroyed.

Jasmine patted her mouth with her napkin and smiled at the servant who was presenting the next course. She wouldn't waste much time on those sorts of regrets. She was a woman with a vivid imagination, and she could accurately predict this group's response in another day or two.

In the midst of the conversation and laughter, Abdul and Omer entered the dining room. Although she was conversing with El-Dabir at her side, Jasmine was aware of the way the big Malounian's gaze found her immediately. She looked up, made her smile welcoming. ''The two of you have almost missed a very fine dinner.''

Abdul swept the table with his gaze. ''The chef appears to have outdone himself.''

''Join us, Tariq.'' El-Dabir's voice was expansive. ''Madame Mahrain has informed us of her intention to return to Tamir tomorrow.''

An imperceptible stillness came over the other man. ''You depart tomorrow?''

Jasmine nodded. "As I told Marakeh, I am already convinced of the merits of an alliance between our two countries. And what I have learned about the Brothers and their objectives only strengthens my opinion."

"Surely you share our pleasure, Tariq." Marakeh's tone was dry, his gaze watchful.

The younger man nodded stiffly. "Of course. This is good news indeed. For both of our countries."

But, Jasmine noted, Abdul lacked the others' exuberance. He sat near the end of the table, and, from what she could observe, rebuffed Omer's attempts to engage him in conversation.

She thought she was the only one to notice, an hour later, Walker excuse himself and depart the room. Her gaze flicked to the window. Darkness was beginning to fall. She knew he would lose no time in retrieving the tracking device. Sipping from her cup of tea, Jasmine admitted to herself that she hoped Walker would remain absent for the rest of the evening. She wasn't eager for any witnesses to the upcoming scene with Abdul. Sending a covert glance at the other man, she found him watching her steadily, no answering smile on his lips.

A frisson of nerves skittered down her spine. There was no doubt in her mind that a showdown with the man was forthcoming. And she wasn't so inexperienced that she underestimated the ire of a spurned would-be lover. Handling Abdul would take all the finesse she could muster.

Taking a shaky breath, she covered her anxiety by reaching for her tea again. She would need whatever fortitude it could provide.

"You are quiet tonight, Tariq." Deliberately, Jasmine sought him out. Once Marakeh had announced his intentions of retiring, the occupants had slowly begun to drift from the dining room. She, Abdul and Omer were the only ones remaining. Including the scientist in her question, she inquired, "Did you have a strenuous day?"

"It was like any other." Abdul dismissed her attempts at conversation brusquely. "It is your day that I am more interested in. You seem to have come to your decision quite abruptly."

The waters had just become choppy. Jasmine treaded them carefully. "I realize I did not finish meeting with each of the individual leaders. However, there has been nothing sudden about my decision. I thought you would be pleased with the outcome. It was your doing, after all, that brought me here."

His heavy-lidded gaze rested on her with a familiarity that made her flesh crawl. "I am happy that you have been convinced of the purity of our goals." He slid a glance at Omer, who hovered uncomfortably at his side. "You must be tired, Sinan. I will see you in the morning."

It was the most abrupt sort of dismissal, but the protest Omer seemed about to make was stemmed after one look at his friend's expression. "Of course, Tariq." Turning to Jasmine, he gave an awkward bob of his head. "A pleasure to meet you, madame."

"And you." Silence reigned until the man made his departure, leaving them the lone occupants of the room. A hum of readiness flooded Jasmine's veins. She had the fanciful thought that they were posed on a stage, with the curtain about to go up.

She prepared to give the acting job of her life. "Really, Tariq, your reaction is not what I expected. I thought you would be elated by my decision. I can assure you that I am prepared to give a positive report to Sheik Kamal on my favorable impressions of Maloun and the Brothers of Darkness."

"You misinterpret my response, Rose." A note of intimacy crept into his tone. "I am thrilled to hear that you have come to a true understanding of our organization. It is your departure that saddens me."

She startled him by closing the distance between them, laying a hand lightly on his chest. "Surely you do not believe that my departure changes things between us."

He was silent for a moment, before a slow smile, unpleasantly lascivious, spread across his face. "I am delighted to hear you say that, Rose." One heavy hand went to her shoulder, brought her close. "We have this night left to us, after all, and with the new alliance you will help forge between our countries, travel between them will not be a problem, will it?"

His lips went to her throat, and with difficulty she quelled the shudder of revulsion that worked through her. She forced an intimate laugh. "I should hope not. I do not want to be parted from you for long." Entwining her arms around his neck, she tipped her head back, looking up at him flirtatiously. "In any case, once the sheik realizes we intend to wed, I know he will do everything in his power to make our betrothal go smoothly."

She could observe the exact second he grasped her meaning. His head lifted and he pulled away to look at her, a wary expression on his face. "Our betrothal?"

With a coy smile, she smoothed her palm over his jaw. "Of course. When you spoke this afternoon about your intentions, I knew at once that we were of like mind." She went up on tiptoe and pressed a warm kiss to his lips. "I had fears of never meeting another man who could make me feel like my dear departed husband did." She ran her fingertip across his lips, eased away. "And now I find myself doubly blessed." As if his silence had just penetrated, she allowed her smile to go wavery at the edges. "Tariq. What is wrong?"

He didn't release her, but there was a distance between them nonetheless. When he spoke it was with the care of a man picking his way through a minefield. "My dear Rose. You know how much I care for you."

Her smile went relieved, and she cupped his jaw lovingly. "And I, you, Tariq."

He took her hand, held her fingers to his lips. "But marriage...that is not in my plans. At least not at this time."

She gave every appearance of a woman in an emotional tailspin. Pulling away, she slipped her fingertips from his grip. "But you said..."

"My intentions are serious." His familiar conceit rapidly returning, he pulled her into his arms again, pressed a warm kiss to her forehead. "Very serious. And I am looking forward to a very...close...relationship with you."

Her words dripped ice. "Are you suggesting...an affair, Tariq?"

With more confidence than perceptiveness, he ignored the warning in her tone. "A mutually satisfying relationship," he assured her. "One where you will want for nothing."

"I misunderstood you earlier today." Her words would have etched glass. "Forgive me for that. But you...you have obviously misjudged me. I am no man's mistress, Tariq. If these are the intentions you spoke of, they are no longer welcome."

When she would have turned away, he reached out, spun her around and gripped her shoulders tightly. Jasmine tensed. "Think about what you are turning down, Rose. I will satisfy you as most women only dream of being fulfilled."

''You dishonor me with your request.'' She remained rigid in his arms. ''Unless you want me to report this behavior to Marakeh, Tariq, I suggest you release me.''

The savage wave of anger that passed over his face was a fascinating study. In that instant she wondered what she would have used for leverage if Abdul didn't fear Marakeh to some extent.

As it was, he stepped away abruptly, as if he no longer trusted himself near her. Carefully gauging his reaction, Jasmine thought it wise to defuse the man's anger. In another moment her eyes were swimming with orchestrated tears. She allowed two dramatic drops to make their way down her cheeks, before she turned and fled. On her way up the stairs she heard him call her name and smiled to herself, not pausing.

In the safety of her room she waited for the house to grow quiet. She didn't dare undress; she wasn't convinced that she'd seen the last of Abdul that evening. She heard his heavy tread on the stairs a half hour after she'd left him. He hesitated outside her door, and she stood still, readying herself to face him again. Then an instant later he continued down the hallway.

A long breath shuddered out of her as she sank onto the side of the bed. She knew just how precarious her position had been tonight, and was all too aware of the narrowness of her escape.

When Walker re-entered his bedroom window, he was attuned to Jasmine's presence long before he laid eyes on her.

The knowledge made him itchy. It had less to do with instinct than it did with a deeper, more visceral awareness. First there was a trace of the indefinable scent she wore, something rare and exotic. Then there was the clutch of

hormones stirring in his blood, the call to his most primal
level.

The feelings were unfamiliar, but undeniable. And because recognizing them made him edgy, he didn't address
her right away. Instead he took his time removing the black
watch cap and gloves he wore.

She broke the silence. "Did you remove the device?"

The realization that he had, for even an instant, been
distracted from the serious matter at hand had him scowling.

"Afraid not."

A beat went by. "You could not retrieve it?"

"I couldn't find it," he said flatly, all his pent-up disgust
apparent in his tone. "And the reason I couldn't find it is
because the damn Jeep wasn't put back into the garage."

"Ah."

Her understanding was apparent in the word. Their pre-
dicament had just gotten a little trickier. He tugged at his
dark pullover, which had gotten filthy from his endeavors
that evening. Yanking it over his head, he freed his arms
and violently tossed the shirt to the floor. "Tariq had
driven Omer and himself. I'm certain of that. I watched
them take off from my window."

"So one of the men took it back to the camp after they'd
finished with it?"

"Most likely. Damn." He sank down onto the bed, and
after a moment, she crossed to join him. "I took the chance
of going out to the building where the weapons are stored,
on the off chance that the Jeep the guards were using was
the one we wanted. Waited through two shifts. Neither of
them was the right one."

He'd taken a helluva chance checking that out for himself, too, but didn't consider the fact worth mentioning.

The vehicles had been parked more closely than he'd liked to the guard at the entrance of the building.

Her voice, when it sounded in the shadows, was calm. "How big a problem is this?"

He thought for a moment. "It won't shake loose from the chassis, I wired it too well for that. Someone would have to be working on the Jeep to find it, and it just received a thorough tune-up earlier today. We'll probably be okay."

The fact that he spoke the truth didn't make it any easier to swallow. Loose ends made him damn nervous. They were sloppy, dammit, and he didn't do sloppy. But having the Jeep disappear was one of those freakish twists sometimes encountered in a mission. He didn't like them, but they had to be accepted, and dealt with. He'd already weighed chances of discovery with the risk of infiltrating the camp again to search the Jeeps there. It hadn't seemed worth it.

"I think you are right. And if the worst happens…" He felt her shrug. "Then we do damage control. At any rate, we are ready to leave tomorrow. Time is on our side."

"You must have done a helluva job on Marakeh this afternoon," he noted. "I think I saw him smile for the first time at dinner this evening."

"Yes, the Brothers of Darkness are convinced that I will go back to Tamir and pave their way for them." Her voice was coolly contemptuous. "A treaty will be forged with Sheik Kamal, he will lower his guard, thus making it easier to destroy him and the people of his country. I am very glad we took this job, Walker. I would hate to think of them getting away with their plan."

Her face was etched against the shadows of the room, and involuntarily he raised his hand, traced her profile with his finger. With the millions of people in this world, what were the odds that this woman sitting beside him would share that almost unmentionable code of honor that plagued him?

Honor. The word didn't sit easily, and most of the time he didn't consider the compunction he had to right some of the wrongs in this world. It could be baffling at times, especially when the situations grew deadly. But the feeling was there, and it was real, for all it remained unspoken. And he realized it was just as real for Jasmine. The knowledge fostered an odd sense of kinship that would be much more comfortable to deny.

"Any difficulties after I slipped out tonight?" The casual question took on a more serious edge when he sensed rather than heard her evasion.

"Nothing I couldn't handle."

"Care to define 'nothing'?"

Her hesitation was barely perceptible. "Abdul's interest in me had to be dealt with. I managed to dissuade his ardor without sleeping with him."

His reaction was immediate and savage. His hand went to her chin, and he turned her face to his, although he couldn't see her clearly. "Don't." That was all he said, all he could manage. There was anger in the word, but it was directed at himself. He didn't like the brittle sound that came to her voice when she said such things. Didn't like the fact that she felt she needed to say them at all.

And he especially didn't like that he'd been the one to put her on the defensive to begin with. "Tell me what happened."

She took a breath. "Nothing happened. Because I managed to bring up the topic most guaranteed to send any man running for the nearest exit. Marriage."

The word hit him like a fastball square in the chest. "Marriage?"

She gave a humorless chuckle. "His reaction was much

the same. When I convinced him I had misinterpreted his intentions, and then grew insulted when he clarified his feelings..." A shrug sounded in her voice. "The scene was easily manipulated."

He felt a keen sense of admiration that was combined with unease. *Marriage.* It was a word that packed a strong enough punch to send him reeling, just thinking about it. He tried to speak, found he had to find his voice first. "How'd you know how to play him?"

Drolly she said, "I could predict his reaction easily enough. It is one universal to the male of the species."

He had the wisdom to leave that remark alone. There was enough truth in it to fit, however uncomfortably. Instead he said, "Well, at least you didn't have to use your stiletto on him. I have a feeling he wouldn't have reacted to that as calmly as I did."

"Ah, but your reaction to that was all too predictable, as well, Walker." There was a hint of pique in her tone, and his mood lightened a fraction.

"I can assure you, there's never been another naked woman who could turn me on even while she was trying to kill me. You're unique in that sense, Jaz." His smile slowly faded as his hand left her cheek and went unerringly to her hair. He found the comb securing it, and with a single tug freed the tresses to fall heavily over his wrist. He combed his fingers through the thick mass, feeling his blood begin to beat in a rhythm that he was beginning to anticipate. Beginning to savor.

Her hand came to his chest, lingered. He liked the feel of her hands on him, too much. When he touched her he never failed to be amazed at the delicacy of her bones, her exquisitely feminine form. She was a woman at ease in her own femininity. She wore trousers when the job necessitated it, but usually he'd noticed that she wore dresses or skirts that showed her mile-long legs to advantage.

Leaning forward, he skimmed his lips along her smooth cheek, took her earlobe in his teeth. Satisfaction filled him as a shudder worked through her, and her fingers on his chest clenched. He could feel the sharp-edged hunger begin to surface again, heightening his other senses, until they all were filled with her.

He laid her back on the bed, and she went with a little sigh that tugged at something deep inside him. Levering himself above her on his elbows, he took one of the ties of her robe in his hand and gave a slight tug. The two halves of the garment parted, and he feasted on the sight revealed to him.

The darkness painted her form with shadows but it was branded on his memory in the most exquisite detail. The taste and texture of her, the scent of her arousal, the sound of her fulfillment.

His blood was already hammering and he'd barely touched her. But last night had been all flash and fury, lightning and electricity. Tonight he'd give her something less familiar, to both of them. Tonight she'd have tenderness from him. Somehow, he'd make it last forever.

And so while his lungs grew thick and his breathing labored, he explored her, his mouth finding every inch on her that elicited a moan, a sigh. Her breasts were full, firm, an erotic invitation. He took her turgid nipple between his teeth and suckled strongly enough to rip a gasp from her throat.

Something darkly male and satisfied curled through him at the sound of her pleasure. It increased his own tenfold, and he switched to her other breast, fingertips teasing the damp nipple he'd just released.

His hand swept down, more demanding now, finding every curve, every hollow. Her hands went to his shoulders and he felt the bite of her nails. The small pain fired his hunger, sparked a visceral longing for more. And then more.

When her hands went to his waistband, he lifted his hips, let her unfasten his jeans before releasing her long enough to rid himself of them completely. Then she was back in his arms, skin to skin, bodies radiating heat. Her hands were too quick for him to temper his response. She traced the crease of his leg, her touch almost unbearably light, before wrapping her fingers around his shaft. He bucked wildly into her touch, one heavy thrust, before shuddering deeply, reaching for his torched control. This was going to end much too soon if Jasmine had her way. Already his vision was graying at the edges, heralding a control that was rapidly spiraling away.

He took her hands in his and rolled with her, first him on top and then her. He could feel the hot molten blood chugging in his veins. Could hear the quick short breaths she took at the exquisite friction of skin against skin.

Sitting up, he braced himself against the headboard and brought her closer so that her knees straddled his hips. When he had her positioned he guided himself with one hand between their bodies, so that he barely entered her. And then, sweat popping out on his forehead, he waited.

Her hands went to his shoulders, and her gaze met his, held. The sight of her mounted above him was almost enough to shred his resolve, but then she began to move.

Her bottom lip caught between her teeth, she took more of him inside her, but only a torturous inch at a time. His eyes slid half shut, listening to the tiny gasps she gave as she moved. When he filled her, his length stretching her delicate softness, he gave a strangled groan and rested his forehead against hers. She was going to kill him. He was certain of it. And in the next instant she very nearly proved him right by lifting herself almost completely off him only to begin again. And then again.

His breath was sawing in and out of his lungs. Her arms went to his neck, her breasts flattened against his chest and she arched against him, taking him halfway inside her before sliding upward again. Not trusting his reaction, Walker fisted his hands on the sheets and fought the savage demand of his body. Tonight was different in a way he couldn't identify, and he wasn't going to change the pace, or to shatter the mood. Instead he withstood the torture and watched her, enthralled, arousal etched on her face as she slid up and down on him.

He could feel her growing damp around him, her rhythm growing quicker, and he had to bite back a harsh groan. The sheet loosened beneath his hands, and the feel of her breasts rubbing against his chest coupled with the pleasure from her repetitive movements was a sensual assault that shattered what remained of his restraint.

She leaned forward, scored his bottom lip with her teeth, her breath all but sobbing from her body. Filling his hands with the curves of her hips he surged upward, swallowing her cry with his mouth over hers. He held there for a moment, trying to make it last, but she was moving frantically on him now, every movement taking him in deeper.

In a sudden burst of desperation he lunged upward again, and then again. His vision had gone to haze and his other senses were honed to fever point. He controlled her movements and set the rhythm, driving himself up inside her, as deeply as he could manage. And when her breath began to hitch and catch, when her moans came faster and her skin grew damp, he lowered his hand to where they were joined and found her, taut and waiting.

He let her climax work over him, milking his own response. And as he closed his eyes and surged toward his own release, he tried to believe that this could be enough.

Chapter 13

The sun was high overhead before either of them stirred.
Turning her head, Jasmine contemplated Walker, who was,
as usual, sprawled out over most of the bed. She was
curled against him, the heavy weight of his arm keeping
her tucked close to his side. She gave herself the gift of a
few precious more minutes, mentally freeze-framing the
moment.

She was a woman who courted danger for a living, but
the biggest risk she'd taken to date was with this man.
She'd stepped into Walker's arms with her eyes, and her
heart, wide open. Of course she'd fallen in love with him.

And of course she would still have to walk away.

Nothing had changed between them, not in any sense
that mattered. And she had entirely too much self-respect
to turn weak and clingy once this assignment was through.
With an ache in her chest she wondered if it would be
another three years before they met up again. And if the

pain of leaving him would have subsided by then, at least a little.

The moment had grown too bittersweet. Slipping from his grasp, she went to her own room, stepped into the shower. Even as she'd made the vow to herself to take her pleasure with Walker, then be the one to leave without a backward glance, she'd somehow known that she wouldn't walk away unscathed. And she wouldn't. Her heart would bear the scars to prove it.

She worked the shampoo into her hair with both hands, as if with the deep massaging motion she could work the man out of her mind. Images kaleidoscoped behind her closed eyelids; pictures of Walker that would never be banished. The most she could hope for was to lock them away in a dark and secret corner of her mind. But her experience from three years ago had taught her that no matter how hard she willed the memories, they responded to no command. They'd pick their time and place to rise, and the anguish that accompanied them would have to be borne. Over and over again.

Turning off the faucets, she squeezed the water from her hair, and stepped out, dried off. Her movements were brisk, economical, as she entered her bedroom, dressed, and then began packing. It would help, she realized, to keep her mind on the task at hand. The most dangerous part of their assignment was still ahead of them. They had to find the lab, destroy the virus, make their escape. There was no room in her head for regrets, so she would push them aside until this was over. Her hands paused in the act of folding a nightgown.

When this was over. Then...then she'd do exactly as she'd promised herself. She'd walk away, head held high.

And heart shattering in a million pieces.

* * *

They didn't get moving until nearly noon. There was a leisurely breakfast to be had, goodbyes to be said. Jasmine had disappeared into the office with El-Dabir, Abdul, and Marakeh for a half hour or so. Walker had put their bags in the car, brought it around front, and then lounged against it, his casual posture at odds with the adrenaline pumping through his veins.

He surveyed the area from behind his mirrored glasses. Was it his imagination, or was there a little more activity than normal? A couple men were near the front gate, and he was certain that within an hour of their departure, a full dozen would be back as the Brothers resumed their normal level of security. No doubt the word was already out and the camp in the hills was probably being dismantled at this moment. He folded his arms, the picture of indolence. The Brothers were most likely readying everything to be returned to normal. He was going to do his best to make sure nothing was ever "normal" for them again.

The front door opened and El-Dabir stepped out with Jasmine, Abdul following closely behind them. He watched as the prime minister bent over her hand, and waited to see the goodbye Abdul would give her. The man's face was expressionless, but Walker figured the guy's pride had taken a hit the night before and he couldn't deny a certain vicious satisfaction at the knowledge.

If there was one thing about this job that he'd be glad to put behind him, it was having to witness the way the man watched Jasmine; with the covetous look a miser gave his storeroom of gold, with more than a little lust layered over it.

"Rose, if I may have a word before you go?"

Walker's gaze shot to Abdul, narrowed consideringly. Jasmine hesitated before conceding, the picture of graciousness. The two strolled a short distance away, and despite Walker's excellent hearing, he was unable to pick up a word they were saying.

He stared hard, but lip reading had never been a particular strength of his. Forcing his muscles to relax, he watched the other man adopt an earnest expression, and a cold blade of ice lodged somewhere in the vicinity of his chest.

Pleading his case, Walker thought with disgust. The guy never seemed to give up. The man put his hand on Jasmine's shoulder, and when she smiled up at him Walker lurched away from the car, yanked open the car door, and slid in to start the ignition. Pretense aside, Jasmine didn't have to drag this thing out, did she? Abdul didn't matter anymore; in another few minutes he'd be out of their lives forever.

That thought didn't satisfy as much as the next. Walker had well-developed sources all over the world. A man like Tariq Abdul may well pop up again in one trouble spot or another. Fingers curling into a fist, Walker gave a thin, feral smile. He'd look forward to meeting the man again. Just once.

The couple were walking to the car now, so Walker got out, went to the rear passenger side and opened the door. He may as well have been invisible for all the notice the pair seemed to take of him.

The Malounian man lifted Jasmine's hand to his lips, his regard soulful. "Until we meet again, Rose."

Jasmine, damn her, was doing nothing to discourage his attentions, if the tiny smile on her lips was any indication. Walker shifted impatiently. "Yes, Tariq, I look forward to hearing from you."

She turned, slid into the car, and Walker slammed the door after her with just a little more force than necessary. The burning in his gut had nothing to do with the searing sun overhead, but he'd be damned if he'd admit to jealousy. He gave a casual wave to the group of people seeing them off, rounded the hood and got into the car. He'd never been jealous of a woman in his life, and he certainly wasn't going to start with Jasmine LeBarr.

Abdul hadn't moved away from the vehicle. Walker wondered if he could run over the man's foot and make it seem like an accident, before regretfully deciding he couldn't.

As he drove slowly toward the front gate, Jasmine opened her purse and took out a small makeup mirror and her lipstick. He waited as she outlined her lips, but there was no sound emanating from the tiny sensor lodged in the tube. The car was clean.

"That was a touching goodbye you shared with Abdul." Walker slowed as he drove through the gates, aware of the two guards watching them turn onto the road. "It appeared as though he's forgiven you."

"The man's ego is incredible." There was more than a tinge of irritation in her tone. "Apparently he reconsidered his options and decided that he only needed a bit more time to convince me of his irresistible charms."

"Sounded like he plans to contact you."

"He plans to contact Rose," she corrected. Dropping the lipstick into her purse, she reached for her sunglasses and slipped them on. "We'll have to make sure she receives an unlisted number. As a matter of fact, it would not hurt if she remained out of the country for several more months."

He nodded. The civilian would be protected, as in any of the assignments he worked on. "The binoculars are under the seat on your side. Use them to keep an eye out for anyone who might get the idea to follow us."

She did as he instructed, scanning the road behind them.

"I am not able to see anyone," she said finally, lowering the glasses. "When will we double back?"

"If it stays clear, I'll give it another twenty miles or so before finding another road that will take us back that way. I don't want to pass the front of the compound this time. I'd rather head north, catch a road west and then go south, staying as close to the hills as I can. It'll take a couple hours, but it's the best way to avoid detection."

"Just tell me when we are far enough away for me to change clothes. This time when the undergarment comes off, it will be for good."

His lips curved. "If you need a hand getting undressed, honey, you know you can always count on me."

Two hours later Walker stopped the car in a heavily vegetated area. Jasmine looked around. "Are we close?"

"This is as close as I'm taking the car right now." Staying as near to the hills as he was, every mile he went he risked damaging an axle. And night would have to fall before they could veer away from the cover the hills afforded and not be detected.

"We'll go the rest of the way on foot." He'd used the high-powered transmitter in his bag as soon as he'd gotten them a comfortable distance from the compound. Once they destroyed the lab, it was imperative that the agent have the ship ready for them. He wanted to be long gone before the Brothers figured out what had happened.

He got out of the car and waited for Jasmine. She pulled the pins from her hair and took a band from her purse. He enjoyed watching her as she swiftly caught the mass in one hand and plaited it with quick expert movements. Restraining her hair that way seemed a shame to Walker, but he supposed it was less bother.

The puerile fantasies he'd harbored had been dashed to

disappointment earlier when he'd discovered that she'd worn the black leggings and shirt beneath her caftan and undergarment. As a striptease, her discard of clothing had left much to be desired, but he still had an excellent imagination that served, a fact he'd reminded her of.

He winced at the memory, rubbed a spot on his side that still ached. The woman had a mean right jab.

He reached into the car to pop open the trunk, then moved to remove a toolbox. Quickly clearing the trunk area of their bags, he went to work removing the false floor.

Jasmine leaned close, watching. "That is cleverly done."

"Comes in handy," he agreed, lifting away the floorboard he'd loosened. He extracted some items from the exposed hidden compartment, mentally taking inventory. Satisfied that all he'd ordered was accounted for, he withdrew a high-powered rifle and scope, assembled it, then handed it to Jasmine. "Know how to use that?"

Her brow lifted in disdain, she reached for the box of ammunition and loaded the rifle, quickly and expertly. Giving a nod of approval, he reached for the second rifle and did the same. He shrugged into the shoulder strap hanging from the rifle, grabbed the binoculars and a canteen, and they started off on foot.

They'd walked twenty minutes before he sighted a building through the field glasses. Leading Jasmine down to the foot of the hills, they moved as close as they dared before dropping to their bellies.

"What do you see?" Jasmine didn't bother to disguise the impatience in her tone, and he hid a grin.

"Looks like our place. Building is good-size. Sixty-by-eighty, I'd figure." He was silent a moment, scanning the area. "Appears to be run by a gas-powered generator.

Don't have to worry about running power lines out here. They probably have a well dug nearby to supply the water.''

"How many people can you see?"

"Half a dozen Jeeps. Three men standing guard outside." He wondered if the guards were on the same rotation schedule as the one maintained around the weapons building. They'd have to be certain of that before making their move after nightfall.

Lowering the glasses, he looked at Jasmine. "Okay, now we go back to the car, make some preparations."

"What kind of preparations?"

Adrenaline pumping, he grinned at her. "The kind that's gonna blow this sucker, and the virus inside it, right off the map."

Equipped with night-vision goggles, Walker kept his gaze trained on the lab as he was rejoined by Jasmine. They'd moved much closer after darkness had fallen. She'd just brought the car to be hidden nearby, so they could access the materials they needed more easily.

"Do you think the lab is equipped with an alarm?"

"I doubt it." Both of them watched the relative quiet of the building. The scientists had left hours earlier, and the heavily armed guards were in the middle of a rotation shift. "With the generator as their source of power, it'd be a waste of time. All someone would have to do is knock out the generator to do away with the alarm. No, I figure the guards supply the security here."

"I want to go inside."

His head swiveled. "Why?"

Using her elbows for leverage, she inched closer to him, reached for the night goggles. "We must make sure we have the right place."

He didn't reply. He couldn't think of any other use for the building they'd found, but he didn't complete his assignments on the basis of assumptions. He'd already planned to take a look inside. It would be the best place to plant the explosive.

"I'll make sure."

"*We'll* make sure."

He wasn't surprised at the correction. He shot her a sideways grin. "Yeah, okay, *we'll* make sure. You planning on taking care of all three guards yourself, or do you want me to give you a hand?"

She gave him a considering look. "You may as well come along and make yourself useful," she said finally. "But try not to get in my way."

He snorted. "I'll see what I can do. I'll take the guards on the north and west. You take the one on the south. Ready? This is how we'll take them out."

And in a low whisper he detailed their plan.

Tariq Abdul frowned as a pounding at the front door began, and, with a glance at his watch, laid down the paper he'd been reading. Some of the other leaders had departed after their guests had; the rest had retired for the evening. Striding to his desk, he slid open the drawer and took out his automatic. Thumbing the safety, he stalked to the door, using the peephole to look out. His anxiety was allayed as he identified the visitors, but he didn't lower the Sig Sauer when he opened the door.

His gaze traveled between Emil, head of security, to the frightened man beside him. Tariq recognized the man as a member who performed mechanical work for them. "What is the problem? Why are you disturbing us so late?"

Emil handed him a clear plastic bag, and Abdul squinted at it. "What is this?" There was an empty three-sided casing, and loose pieces of a mechanism he couldn't identify. His gaze shifted to the security chief. "Explain yourself."

"This device was found on one of the Jeeps this evening."

The chief gave the mechanic a shove, and he stammered out, "That is right, sir. One of the Jeeps had a flat tire and while it was being changed, this mechanism was found. I did not know what it was, but I took it to security right away." His head bobbed eagerly, his expression hopeful.

Abdul studied the man for a moment before switching his attention back to Emil. "And you took it apart?"

The man's onyx gaze gave nothing away. "I have never seen anything like it. But I suspect that it is a tracking device of some kind, one that would transmit to an outside power source. I thought you would be interested to know that it was found on the Jeep you used yesterday."

Impatience drained away, to be replaced with suspicion. And a sudden, simmering rage. "The Jeep I took with Omer?" At the man's nod, Abdul shot a deadly look at the mechanic. "Was it not your duty to go over that Jeep thoroughly?"

Accurately reading the menace on Abdul's face, the mechanic cowered. "I did, sir. I spent hours getting it into perfect running condition."

"And yet you did not find the device in your work."

"It was not there when I left it, sir. Perhaps it belongs to the Englishman."

Abdul stilled. "The Englishman?"

"Yes, sir. He was in the garage washing the visitor's car while I worked."

Tariq Abdul found stupidity as enraging as incompetence. His hand moved in a sudden savage action, bringing the gun across the man's temple. "Idiot!" he hissed. The mechanic slowly crumpled to the ground and Abdul kicked him hard in the ribs. Then, and only then, he looked at the impassive face of his security chief. "I want every member of our troops rounded up and fully armed. You have fifteen minutes."

Since the encampment had been moved that very afternoon from the hills back to the compound, the time frame wasn't unreasonable. The man inclined his head. "Where will we be heading?"

"To the lab." Rage roiling in his veins, Abdul strode to the stairway.

"What do you want me to do with him?" Emil called after him, gesturing to the unconscious mechanic.

Abdul didn't bother turning around. "Shoot him."

The first guard was dispensed with quietly. He'd cooperatively crumpled after one well-placed blow. Walker quickly slapped a piece of duct tape over his mouth and bound his arms and legs. Then he rose, a silent shadow in the night, and slipped around the corner to see Jasmine kick the rifle from the second guard's hands. The man dropped to combat stance and rushed her. Muscles bunched, Walker tensed to go to her aid, but it wasn't necessary. Jasmine let the man get within range and then leaped, as graceful as a ballerina, one foot connecting with the man's chin, snapping it up and back. He hit the ground heavily, and Walker allowed himself a quick grin as he readied for the next guard. Seeing Jaz in action was quickly becoming one of the highlights of the mission.

He banged on the side of the building and waited for the sound to bring the other guard to investigate. When the man rounded the corner, the barrel of Walker's rifle pressed against his forehead. Without a word Jasmine was at the man's side, divesting him of the gun and competently binding his hands. She slapped a piece of tape over his mouth, cutting short his curses, and reached into the pocket of his *jellaba,* searching for a set of keys.

Not finding any, she went to the next guard and searched him. Discovering a large key ring, she rose and tossed it to Walker, who caught it in one hand. "You do the honors."

He handed her the pocket flashlight and, as she held it steady, unlocked the door and pushed it open. They stepped through it together, and Jasmine swept the area with the beam. "It looks like we've found it."

To his admittedly unscientific eye, the lab looked first-class. There were row after row of tables, topped with microscopes, culture ovens, and other apparatus he couldn't even begin to identify. Heading over to one of the tables, he laid down the explosive device, with all the care it warranted.

"Ready?" She nodded and he took her arm, guiding her back out the door. "We'll bring the car up, take the guards to the foothills and dump them." His grin was quick. "And then we're out of here, sweetheart. It's as easy as…"

She stopped abruptly in the doorway of the lab and he bumped into her from behind. Switching off the flashlight, she reached for the high-powered night binoculars hanging around his neck. Seeing the same thing she had, he grabbed the glasses from her, took a closer look. Her voice was dry as a bone. "Looks like we have company."

"Son of a bitch." Curses tripped off his tongue, even as he shot into action. There were too many Jeeps for him to count, all hurtling forward without headlights. He couldn't tell for sure how many men were coming, but every Jeep looked full.

"Out the back. Move." He grabbed Jasmine's hand and

together they ran for the rear exit. She fumbled with the lock, then the door was pushed open and they both ran like hell for the cover of the vehicle.

''If we can make it to the car maybe we can outrun them,'' she shouted.

At that moment the Jeeps turned on their headlights, spotlighting the area around the lab. Walker heard shouts, knew they'd been spotted. Dust kicked up near them. They were being shot at. ''Hit the dirt and cover your ears,'' he yelled. Reaching into his pocket, he removed the remote to the explosives, held it behind him and pressed the button.

Time clicked into slow motion. He dove after Jasmine, rolled with her, shielding her body with his. The shouts and shots dimmed…he pulled his arms over his ears…and a huge explosion rent the night. The blaze was immediate, far-reaching and searing. Even from this distance he could hear the crackle of the flames, feel the reach of the awesome heat.

When he was assured that there would be no more falling debris, he rolled off Jasmine, turning her face to his. ''Are you all right? Jaz!''

She blinked up at him, dazed but alert. ''I am fine.''

He gave her a quick once-over, to assure himself of the truth of her words, then pulled her close for a brief, hard kiss. ''Then let's keep running, honey.'' He rose, grabbed her hand and heaved her to her feet. Giving her a light push, they headed for the huge boulders amid the trees. Ducking behind one, he hauled up the night binoculars, took a quick assessment.

He figured the explosion had taken out fully half of the Jeeps and troops, but he could see Abdul, standing at the rear of the remaining vehicles, screaming orders.

''What about the car?''

He spared a quick glance at Jasmine, wishing he didn't have to tell her what he'd seen. "It's riddled with bullets, the tires are shot out. We wouldn't get a mile in it before they caught up with us."

She blinked once, comprehension filling her face. Her voice amazingly calm, she said, "What do we do now?"

He turned his attention to reloading the rifle. "You fall back. Stay down, head up the hills and make as good time as you can."

"And what about you?"

He gave her a quick look and delivered the lie convincingly. "I'll cover you, follow when I'm able. Go on now." He jerked his head in the direction of the upper hills. "I'll be along."

There was a moment of silence while she surveyed him, a moment in which he had no idea what was going on in that beautiful head of hers. But the last thing he expected to hear her say was, "And what is option two?"

He scowled. "There is no option two. Now move your ass, Jaz. That's an order!"

Calmly, she shrugged off the shoulder strap of her rifle and picked up the field glasses. "We will both stay."

Duty, honor...all were forgotten as an unfamiliar cold-edged fear coiled and struck inside him. He grabbed her shoulder, shoved his face close to hers and shook her. "You don't have a choice! Get moving. I'll be along as soon as..."

She pulled away from him, brought the glasses to her face and studied the scene beyond them. He thought he saw her swallow hard once, but her hand when she lowered the glasses was steady. "We will stay together. We are partners, remember?"

His stomach took a quick vicious lurch. His best chance

of getting her out of this alive was getting her to head out alone. "Dammit, Jaz..."

A shot kicked up dirt close by. Walker grabbed the glasses, saw that the remaining troops had fanned out. Jasmine reached for her rifle, sited carefully and fired. A man dropped, screaming loudly. Then she looked coolly up at him. "Well? Are you going to make me hold them off on my own?"

A boulder lodged in his throat, and he knew the struggle was over. Hell, it hadn't even begun. There was no moving the woman, no forcing her to relative safety. He grabbed his rifle, waited for a shot at the man closest to them and fired.

Ducking back down, he said, "We don't return fire. Save your shots and make them count. We'll pick off the closest ones, one at a time."

He didn't mention the dismalness of their situation. Didn't mention that they were greatly outmanned, outgunned and that it was only a matter of time until the troops surrounded them. He didn't have to. She was intelligent enough to have figured out the situation on her own, and still she'd chosen to stay and take her chances.

They took turns shooting, using their ammunition sparingly. And knowing that he faced almost certain death, it was both heaven and hell for Walker that Jaz was there beside him.

Chapter 14

Walker dropped the field glasses, squeezed off a shot. When he heard a curse, he smiled grimly. Abdul, the son of a bitch, had chanced just a little too close. If Walker was going down, he was going to be damned sure to take the arrogant Malounian with him.

Hunched behind the boulder, he searched the ground blindly with his hand. "Ammo."

Jasmine glanced at him, face sober. "Gone."

He took a deep breath, nodded. Grabbing the last of the rifles he'd taken off the lab guards, he raised his head above the rock again, prepared to fire.

The night was alive with sounds. The second explosion, of the gas generator, had rained scalding scraps of metal on the troops. The screams of the dying and the shouts of the men below mingled with the gunfire hadn't ceased since they'd fled the lab.

And through it all his mind circled determinedly for a way to get Jasmine out of this. They were going to have to make their move while they still had the cover of darkness. Which meant he was going to have to buy them some time.

There was a small rustle of sound and Walker reacted without thinking. Whipping the rifle around he shot the man who'd ventured closer than the others, all the while coolly examining their options.

They were depressingly limited.

The ship he'd arranged to pick them up wouldn't be able to wait around for long. He'd need the transmitter to call the contact, arrange for a different pickup. And he needed a few of the other supplies that remained near the car.

Jasmine rose, fired, and dropped back down beside him in one smooth movement. He glanced at her, his gut clenching once at the impassive determination of her expression. "You ready to get out of here?"

She glanced at him. "Are you coming with me?"

He released a short laugh at her words. She couldn't have said any plainer that any renewed attempts to get her to flee alone would meet with failure. "Yeah. We'll go together."

She nodded once. "Then I am ready."

"I need to get to the car. I've got a few other things in the supplies that I might be able to buy us some time with. Think you can cover me while I try to reach it?"

He saw her swallow once hard, then measure the distance between them and the car with her gaze. But her voice when she answered was calm. "Of course. Do you think you can try and not get yourself killed?"

He laughed again, grimly amused. No doubt there was something desperately wrong with a man who would feel so pumped in a situation as deadly as this one. He credited that emotion to the woman crouched beside him.

"Don't fire until you have to. The longer it takes them to determine that we're on the move, the better off we'll be. When I get closer to the car you can spray some fire in front of me while I'm on the run. Ready?"

But her attention had shifted from him, her head tilted. An instant later he realized what she was listening to. There was a new sound layering over the others. One he couldn't identify at first, one too unexpected to contemplate. He and Jaz looked at each other, stunned. It sounded like the whirring of chopper blades.

The noise was followed in the next moment by a barrage of gunfire. "Stay down." He grabbed Jasmine's head and pushed to be certain she obeyed. Chin to the ground, he peered around the rock, glasses in hand. Several black choppers were silhouetted against the night sky, and explosions sounded, one after another.

Grenades, followed by more gunfire. The helicopters swooped and followed the fleeing troops. Black-clad figures dropped from lines out of the choppers, appearing to fall from the sky. Each one hit the ground running, weapon raised.

It was over in moments. Dozens of the men swarmed the area, taking captives and chasing those who'd turned to flee. Night binoculars to his eyes, Walker struggled to make sense of the scene. It wasn't until he'd caught sight of a familiar figure that comprehension dawned. And with it, a sense of relief flooded through him.

Grinning, Walker lowered the binoculars. "C'mon, honey." He hauled Jasmine up, gave her a delighted kiss. When he lifted his head, she was looking at him as if he'd lost his mind.

"Walker, what is going on?"

Nudging her forward, they walked out of the hills toward the newcomers. "In America we'd say the cavalry just arrived."

"You owe me big for this one, James."

Walker returned the huge blond man's hug, thumping him on the shoulder. "Are you kidding? We had the whole thing under control."

"Uh-huh." Covert Intelligence Officer Reed Galloway rocked back on his heels and cast a gaze at the troops his men had gathered up. "I could see that. I really could. If I'da known you was the one they was shooting at, I mighta called the rest of the fellas off."

Sensing Jasmine's confusion, Walker made introductions. "Jasmine, this is Reed Galloway, master of showing up where he's least expected. That speech impediment you hear in his voice is called a Georgia accent." He absorbed Reed's punch in the arm with a grin. "Reed, Jasmine LeBarr."

The man swept the black watch cap off his head, his gaze lingering a lot longer on Jasmine that Walker thought necessary. "You are a sight for these poor eyes, ma'am."

"What brought you here?" Walker distracted him by asking. "I had a ship waiting at the shore, but our departure was, uh, delayed for a while."

Reed replaced his hat on his head, looked at the scene beyond them. "Fact of the matter is, we were looking for a lab operated by the Brothers of Darkness." He nodded in direction of the building, which was still burning wildly. "That it?"

Walker nodded.

His grin delighted, Reed said, "Guess you beat us to it, then. Least we could do in return is save your butt afterward."

"Yeah, yeah. You in charge of the operation?"

Reed shook his head. "Just along for the ride on this one." He turned, gestured to a tall, dark-haired man, who came to join them. Walker felt a jolt of recognition, but it was Jasmine who spoke first.

"Rashid. It is a pleasure to see you again. And *alive.*"

Sheik Rashid Kamal bowed low over Jasmine's hand, his dark eyes twinkling. "Jasmine LeBarr. I pride myself on not being easily surprised but it is a shock finding you here."

Galloway introduced Walker, and he shook hands with the young sheik. "Rashid. Your father will be greatly relieved to hear of your well-being."

"Yes, I owe my father a few explanations." He turned to the burning lab, then shot a questioning look at Walker. "The virus?"

"Destroyed. And another forty-two kilometers due northeast you'll find the compound that houses the Brothers, with a large building filled with weapons and ammunition. The organization was selling them to terrorist groups to finance their own operation."

Rashid's face lit up. "We will have to relieve them of those weapons. It would be a shame to leave the job half done."

"My thoughts exactly." Walker noticed Jasmine beginning to slip away and reached out, caught her hand. "Where are you going?"

The three men looked at her expectantly. Jasmine opened her mouth and then closed it. Finally she said, "I need to get something out of the car."

"What? I'll be transferring our stuff to one of the choppers in a few minutes." To her dismay, he fell into step beside her. "Tell me what you need and I'll get it for you."

"That's all right." Her step quickened and she wondered if the man could possibly be as obtuse as he pretended. "I'll only be a minute."

"I don't want you lifting anything, Jaz. As a matter of fact, as soon as we get back to the States, you're getting checked out by a doctor. You took a nasty spill back on the hill."

She clenched her teeth and walked faster. "I don't need a doctor, I just need a little privacy."

"Privacy?"

His confusion showed in his tone, so she whirled on him, hating the flush that scalded her cheeks. "I need a rest room, Walker, and since I do not see one in the vicinity, I need some privacy. Have I made myself clear?"

She hoped, she really hoped, that he didn't make the mistake of smiling. It would be a shame to have to hit him again.

"Ah, crystal-clear." And although there was a hint of amusement in his voice, he was wise enough to keep it from showing in his face. "I'll just wait for you over here." He made a production of turning his back, and she stalked away, head held high, mortification keeping her spine stiff.

She found a private area to relieve herself, choosing a spot that was well away from where Walker stood. Minutes later she was picking her way back down the hillside, taking care with her footing. The last thing she needed was to take a tumble and skid down the hill to land at Walker's feet. She would...

Before she could complete the thought she was pulled off her feet, and a hand clamped over her mouth. A heavy body wrestled hers to the ground and her eyes widened disbelievingly.

Tariq Abdul bared his teeth, his face twisted with rage. "And what a prize I have caught here, Rose." He ran his hand over her form insultingly, lingering on her breasts and the notch between her thighs. She squirmed wildly, but couldn't free her hands.

"You have cost me much." The almost-conversational tone was all the more chilling for being completely expressionless. His robe was soaked with blood. He'd fashioned a makeshift bandage around the wound, looping it over his shoulder and knotting it under his arm.

"My reputation is in ruins because of you. Do you think Marakeh would forgive such a grievous lapse in judgment? It was my idea, after all, to bring you to the compound." His free hand went to Jasmine's throat and he squeezed, all the fury apparent in his face reflected in his threatening touch. "I should kill you right here for that alone."

Spots danced in front of Jasmine's eyes. Her struggles grew weaker as her lungs screamed for oxygen. When he loosened his fingers a fraction, she went limp, all her strength expended on sucking in much needed air.

"You will pay for your part in this. You will pay over and over again. And you will help me regain everything you took from me. How much is your life worth, Rose? How much will the sheik pay for your safe return?" He was playing with her now, his face stamped with cruelty. He allowed her to fill her lungs, one desperate gasp, and then another, before slowly cutting her oxygen off again. "You had better hope that Ahmed Kamal values you highly. And hope that I can keep from killing you while we wait for your ransom to be paid."

One of her hands crept toward the back of her thigh. His weight made it difficult to move. Her weakness made it even more so. His fingers tightened on her throat again. "How will we spend the time while we wait, hmm? You will please me, in every way possible, or you will be delivered to the sheik one piece at a time."

Her vision went hazy as he squeezed again. She clawed for the sheath, used every bit of her remaining strength to free the knife.

The stiletto flashed through the air and sliced Abdul's cheek, causing him to curse and let go of her, clutching the wound. She rolled away, struggled to her feet and turned as he grabbed for her again, cutting him this time on the hand.

"Bitch!" The venom on his face, in his voice, told Jasmine she didn't have a prayer if she failed. Nothing on earth would keep this man from killing her. She backed away carefully, stumbling a little on the rocky soil. Abdul looked at the blood on his wrist disbelievingly before rushing toward her. Jasmine danced away, her movements uncoordinated from lack of oxygen. She slipped, and he lunged forward, grasping her wrist that clutched the stiletto.

He squeezed and she could feel bone grind against bone. The knife dropped from her nerveless fingers and he slapped her, hard enough to rock her head back and drive her to the ground.

He disappeared then. No, he rolled to the side. She shook her head. Her vision was blurred—nothing made sense. When it cleared she saw two bodies entwined, arms flying. Walker and Abdul.

She scrambled to her feet, swayed. Walker was on top of Abdul, and the fight was streaming out of the Malounian as Walker landed one blow after another.

His face was a mask of grim purpose. He struck the man with methodical precision, and she knew from the light in his eyes that he was beyond stopping.

"Walker." She stumbled to his side, stilled his movements by the simple action of leaning over him, holding him tight. "Stop. Enough."

It took long moments for her words to reach his rage-fogged brain. She could almost watch the journey as comprehension returned to his face. When it did, he rose and caught her to him tightly. "He hurt you."

She flinched when he touched her neck, where she could already feel the bruises blooming.

"Not anymore." She grasped his wrist, held on tight. "It is over." And when he wrapped his arms more closely around her, she went willingly, laying her head weakly on his chest. It really was over now. In every way.

"Another successful mission." Dirk's proud look took in both of his protégés.

Walker and Jasmine sat side by side on the overstuffed couch, and she had an odd sense of déjà vu. It was in this very room that her latest encounter with Walker had begun. And it was here that it would end. The quick slice of pain that accompanied the thought produced an all too familiar ache.

"And Rashid was working undercover for the U.S. government?" the man continued, shaking his head. "Never heard a whisper of that, I can tell you."

"Nice to know some secrets can still be kept in this world," Walker drawled. "I doubt Sheik Kamal will be too happy with his son's alliance with the U.S., or the scare he put the family through, but he can't argue with his motivation."

"Rashid heard hints of the Brothers of Darkness's plot while he was in Maloun on business for his father months ago." Talking about the assignment, Jasmine discovered, was one way to take her mind off the throb in her heart. "He shared his intelligence with the U.S. government and has been heading up a team ever since, trying to locate the virus and destroy it."

"They made nightly forays over the landscape surrounding the compound, trying to discover the lab's whereabouts." Walker leaned back against the rich leather. "The wooded terrain made it difficult to spot from the air. The Brothers had a damn-near-perfect spot for it. But they sighted the explosion and fire and came down for a closer look." He shot a grin at Jasmine. "Lucky for us."

Because it would be expected, she returned his smile, hoped it looked natural. Shifting her attention to the older man again, she said, "Sinan Omer was one of those killed in the blast."

Interest sharpening his voice, Dirk asked, "The U.C.L.A. scientist?"

"He had fled the U.S. fearing he would be convicted for shooting at Princess Christina. He had been a sympathizer of the Brothers of Darkness, although not trusted with its long-range goals. Nonetheless, the Brothers were willing to use him to help them finish the virus." She frowned then, asked Walker a question that had been bothering her. "Reed Galloway said Abdul would stand international charges for attempted murder. But what about Marakeh? And the other leaders of the Brothers?"

Exchanging a look with Dirk, Walker said, "I don't think we'll have to worry about them escaping justice. Marakeh was caught with the building full of weapons on the compound. He must have heard the explosion and had erased the computer files. But we've got an expert retrieving them. Once the arms sales records on there are recovered, I think international law will take care of him, too."

Seeing the relieved expression on Jasmine's face, Walker went on. "United Nations has been alerted to the plot they were working on, and Maloun will be under international scrutiny for a long time to come. Even if Marakeh and his partners weren't charged, with the virus and the lab destroyed, their source of income gone, I think their operation is shut down for good.''

It wasn't quite the nice neat ending that she'd hoped for, but Jasmine knew she'd have to be satisfied with it. She'd learned long ago that life rarely approached perfection. And if she'd needed further proof of that fact, there was the relationship between her and Walker.

He'd barely left her side for a moment since Abdul had been captured. She recognized the care with which he treated her, identified his grimly concerned glances at the bruises on her throat, her wrist. But try as she might, she couldn't convince herself that he felt anything other than the concern he'd feel for any of his colleagues. He'd recently gone in to a building set to detonate for one of his team solely from a sense of responsibility.

A feeling of responsibility would never be enough for her.

Last night he'd defied convention and crawled into her bed in the sheik's palace. But he'd done no more than hold her, and they'd fallen asleep in each other's arms. In the morning he'd been gone, and even though his absence heralded a far more permanent one, she'd been relieved. There was no room for emotion as they disentangled themselves from each other's lives. It would be uncomfortable for both of them. She would spare them both that, if she could.

There was a knock on the office door and a man entered, exchanging a greeting with Dirk. Jasmine looked at him curiously. There was something the slightest bit familiar about him, although she was certain she'd never seen him before. Under six foot, with dark hair silvered by age, his piercing blue gaze missed nothing as it touched on her then slid to the man beside her.

Belatedly, Jasmine became aware of the stillness that

had come over Walker. Turning to him, she was shocked by the closed expression on his face.

"What the hell is he doing here?" Ignoring the newcomer, he addressed Dirk, and Jasmine found herself just as eager for an answer. It wasn't forthcoming.

"You don't mind giving Walker and me some privacy, do you, Dirk?" That bright blue gaze turned in her direction. "Miss LeBarr?"

Silently she rose, as did Dirk. Walker stood, as well. "That's not necessary. I said everything I had to say to you a long time ago."

The antipathy in Walker's tone had Jasmine's eyes widening. Dirk placed a hand at the base of her back and steered her toward the door. As they passed through it she heard the other man say, "A half hour of your time, Walker. That's all I'm asking."

In the hallway, with the door closed on the drama being played out in the office, Jasmine turned to Dirk. "Who was that man?"

"Richard Sutter. He's an old friend of mine."

She gave the door one more look, then released a breath. They'd reported back to Dirk on the mission, and it was glaringly obvious that there was no reason for her to put off the inevitable any longer. Dragging it out wouldn't make the pain easier, or gentler. "Would you mind calling me a cab, Dirk?"

"A cab?" Her words distracted the man's attention from the closed door in his office. "Where to?"

"The airport." She gave him a smile that she hoped didn't look as forced as it felt.

"But I thought..." His gaze swung from her, to the direction of office, and back again. "Well, no matter what I thought. I guess I was wrong." His mouth lifted in that lopsided smile that was so dear to her. "Where are you going, sweetheart?"

Her breath released on a sigh, the decision being made at that exact moment. "Home." Pain mingled with trepidation. "I'm going home."

"A half hour is a lot to ask. It's more than you ever gave me, isn't it?" Walker made no apologies for the barb in the question, but the other man's slight wince of reaction surprised him.

"We've covered that territory before. The first time when you were sixteen, I believe." The man's smile held more than a hint of nostalgia. "God, you were such a punk."

The memory held no warmth for Walker. What he'd been was a delinquent, a step away from reform school. He imagined in the current climate of zero tolerance for juvenile crime, he'd have been closer to prison. The fact that he'd avoided both had everything to do with Dirk Longfield, and nothing to do with Richard Sutter.

It had been late, much too late to try to wield some control over a sixteen-year-old, hell-on-wheels kid reacting to the death of his mother and the disinterest of his stepfather.

"None of our meetings have been overly friendly. I didn't need a ready-made father when I was sixteen, and I don't need one now. If you've come hoping for a family reunion, you're going to be disappointed." The look he sent the other man was chilly. "How'd you manage to track me down here, anyway? What's your relationship with Dirk?"

An uncomfortable vise squeezed Richard's chest. It layered over a tinge of real irritation. The latter emotion was far more comfortable than the former. "You've got a hard head, Walker. That may well be your only flaw as an agent.''

Walker didn't miss a beat. Flicking a glance at him, he said flatly, ''What are you talking about?''

An absurd sense of pride filled Richard. Damned if he didn't believe the kid was every bit as good as he'd heard. Better. ''Let's not waste time. Dirk and I go way back, from before you were born. It wasn't Dirk who requested you for the Maloun mission. It was me.''

Silence stretched. The two men's gazes held, battled. ''Good work on that, by the way. It sounds as though you've dealt a crippling blow to the power of the Brothers of Darkness. Their cell near L.A. has been dismantled as a result, did you know that?''

Walker stared hard at the other man, struggling for comprehension. ''Explain.''

The word was flat, a demand more than a request, but Richard knew he had Walker's attention now, and he was satisfied with that for the moment. Acceptance, if it came, would be far more precious. He sat back on the couch, hooked one foot over his knee. ''I'm going to have to go back into history a bit to explain.'' He watched his son carefully. ''Beginning with Annabelle.''

''Leave my mother out of this. Leave *us* out of this.'' Walker jammed his fists into his pockets. The anger spurting inside him was all too familiar, all too useless. It solved nothing. It never had.

''I can't leave Annabelle out of this. I wouldn't if I could. I loved her.''

''You abandoned her.'' The correction was swift and rapier-sharp. ''You walked out and never looked back.''

Richard sighed. The familiar argument affected him more deeply than Walker could know. ''After Nam, I roamed the country trying to find what I was looking for.

I found it in Clear Springs, Nebraska, when I met your mother.''

"Then got her pregnant and deserted her." Walker wasn't giving an inch.

"You never believed this, but I didn't know she was pregnant when I left. I'd been contacted about a job. It would pay well...well enough to set me up in any career I chose...well enough to ask Annabelle to marry me. I took it." So far he'd told Walker nothing he hadn't told him before, with a decided lack of success. He gave him more now. "The contact was Jonathan Dalton."

Walker's gaze whipped to his. Dalton? The seasoned mercenary had a reputation in his line of work as one of the top hired guns in the world. The pieces were starting to come together, but he was still grappling with the total picture. "You're in the business."

Richard gave him a small smile. "In a manner of speaking. I couldn't share the nature of the job with your mother, but I promised her I'd come back. I intended to."

"What was the job?"

It had been nearly thirty years ago, but the memories hadn't faded. Richard remembered every mission clearly, this one perhaps the most vividly of all because of the way it had ended. And what it had cost him. "There was a civil skirmish in Pakistan. The deposed shah's family had been kidnapped and we organized a search-and-rescue mission behind enemy lines. We got the family out, but I was captured. It was three months before a team could get me out."

Walker's gaze dropped to Richard's hands, finally understanding the faded network of scars that marred them.

"Captivity changes a man. I wasn't fit to go back to your mother then. I couldn't let what had happened to me sully her." Richard worked his shoulders, as if he could shrug off the memory. His team had made certain he'd gotten counseling, forced him back into the field to regain critically damaged esteem. But there were some things they couldn't help him with.

"I believed in the cause, and owed a giant debt. I thought of Annabelle..." His face softened. "I still think of her...but when I heard she'd married Hank James, well, I figured she was better off. You already had a father."

Walker snorted. Hank James had never been interested in playing that role in his life.

"Just like I told you before, I never knew you existed until your grandmother contacted me."

The walls of the office seemed to be closing in. Walker paced faster. "When you showed up out of the blue like that, I thought..."

Richard's smile was wry. "I know what you thought. You were pretty articulate." And although the animosity had faded over the years, the rejection never had. It was a curious thing to a man who'd spent his life dodging bullets that that dismissal could be as painful as it had been. Still was.

"I wasn't free to explain then, not fully. But you live this life, Walker. You understand how difficult it would be to put a woman through it."

Walker had a single, fleeting vision of Jaz before he answered. "You must have gotten over that. You married Mary Beth...had the girls."

"Not until I was out of the field for the most part. My role has mainly been in the contact, planning stages."

"Your role?" There was too much information coming, and much too fast. "Your role in what?"

"The Noble Men." Richard interpreted the shock on Walker's face. Understood it. "Head of intelligence. It was the Noble Men who got me out of that hellhole I was held in. It was to their cause that I dedicated myself to for my entire adult life. I have regrets—you and Annabelle being chief among them—but I can't regret my life's work when I can see its results every day.''

"The Noble Men.'' Walker had finally come to a halt. "Jeez. I thought they were a myth.''

A small smile curved the other man's mouth. "We're very real, I can assure you, even though we're aging.'' His gaze was steady, revealing nothing of his trepidation. "As a matter of fact, I'm ready to step down. Mary Beth has been after me to retire and all that's waiting is finding the right replacement.'' His meaningful pause was impossible to misinterpret.

"Me?'' Walker stared in amazement. "You want me as head of intelligence for the Noble Men?''

"The second generation of Noble Men,'' Richard corrected. "Dedicated to the same principles as the first. You're an expert, Walker. I've followed your career all along. There's never been a mission where you haven't done me proud.''

"Is that what this last assignment was about? Some sort of test for me to prove myself?''

Richard shook his head. "It was about getting the best man for the job. You were it. And you're the best for this one.''

A thought occurred to Walker then. "When I met Dirk…did you arrange that, too?''

The idea produced a loud laugh from the older man. "Did I arrange to have you break into his home, try to rob him blind, and get caught, you mean? I'm afraid I lack that kind of imagination. Dirk doesn't know about our relationship. But when he started teaching you the trade, you can bet I was watching with keen interest.'' The pride he felt couldn't have been suppressed from his voice if he tried. "You're a natural."

Walker rolled his shoulders, wondered why the compliment should matter. Oddly enough, it did. "Yeah, well, seems like it must run in the genes."

The meeting had gone better than Richard had any right to expect. But he wouldn't be satisfied until he'd gotten the answer he'd been waiting for. "And the job? Head of intelligence?" In the ensuing silence he said, "I'm looking forward to a lifetime of leisure in the trout streams."

Slanting him a look, Walker inquired, "Do you even know how to fish?"

Honesty compelled the other man to admit, "Well…no. But that just means I have a lot of catching up to do. Can't wait around much longer for your answer."

"How can I turn it down? The Noble Men…they stand for everything I believe in."

At Walker's words, a breath Richard hadn't been aware of holding was released. He rose, grasped his son's hand, and looked him in the eye. "I have every faith in you, Walker. And I hope…" He searched for the words, found them difficult to say. "I hope this will be a turning point for our relationship."

Walker returned his father's handshake, trying to sort through the welter of emotions. "I can't promise a rush to any long-lost familial feelings. But you have my respect, sir."

The word meant more to Richard than he could say. "That respect is returned, Walker. Tenfold." His glance went to the door, and grew thoughtful. "I'm going to take advantage of our newfound truce and offer you a piece of advice. If you find a woman who could accept your job…understand it…you'd be wise not to let her go."

Again an image of Jaz flashed across Walker's mind,

and his gaze followed his father's to the door. "I'm not...there's no one like that." And there wasn't, was there? He and Jaz...well, they'd set up the parameters for their relationship well before this point. They'd both gone into it with similar expectations for how it would end. Jaz wouldn't thank him for changing the rules of the game at this point. He was almost certain of that.

But he was equally certain that there was something very rare on the verge of slipping from his reach on the other side of that door.

Chapter 15

Jasmine stood on the porch, surveying the polished teak doors in front of her. They hadn't changed in her long absence. She gave herself a moment to wonder if everything behind them remained just as unchanged, before she raised her hand, rang the bell.

Her silent question was answered a moment later when a serious-faced woman opened the door, swept her with an imperious gaze.

"Have they relegated you to housemaid, Sihri? You didn't used to deign to perform such menial tasks."

At Jasmine's teasing words the woman's eyes widened, and she took one step forward before hesitating. "Jasmine. You are home?"

The word sent an odd thread of bittersweet longing twisting through her and Jasmine stepped through the door and into the woman's outstretched arms. "I am visiting only. But yes." Her eyes slid shut as she gave the housekeeper a long squeeze. "I am home."

"Your mother will be overjoyed. I must fetch her right..." Sihri's gaze narrowed as it zeroed in on the bruises at Jasmine's neck, then she stopped and painted her with an all-over look that missed nothing. "You are hurt?"

She should have waited for the bruises to fade if she'd wanted to avoid answering questions, but Jasmine had thought...she'd known that if she waited at all she'd change her mind about coming. And this time...after all these years...she hadn't wanted to change her mind.

"Sihri, who is at..." Bianca LeBarr stopped short in the large entryway, her beautiful face shocked. Then a tiny smile began to tremble at the corners of her mouth. "Jasmine? Oh..."

They met each other and clasped tightly, and at her mother's embrace a small part of Jasmine's world tilted upright again. Bianca straightened, held her at arm's length for a moment while she gazed wondrously at her before catching her close again. "Jasmine." Her voice was choked. "I was not sure you would ever return again."

"I visited, Mother."

They broke apart, but Bianca linked arms with her, as if afraid if she completely let her daughter go she'd disappear again. "Once. Three years ago." Walking to the sitting area, she made no effort to keep the reproach from her voice. "And you did not stay long."

"I was not welcome." It was odd how the words could slice open a wound she'd thought long healed. A wound that still throbbed after all these years.

Her mother's face was troubled. "Your father did not mean those things he said. And it will be different this time, you will see. He has changed, Jasmine." She caught the skeptical look on her daughter's face, and reached out, ran a loving hand over her cheek. "He has. The two of you are just too much alike."

"Alike?" Nothing her mother could have said could have offended her more. "I am nothing like him."

With the certainty of a woman who loved them both, Bianca shook her head in frustration. "Neither of you give an inch. Each would rather walk away than reach compromise."

"There was no compromising with him when I was eighteen." The memory still burned. "He wouldn't listen to either of us."

"And so you left."

Old memories shot through her, still charged with emotion. "Better to leave than to be bartered off to a man three times my age in what amounted to little more than a business merger."

Her mother winced, but she couldn't dispute the facts. Jasmine still remembered hearing her parents argue over it, but her mother had been unable to sway her husband. It was recognition of that fact that had sent her fleeing her home. She'd known even then that to shackle herself to such an empty life would have driven her mad.

"Your father was wrong. He realizes that now." At Jasmine's raised brows Bianca angled her chin, smoothed back her hair. "He has not admitted it out loud, but he knows it all the same." She reached for her daughter's hand, held it tightly. "But when you visited three years ago, you were both wrong. Trampled pride can be a huge obstacle to love, Jasmine. If you haven't learned that yet, you have a long road ahead of you."

The words arrowed through her cleanly. "Yes," she answered, her thoughts full of Walker. "I've learned that."

Her mother covered her hands with both of hers and they exchanged a look that spoke volumes. But the moment was interrupted in the next instant by the voice of a newcomer.

"Jasmine."

Stiffening, Jasmine turned her head to see her father standing in the doorway of the room. An eerie sense of calm overtook her then. She recognized it as the same sensation she had on an assignment when things took a turn for the deadly.

Which was ludicrous, of course. The only danger her father posed was emotional.

"Hello, Father." She watched him enter the room in his familiar ramrod gait. His almost-military bearing made him appear taller than he really was, and coupled with his stoic countenance a person could be forgiven for believing Ramin LeBarr incapable of feeling at all.

"Your mother has missed you. You should have visited more often."

Jasmine heard her mother's frustrated sound, but didn't remove her gaze from her father. "I think we both know why I kept my visits minimal."

To her shock, there was a flicker of expression across his face. In the next moment it was gone, leaving her to wonder if she'd ever seen it at all. "Have you seen your sister yet?"

At the innocuous question, Jasmine slid a glance to her mother and then back to him. "No. I have not had a chance to say hello to Amir or Kalla."

"Amir is away at university. You will stay long enough to visit with him, I hope. Kalla will return shortly. She is running an errand."

A sense of unreality settled over her as they engaged in the stilted conversation. The words themselves weren't so strange, as was the fact that her father was standing in front of her engaging in small talk. She'd never known him before to sound so conciliatory. Silence stretched, and she felt the subtle pressure as her mother's hands squeezed hers.

"I look forward to seeing them." She maintained eye contact with her father, having learned something in the past few years about taking risks. "I have missed my family."

Ramin inclined his head. From his impassive expression one could be forgiven for believing he was speaking to an acquaintance. Unless one saw the hand lying against his side, fingers rubbing against the palm in an uncustomary act of nerves. "I have a meeting I must go to. I will be back in time for dinner."

Since the words were clearly aimed for his wife, Jasmine remained silent. But before he turned to leave the room his gaze found her again. And emotion was allowed to creep into his voice for the first time, squeezing her heart. "Jasmine. You are welcome here."

"Will you show me how you keep your hair in that twist, Jasmine? Mine is forever slipping out. By the end of the day I look like I have a mop perched on top of my head."

Jasmine smiled at her fifteen-year-old sister's dramatic tone. "Of course, Kalla. I'll show you how to put the pins in tightly. Of course," she teased, "I can't do anything about that mop you were born with."

She ducked the small pillow her sister tossed at her and chuckled. Her siblings had grown up in her absence. When she'd visited Amir, her nineteen-year-old brother, at the local university, she'd gone expecting the boy she had left and had found in his stead a young man. And her sister was growing into a young woman, with all the accompanying insecurities of fledgling femininity.

Her throat grew tight, and she covered her emotion by crossing to the dressing table to arrange Kalla's hair. When she'd fled her home and her father's domination, there had been a high price for her freedom. Besides the personal risks she'd taken, she'd missed being part of the family, watching her siblings change as they aged. Phone calls had been poor substitutes for the close contact she'd craved.

This time, however, was different. Or maybe *she* was different, Jasmine thought. Her brush with death had given her a deeper appreciation for what she would have left behind on this earth, and compelled her to try, one more time, to come to some sort of accord with her father. And to her shock, her attempt was meeting much more success than she'd had any right to expect. Although her father remained stiff and formal with her, he was at least speaking civilly and had refrained, for the most part, from directing her on how to live her life.

Of course, she thought ironically, she hadn't been there long yet. Nor had she made the mistake of giving either of her parents a suspicion as to the true nature of her job.

"Do not part it." Kalla was giving rapid-fire instructions as she twisted her head this way and that to survey her image in the mirror. "I want it pulled straight back like yours. Oh…I see what you are doing. Mina Uehllah wore her hair like this in her wedding. She looked beautiful, but she married a man who looked like an ogre." She scrunched up her nose in imitation, eliciting another laugh from Jasmine. "I would never marry such an ugly man. I will be much too busy getting my journalism degree and making a career for myself with a major newspaper. Only then will I allow myself to fall in love. Have you ever been in love, Jasmine? Is it wonderful?"

Jasmine's hands faltered, her sister's words twisting the blade that seemed permanently lodged in her heart. "Yes.

Yes, it is wonderful." Kalla was far too young to hear about the pain that accompanied love. And Jasmine was far from an expert in the matter, in any case. Not only had she fallen in love after promising herself not to, she'd managed to pick a man who didn't love her back.

To change the subject, and to give the tightness in her chest a chance to ease, she asked, "What do Mother and Father say about *you* going to university?"

Kalla gave a shrug, far more interested in the hairstyling than in the reason behind her sister's question. "Mother will convince Father. I heard them talking one day and Mother said he must not make the same mistakes with me that drove you away." Her gaze met Jasmine's in the mirror. "What mistake was she talking about? Did Father refuse to allow you to attend university?"

"We argued," Jasmine evaded. If her siblings didn't know the truth about why she had left, she wasn't going to tell them. There would be no need, if her mother was smoothing the way so things would be different for Kalla. And if not... Jasmine finished with the hairdo, laid down the brush. She'd been too young, too inexperienced, to fight her father and had chosen to run instead. But she'd fight him for Kalla, if need be. Her sister would have everything her father had denied Jasmine.

Surveying her hairstyle, Kalla bounced from the seat, then gave her a delighted hug. "It is perfect! I will practice every day until I learn to do it just like you do."

A knock sounded at the door and Sihri poked her head in. "There is someone here who is most insistent about seeing you, Jasmine."

Puzzled, Jasmine followed her out the door. "Who is it?"

Sihri gave a sniff. "He would not give his name, but he

is a very dangerous-looking man. I would prefer that you did not see him without your father present.''

''Do not worry. I have been taking care of myself for a very long time now.''

The old servant gave her a disapproving look, then planted herself, arms crossed in a no-nonsense pose, in the high-arched entrance to their main room.

The woman's behavior was a minor annoyance, and a reminder of a time when her freedom had been much more restricted. Jasmine rounded the corner and stopped short, her heart doing a dizzying somersault.

''Walker.'' The word was little more than a whisper trapped in her throat, but he turned at the sound, looking almost as stunned as she. In the five days since they'd parted he'd returned his hair to its familiar jet-black color and discarded the contacts. His piercing blue regard was as lethal as she remembered. It still had the power to leech the strength from her knees and cause little flutters of nerves to ripple in her stomach.

Because the ripple threatened to become a quake, she sank down into a chair, gestured for him to do the same. ''Why...'' Too cowardly to pursue that line of questioning, she chose another. ''How did you find me?''

''I almost didn't.'' His hands shoved deep into the pockets of his black dress slacks, he ignored the chair she indicated and prowled the room. ''When you ran away from Dirk's place, you told him you were going home.''

He'd managed to find a way guaranteed to help her combat her jittery nerves. ''I did not,'' she corrected precisely, '''run away' from Dirk's.''

''I checked your Philadelphia apartment. And your London condo. You weren't at either, so I had to do some digging.'' He scanned the well-appointed room before turning back toward her. "I never expected to find you in a place like this."

Acutely aware of the servant standing nearby, Jasmine said, "Sihri, you may leave us now."

A mulish expression settled on the older woman's face. "Jasmine, that would not be…"

"Now, Sihri." The whip in her voice surprised them both, and had the servant turning, leaving the room in a huff. When she'd departed, Jasmine found it difficult to look at Walker again. Yet it was impossible to look away.

The short-sleeved white shirt he wore was open at the neck, exposing his tanned throat. He wore sandals, and his sunglasses were tucked into the pocket of his shirt. He looked big, handsome, and, Sihri was right, a bit dangerous. He also looked more than a little ill at ease.

"This is your house?"

"It is my family's home."

"Your family." He removed one hand from his pocket to jam it through his hair. His journey had taken him across two continents. But never had he guessed he'd find her looking right at home in the midst of all this splendor. Never guessed that she'd been born to it.

The reasons that had brought him here had never seemed shakier. "I guess I figured you'd grown up much like I did." He frowned, remembering. "From things Dirk said…and you mentioned what you'd learned on the streets of Morocco…"

"My father is a very traditional man. Was very traditional," she corrected. She hoped that was changing. "When I was seventeen he picked out the man I was to marry. I insisted on having a choice, but he would not relent." She shrugged. "I left home. It was after that that Dirk found me on the streets."

Walker could have reflected for a moment, how Dirk

Longfield had had a hand in both of their lives, irrevocably shaping them, but there was a dangerous set of nerves spiking in his veins. They didn't allow for distraction. "Your coming home...does that mean you've changed your mind about the marriage?"

Amazingly, temper flared into her face, and he almost grinned. The sight of Jaz in a snit was usually too good to be missed.

"What do you think? Do I appear to be a woman ready to let a man run her life?"

Something in his throat eased. No. No, she didn't. Although she was the most incredibly feminine woman he'd ever met, there was nothing the least bit submissive about her. "I guess not."

"You could not have come all this way to ask me that question."

"No, it was another question I came to ask." His gaze was sober now, direct. "Why'd you leave like that? You were gone before I even got done talking to Sutter."

It was her turn to look away. "I-it was what we had agreed, was it not? There was no reason to stay. We both knew how it would end. You were very clear. We would walk away after it was over."

Wincing a little, he said, "Yes, that's what I wanted." And saw her wince in turn. "But finding you gone changed all that. Hell—" He thought of the half-formed resolve he'd had when he'd strode from the office. "If I was honest, it changed long before that."

He wasn't a man used to introspection, the weighing and cataloging of emotions. Feelings got in the way in his line of work, and they were an indulgence he couldn't afford. Or so he'd always thought.

"Three years ago the night we spent together blew me away. Finding you gone the next morning was almost a relief because I was so damn spooked by what I was feeling. When I learned about the Star, it was easier to think the worst of you than to believe a woman had really gotten to me.''

He looked at her, her beautiful face full of questions, and hoped she shared at least a fraction of the emotional turbulence that was rocking him. ''Do you remember standing with me on the path outside the Brothers' mansion? Presenting me with the keys you'd lifted from my pocket?'' He barely waited for her nod before going on. ''I think it was then that everything changed. You picked my pocket, and ended up stealing my heart.'' He noted the absolute stillness on her face, and panic streaked up his spine. ''Maybe more than you bargained for, but there it is.''

Driven to move, to touch her, he crossed the room, took her hand and tugged her to her feet. ''I only have the dimmest idea of what love is, Jaz.'' He thought of his mother, dead too young, and his grandmother, old before her time. ''So you'll have to forgive me if I didn't recognize it until it was almost too late. I love you, Jaz.'' Saying it was at once liberating and terrifying. And the moments before she responded were the most hellish he'd ever experienced.

''I fell in love with you three years ago.'' The simple words, heartfelt, dealt a hammer blow of reaction that nearly buckled his knees. She turned her face up to his, expression radiant. ''Not for the first time in our relationship, you were a bit slower than me. This time, however, the cost will not be so high.''

Relief coursing through him, he pulled her close for a bruising kiss. Lifting his head, he said aggrievedly, ''If we're going to be married, you're going to have to stop rubbing it in that you swiped the Star of Benzia right out from under my nose."

She blinked. "Married?"

He ran a finger down her cheek. "Full partners, in every way. First marriage." A surprisingly old-fashioned custom for someone with little use for them, but nothing else would satisfy him. "And as far as work goes…I've accepted an offer to join the Noble Men." He heard her gasp, seconded the emotion behind it. "It's a big job. It'd be better to have a partner."

Her expression was dazed. "But how…why…?"

"I'll tell you all about it. And then you can tell me how you managed to circumvent the security around the Star and make off with it."

Dark eyes sparkling, Jasmine cocked her head. "I do not know, Walker. Some secrets really should not be revealed—even between a husband and wife."

His lips found hers again. "You'll tell me one of these days." The confidence he felt rang in his voice. He had a lot of faith in his persuasive powers and plenty of time to finesse the information from her.

In fact, he had a lifetime.

*   *   *   *   *

Be sure to watch for
HARD TO TAME
by Kylie Brant,
the next exciting tale in her
CHARMED AND DANGEROUS
miniseries, available in January
from Intimate Moments.
And now, here's a sneak preview of
BORN ROYAL

by Alexandra Sellers,
the explosive conclusion to
Intimate Moments's riveting,
FIRSTBORN SONS
series, on sale next month!

Prologue

Prince Rashid Kamal stood on the broad balcony of the palace smiling and waving as the love-roar of the crowd swelled almost to pain level and broke over his head.

Below the balcony, the huge, leafy square writhed ecstatically in the burning sunshine as the people cheered, shouted, laughed, sang, danced and kissed each other.

He was home. Their handsome Crown Prince, whom they had mourned as lost forever, had returned. And better still, he had returned a hero. As the man who had organized and masterminded the downfall of that band of murderous terrorists, the one so fearful no one liked to say its full name, but only called them *Al lkhwan*. The Brothers.

Now the people need not live in fear of the threatened chemical attack. It was said he had found the actual laboratory where the filthy poisons were being made, and that the entire store of the evil virus had been destroyed.

No one needed to be told where the first attack would have occurred. But a country storyteller, who had a sizable group entranced with his version of the prince's great exploit, told them anyway.

"Of course they would have attacked here in the islands of Tamir first," he asserted in a terrible voice, and his audience gasped and nodded. "Such monsters as these are drawn to destroy truth and nobility, for they know instinctively there is no coexistence between evil and good.

"And for a certainty they would have come here, to the big island—and to this city, Medina Tamir. Perhaps even in this very square they would have released their foul poison, hoping to destroy the Kamal family and put their own puppet in Ahmed's place!"

His audience of mostly city dwellers shuddered in horrified delight. The country people had a point—this was much more entertaining than the dry facts in newspapers or on television.

"And only when we died would the world have been alerted and begun to take action," the turbaned, white-bearded ancient said, conveniently omitting the fact that the mission Prince Rashid had headed had been a joint one involving many nations. "Too late for Tamir. But what need have we of the world, when we have a prince such as Rashid? Brave, intrepid…"

The cheers redoubled as Prince Rashid was joined on the balcony by the rest of his family. The silver-haired King Ahmed, lovely Queen Alima, handsome Prince Hassan and his sisters, the beautiful and headstrong Princess Nadia, gentle, smiling Samira, and Leila—the youngest and, some argued, the loveliest.

It was Nadia who stood closest to Rashid as the family took their places, smiling and waving to the delirious citizenry. She glanced down at the crowd around the storyteller in the square, and pointed him out to her brother.

"By the end of the week you'll have done the deed

single-handed,'' she remarked in an ironic aside. ''Flying on the back of a giant bird—the Natobird, no doubt—and with the sword of your ancestors. I suppose they'll call it the Kalashnikov-sword—raised high, you dispatched the monsters after a fight to the death and won your way to the coffers wherein lay the terrible poison. You threw magical powder on the poison to render it harmless.''

Rashid laughed. ''Well, if my mythical powers win the people to my side when I'm proposing a shift in foreign policy, among other things, I won't object.''

Nadia flicked him a look. He should have known she would be quick to pick up on that hint. ''Other things? As for example?''

Rashid shook his head, turning to lift his hand again and smile. The sun was high in the blue sky, burnishing the thick black curls, enhancing the glint in his dark eyes and the white, even teeth. The crowd swayed with reaction.

There was no one, Nadia reflected, whom he did not, one way or another, seduce. He had much more charisma than their rather severe father. It was no wonder that the people had been brokenhearted when Rashid went missing.

As for her, it had been like losing a limb. The miracle of having her brother back from the dead had not worn off yet. Maybe it never would.

'''Among other things,''' Nadia repeated musingly, sliding an arm through her brother's. ''Now, what else would you be *proposing* besides a shift in foreign policy?'' He was silent. ''So the baby really is yours? I wondered.''

His gaze turning inward, Prince Rashid absently waved and smiled. The crowd cheered. He thought of Princess Julia's soft cry when his hands were on her, when what was going to happen was inevitable. *Rashid, I'm—I'm a virgin...*

He had not believed her. Other women had said it to

him at such a moment, he had never understood why. Hoping to make his passion hotter, perhaps.

But it was true. When he realized it, too late, it had struck him a blow like nothing else he had experienced. A virgin. After all this time, she was a virgin.

"Yes, it's mine," he said.

He thought of the way she had melted at his touch, saw her face in his mind's eye, those full lips stretched with desire. He had lost control.

"It will put an end to the feud, won't it?" Nadia commented. "If marriage is what's in your mind."

Had it been his subconscious mind understanding that the one unanswerable way to bind them together was a child? Was that the reason such powerful desire had swept him, blinding him to every other consideration? His one chance offered, and he had taken it.

Now it wasn't a question of *if* he'd marry Princess Julia Sebastiani, but *when*...

Silhouette®

INTIMATE MOMENTS™
is proud to present

Romancing the Crown

*With the help of their powerful allies,
the royal family of Montebello is determined
to find their missing heir. But the search for the
beloved prince is not without danger—or passion!*

This exciting twelve-book series begins in January and continues throughout the year with these fabulous titles:

Available at your favorite retail outlet.

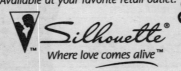

Silhouette®

Where love comes alive™

CALL THE ONES YOU LOVE OVER THE HOLIDAYS!

Save $25 off future book purchases when you buy any four Harlequin® or Silhouette® books in October, November and December 2001,

PLUS

receive a phone card good for 15 minutes of long-distance calls to anyone you want in North America!

WHAT AN INCREDIBLE DEAL!

Just fill out this form and attach 4 proofs of purchase (cash register receipts) from October, November and December 2001 books, and Harlequin Books will send you a coupon booklet worth a total savings of $25 off future purchases of Harlequin® and Silhouette® books, AND a 15-minute phone card to call the ones you love, anywhere in North America.

Please send this form, along with your cash register receipts
as proofs of purchase, to:
In the USA: Harlequin Books, P.O. Box 9057, Buffalo, NY 14269-9057
In Canada: Harlequin Books, P.O. Box 622, Fort Erie, Ontario L2A 5X3
Cash register receipts must be dated no later than December 31, 2001.
Limit of 1 coupon booklet and phone card per household.
Please allow 4-6 weeks for delivery.

**I accept your offer! Enclosed are 4 proofs of purchase.
Please send me my coupon booklet
and a 15-minute phone card:**

Name: _____

Address: _____ City: _____

State/Prov.: _____ Zip/Postal Code: _____

Account Number (if available): _____

---

097 KJB DAGL
PHQ4013